Edward Marston was born and brought up in South Wales. A full-time writer for over forty years, he has worked in radio, film, television and theatre and is a former chairman of the Crime Writers' Association. Prolific and highly successful, he is equally at home writing children's books or literary criticism, plays or biographies.

edwardmarston.com

By Edward Marston

THE BRACEWELL MYSTERIES

The Queen's Head • The Merry Devils • The Trip to Jerusalem
The Nine Giants • The Mad Courtesan • The Silent Woman
The Roaring Boy • The Laughing Hangman • The Fair Maid of Bohemia
The Wanton Angel • The Devil's Apprentice • The Bawdy Basket
The Vagabond Clown • The Counterfeit Crank • The Malevolent Comedy
The Princess of Denmark

THE RAILWAY DETECTIVE SERIES

The Railway Detective • The Excursion Train
The Railway Viaduct • The Iron Horse
Murder on the Brighton Express • The Silver Locomotive Mystery
Railway to the Grave • Blood on the Line
The Stationmaster's Farewell • Peril on the Royal Train
A Ticket to Oblivion • Timetable of Death

Inspector Colbeck's Casebook:
Thirteen Tales from the Railway Detective

The Railway Detective Omnibus:
The Railway Detective, The Excursion Train, The Railway Viaduct

THE CAPTAIN RAWSON SERIES

Soldier of Fortune • Drums of War • Fire and Sword
Under Siege • A Very Murdering Battle

THE RESTORATION SERIES

The King's Evil • The Amorous Nightingale • The Repentant Rake
The Frost Fair • The Parliament House • The Painted Lady

THE HOME FRONT DETECTIVE SERIES

A Bespoke Murder • Instrument of Slaughter
Five Dead Canaries • Deeds of Darkness • Dance of Death

THE BOW STREET RIVALS SERIES

Shadow of the Hangman

The Counterfeit Crank

An Elizabethan Mystery

EDWARD MARSTON

Allison & Busby Limited
12 Fitzroy Mews
London W1T 6DW
allisonandbusby.com

First published in 2004.
This paperback edition published by Allison & Busby in 2015.

A CIP catalogue record for this book is available from
the British Library.

ISBN 978-0-7490-1846-7

Typeset in 10.5/15.8 pt Sabon by
Allison & Busby Ltd.

The paper used for this Allison & Busby publication
has been produced from trees that have been legally sourced
from well-managed and credibly certified forests.

Printed and bound by
CPI Group (UK) Ltd, Croydon, CR0 4YY

To Stuart Krichevsky

These that do counterfeit the crank be young knaves and young harlots, that deeply dissemble the falling sickness. For the crank in their language is the falling evil.

THOMAS HARMAN, *A Caveat for Common Cursitors*, 1566

A slipper and subtle knave, a finder-out of occasions, that has an eye can stamp and counterfeit advantages, though true advantage never present itself; a devilish knave!

WILLIAM SHAKESPEARE, *Othello*, 1604

Chapter One

'What ails you?' asked Nicholas Bracewell, peering at his friend with concern.

'Nothing,' said Edmund Hoode. 'Nothing at all.'

'Your face is pale and drawn.'

'I am well, I do assure you.'

'Your eyes are bloodshot.'

'Pay no heed to that, Nick.'

'Are you in pain?'

Hoode shook his head. 'No, no.'

'Yet I saw you wince even now.'

'Only because of the mistakes I made in that last scene.'

'That, too, was unlike the Edmund Hoode I know. You so rarely make mistakes.'

'Even the best horse stumbles.'

Hoode smiled bravely but Nicholas was not fooled. The company's book holder had worked so closely with his friend over the years that he could always tell what the latter was thinking and feeling. Something was amiss. Hoode, the resident playwright with Westfield's Men, was also a gifted actor and he was rehearsing a role for the first performance of *Caesar's Fall*, a play by a new dramatist. Known for his reliability, he was uncharacteristically hesitant that morning, forgetting lines, inventing moves that had not been specified and, at one point, clumsily knocking over a piece of scenery in the Forum. They were in the yard of the Queen's Head, the London inn where the company was based, and where they had to compete with the pandemonium of the market outside in Gracechurch Street. The sky was overcast. A cool breeze was blowing yet Nicholas thought he saw beads of sweat on Hoode's brow.

'Do you feel hot, Edmund?' he said.

'No more than usual.'

'Not troubled by a fever, I hope?'

'All that troubles me is this damnable memory of mine. It keeps failing me, Nick, and I'll not abide that. I must serve the playwright much better than this.' Hoode turned away. 'Forgive me while I con my lines.'

Though he unrolled some parchment to check his speeches for the next scene, he really wanted to escape Nicholas's scrutiny. Edmund Hoode felt distinctly unwell, but, not wishing to let the actors or the playwright down, he was being stoical, forcing himself to go on and trying to ignore the growing queasiness in his stomach. His head was pounding and sweat was starting to trickle down his face. He wiped it off with a sleeve.

Nicholas was not the only person to be worried about him during the break in rehearsal. Michael Grammaticus, author of *Caesar's Fall*, looked even more anxious. He came across to the book holder.

'What is wrong with Edmund this morning?' he wondered.

'I wish I knew, Michael.'

'Does he always stumble so badly through a part?'

'No,' said Nicholas. 'It's a matter of pride with him to learn his lines. Edmund has great faith in your play. He strives to do his utmost on your behalf.'

'He has been my greatest ally.'

'How so?'

'Without his help, *Caesar's Fall* would never have reached the stage.'

'You wrote it, Michael,' Nicholas reminded him.

'Yes,' agreed the other, 'but Edmund Hoode inspired it. Do you know how often I sat up there in the gallery, watching a performance of one of his plays and marvelling at its quality? It was he who first fired my ambition. Edmund was my teacher and the Queen's Head, my school. I dreamt of the day when I would emulate him as an author.'

'That day is at hand. Your play is set fair for success.'

'Not if someone blunders through the role of Casca like that.'

Michael Grammaticus shot an anxious glance in the direction of Hoode. *Caesar's Fall* was his first venture into the world of theatre and he had set great store by it. Having been taken up by the finest troupe in London,

11

he wanted to forge a partnership with them that would go well beyond the tragedy they were about to perform. Grammaticus was a tall, spare, phlegmatic man in his late twenties with a scholarly stoop and a habit of squinting. A graduate of Cambridge, he was steeped in learning, highly conscientious and – on the evidence of *Caesar's Fall* – a talented playwright.

Nicholas understood why the man was so tense and nervous. The performance of a new play was always fraught with difficulty because the actors were translating it into live performance for the first time without having any idea how it would be received. On their makeshift stage in the inn yard, Westfield's Men had launched many new works and not all had found favour. Some had simply bored the spectators, others had aroused them to such a pitch of anger that they had yelled abuse, hurled food and other missiles at the cast or just walked out in disgust. On such occasions, the first performance had also been the last. Grammaticus did not wish his play to meet that fate.

'What is your opinion, Nick?' he asked. 'Does the piece *work*?'

'It works very well, Michael. You could not have a more commanding Caesar than Lawrence Firethorn and he is ably supported by all the company. Have no fears,' said Nicholas, putting a hand on his shoulder. 'I sense that we may have a triumph on our hands. The story may be old but you have given it new life and direction. I have no qualms about what will happen when we present it before an audience.'

Grammaticus was relieved. 'That contents me more than I can say.'

Nicholas Bracewell was the book holder and, as such, only a hired man with no financial stake in the company, but the newcomer had soon discovered how central a figure he was. Lawrence Firethorn, the actor-manager, might dazzle on stage along with the other sharers but it was Nicholas who controlled things behind the scenes and who helped to keep the troupe at the forefront of their profession. He was the solid foundation on which everything else rested and Grammaticus had especial reason to be grateful to him. Before buying a new play, Firethorn always sought Nicholas's advice and the book holder had given his unequivocal approval to *Caesar's Fall*. He had also devised some of its most dramatic effects on stage, enhancing its impact in the process.

'Is Edmund ill, do you think?' asked Grammaticus.

'He denies it, Michael.'

'What else could make him so disordered?'

Nicholas heaved a sigh. 'There is one explanation.'

'Pray, tell me what it is.'

'Edmund is in love. He is ever inclined to wear his heart on his sleeve and there are times when it is too heavy to carry. Edmund gets distracted. But he will do his duty when the play is staged,' Nicholas assured him. 'Put him in front of an audience and a hundred unrequited loves would not divert him.'

'I hope that it is so,' said Grammaticus, screwing up his eyelids. 'Casca is not a large role but it is an important one.'

Nicholas gave a nod of agreement then picked up a signal

from Lawrence Firethorn. It was time to resume. The book holder checked that the correct scenery had been set up on the stage then he called the cast to order. After reading his lines for the last time, Hoode thrust the scroll inside his doublet. He looked paler than ever and seemed to be in some distress, but he was determined to soldier on. They were about to rehearse the assassination of Julius Caesar. Before they did so, Firethorn issued a stern warning.

'Strike as if you mean to kill,' he ordered, 'but be sure to move away once you have used your daggers. Above all else, I must be *seen*. Do not dare to cheat the audience by blocking their view, or you'll answer to me. A mighty emperor deserves a memorable end. That is what they will get.'

'Do not linger in the throes of death,' said Barnaby Gill, waspishly. 'You took so long to expire in *Antonio's Revenge* that we could have played the entire piece through again before you hit the ground.'

Firethorn stood on his dignity. 'I am famed for my death scenes.'

'Only because they outlast anyone else's.'

'Be silent, Barnaby. Curb your jealousy of a superior actor.'

Gill smirked. 'I've yet to meet one – alive or dead.'

'I bestride the boards like a giant.'

'That explains why you lumber so and get in everyone's way.'

Nicholas clapped his hands to interrupt them before another row was sparked. Barnaby Gill was the established clown in the company, second only to Firethorn in terms of talent and able to control an audience with equal skill. Though they worked together superbly on stage, the two men were sworn enemies once they stepped off it, forever indulging in verbal duels as each tried to seize the advantage. Edmund Hoode was the usual peacemaker between them but he was not even aware of their heated exchange this time. It was the book holder who turned their minds to the rehearsal.

The scene began with the entry of the conspirators. Brutus and Cassius instructed the others and reminded them of the magnitude of Caesar's faults. Their manner changed when the remaining members of the Senate came in, and they gave no hint of their murderous intent. Mark Anthony had a brief conversation with Casca, and Nicholas was pleased with the way that Hoode declaimed his lines. He appeared to have shaken off his earlier problems and spoke with confidence. Wearing a toga over his doublet and hose, Julius Caesar then entered like a conquering hero, treating the senators with weary condescension as they tried to press him with individual petitions.

Even in rehearsal, Firethorn was supreme, moving with imperious strides, using peremptory gestures to keep the senators in their place and investing his voice with an authority that reverberated around the inn yard. While the arrogant Caesar praised himself extravagantly for having done so much for Rome, the conspirators moved into position. One moment, Firethorn was the head of a vast empire, the next, he was the victim of a brutal attack as no less than eight senators produced daggers from their robes in order to stab him. Casca was the first to strike, then, in quick succession, came the flashing blades of Cassius, Trebonius, Decius Brutus, Metellus Cimber, Cinna, Caius Ligarius and, finally – to Caesar's utter dismay – the trusted Brutus. As the conspirators drew back to allow Firethorn to play his death scene, however, they revealed that one body had already fallen to the floor.

In the hurly-burly of the assassination, Casca had collapsed. Edmund Hoode was no longer playing a part. Sensing that he was seriously ill, most of the actors abandoned their roles to crowd around the prone figure and Julius Caesar became aware that the agonising death he was undergoing with such ear-splitting groans had no audience at all. Instead, everyone was looking at Hoode. Enraged that his thunder had been stolen, Firethorn tore off his toga, flung it to the floor, and turned to confront the other actors.

'God's tits!' he howled. 'This tragedy is called *Caesar's Fall* and not *The Death of Casca*. Remember, if you will, that *I* have the title role here and I'll not be eclipsed by anyone else in the play.' He glared at the Roman senators. 'Which one of you blind and brainless idiots stabbed the wrong man?'

But nobody was listening. They were too alarmed by Hoode's sudden collapse. Nicholas dashed across the stage and knelt beside his friend, easing him gently on to his back and placing a hand on his fevered brow. Hoode was completely unconscious. His breathing was uneven and there was a strange smell on his breath. Michael

Grammaticus clambered on to the stage. His face was a study in apprehension.

'What happened?' he asked. 'Is he unwell?'

'Yes,' said Nicholas, solemnly. 'He needs a doctor.'

'I'll fetch one with all haste.'

Grammaticus rushed off at once and left them to make Hoode as comfortable as they could. Fury now spent, Firethorn was as sympathetic as anyone, bending solicitously over his friend and imploring him to say something. Edmund Hoode, however, was beyond the reach of words. Retrieving the discarded toga, Nicholas rolled it up to make a cushion for the patient's head, then urged everyone to stand back in order to give him plenty of air.

The rehearsal was over.

Alexander Marwood was trapped. The landlord of the Queen's Head had long ago discovered that he was in the wrong occupation and the wrong marriage. Small, skinny, ugly, misshapen and balding dramatically, he had the face of a diseased ferret, but it was his nature that was unsuited to life in a boisterous tavern. He abhorred crowds and despised drunkenness yet he was at the mercy of both on a daily basis. If he had been happy in his private life, he might have borne it with resignation but he was locked in a joyless union with his wife, Sybil, a stone-faced harridan who was skilled in the black arts of marital persecution. Marwood's soul had shrivelled inside him.

'I should never have taken this hellish place on,' he confessed.

'But it's a fine inn, Alexander, with a good reputation and regular custom.'

'I always wanted a quiet life.'

'Ah, well,' said Adam Crowmere with a chuckle, 'you should not have come near London if you sought tranquillity. Here's life, here's bustle, here's the biggest and most exciting city in the whole of Europe. Would you really choose to waste away in some dull country backwater? Come, Alexander, tell the truth. Being here in the capital has many consolations. Think how blessed you have been in your chosen bride, for instance. Sybil must bring great comfort to you.'

Squirming inwardly at the mention of his wife, Marwood did not trust himself to reply but his face was eloquent. Three separate nervous twitches broke out to animate his features, each moving rapidly and indiscriminately from nose to cheek, from chin to ear, from eyebrow to forehead, from lip to lip, until all three coalesced on his pate and made it ripple. Marwood smacked his head with an irritable hand but it only made the waves roll more swiftly across his skull.

'I'll wager this,' said Crowmere, patting him familiarly on the back. 'You and Sybil will miss the Queen's Head. No sooner will you reach Dunstable than you'll wish that you were back here again.'

'I doubt that,' replied Marwood, testily. 'I'll be too busy breathing fresh air again and enjoying a life where I am not at the beck and call of every fool, knave and drunkard who walks through my door. Be warned, Adam. The Queen's

18

Head is no Garden of Eden. The sweepings of London come into this tavern.'

'As long as they can pay for their ale, they'll be more than welcome.'

Crowmere was a fleshy man of medium height with a geniality that shone out like a beacon. Still in his thirties, he was an experienced innkeeper with a knack of increasing the profits in every establishment that he managed. Given the opportunity, he had been more than ready to desert his own tavern in Rochester for a short while in order to take charge of the Queen's Head. Adam Crowmere felt that he would be in his element. The two men were standing in a private room at the inn while they discussed the terms of their agreement. Marwood could not believe that anyone would undertake the task with such patent enthusiasm.

There was a tap on the door. The landlord opened it to admit Nicholas Bracewell.

'Ah,' said Marwood. 'Come in, sir. Your name was on my lips even now.'

'Master Firethorn has sent me to pay the rent,' explained Nicholas, handing over a purse. 'I would have come earlier but one of our fellows was taken sick and we had to carry him back to his lodging.'

Marwood was bitter. 'Only one of you? If prayer had any value, the whole company would be struck down. This is the bane of my life, Adam,' he went on, turning to his companion. 'As I told you, I am condemned, for my sins, to have this accursed theatre company clinging to my back like a ravenous ape that feeds off my flesh.'

'Westfield's Men are not accursed,' said Crowmere, beaming at Nicholas. 'They are the jewels of their profession. I saw them once at Rochester and they played such a sprightly comedy that I laughed for a week.' He offered his hand. 'I am Adam Crowmere and I'm happy to meet any member of so illustrious a troupe.'

Marwood introduced the two men properly, then stunned Nicholas with the news that he and his wife were quitting London for what might be a matter of some weeks. The landlord's elder brother was desperately ill in Dunstable and they were rushing to be at his bedside. While they were away, the affable Crowmere, a cousin of Sybil Marwood's, would look after the Queen's Head. Nicholas concealed his delight behind a frown.

'I am sad to hear that your brother is not well,' he observed.

'Reuben is at death's door,' declared Marwood with a notable lack of anything resembling brotherly affection. 'but it may take a while before it creaks open to let him through. It falls to me to keep a vigil.' He weighed the purse in his hand. 'I must go and enter this into my accounts. I'll leave you to become more closely acquainted.'

'Thank you,' said Nicholas. He waited until the landlord had gone. 'I own that I expected more grief from the brother of a dying man.'

Crowmere smiled. 'All that grieves Alexander is the fact that he and Reuben fell out with each other many years ago. He's hurrying to Dunstable to repair the rift so that his brother will remember him in his will. Reuben Marwood is a wealthy man.'

20

'How long will our landlord be away?'

'Long enough for me to make my mark at the Queen's Head.'

'I am glad to hear that you take a more kindly view of our presence here. Where our landlord is concerned,' said Nicholas, tactfully, 'I fear that it has never been a true meeting of minds.'

'Alexander hates you,' said Crowmere, frankly. 'Before you came in, he was telling me that Westfield's Men were detestable vermin, but that a certain Nicholas Bracewell was the least detestable of them.' He gave a ripe chuckle. 'Coming from him, that's praise indeed.' His face clouded. 'But you say that one of your fellows has been stricken. Not the great Lawrence Firethorn, I hope?'

'No, no, he has the constitution of an ox.'

'Nor that clown of yours either, I trust? Barnaby Gill made me laugh until I felt I was about to burst. I'd hate to think that he has been carried off to his bed.'

'Master Gill is not the invalid,' said Nicholas. 'If either he or Master Firethorn had been taken ill, our chances of staging a new play tomorrow would disappear. Nobody could replace them in time. Casca, a much smaller role, can be substituted and he will need to be for Edmund Hoode is far too sick to perform.'

'What's the nature of his sickness?'

Nicholas gave a shrug. 'That's what troubles us. We do not rightly know. The doctor, too, is mystified. All that he can do is to ease Edmund's pain with medicine.'

'I hope that he soon recovers,' said Crowmere with

21

obvious sincerity. 'But I'm delighted to hear that you will be staging a new play here tomorrow. That will bring the crowds flocking to the Queen's Head.'

'We never lack for spectators.'

'I wonder that Alexander does not treasure Westfield's Men for increasing his takings every time they perform at the inn.' He raised a bushy eyebrow. 'How will his departure be greeted?'

'With some relief,' admitted Nicholas.

Crowmere laughed. 'And no small amount of celebration, I think.'

'I'll not pretend that our absent landlord will be mourned.'

'Would that my arrival will also be a cause for joy! I'm no enemy to your endeavours, Nicholas, be certain of that. Look to me for any help that you need. Where you once found coldness, you'll now meet nothing but encouragement.'

'That's good news indeed.'

'Then here's better to take back to your fellows,' said Crowmere, hands on hips. 'When Alexander is safely on the road, I plan to treat you in the way that you deserve, and to that end, I'll invite the whole company – nay, and your patron as well – to a feast under this roof at my expense.' He grinned amiably. 'Will this content you, my friend?'

'Very much,' said Nicholas, unable to believe what he had heard. 'I see that I was mistaken in you, sir. You are no new landlord – you are a gift from God.'

* * *

Superstition ruled the lives of the actors. They were always looking for signs, portents, tokens, auguries, and anything else that might be construed as a harbinger of good or ill fortune. Edmund Hoode's mysterious illness was seen by most of them as an evil omen, a clear warning of imminent disaster. *Caesar's Fall*, they believed, was doomed and they were helpless to avert that doom. Even though the final rehearsal went exceptionally well, voices were still raised in consternation.

'Trouble lies ahead,' warned Barnaby Gill. 'I feel it in my water.'

'I see it in the stars,' said James Ingram. 'They foretell catastrophe.'

'*Caesar's Fall* will be our collapse as well,' decided a mournful Frank Quilter. 'There is something about the piece that presages danger.'

'Yes,' said Owen Elias, scornfully. 'It is because you three merchants of misery are in the cast. Hell's fire! Why talk yourselves into defeat when we have such a strong chance of victory? If we had to rely on Barnaby's piss, James's stargazing and Frank's instincts, we'd never stage *any* play with success. Weak minds are prey to foolish fears.'

'Do you call Edmund's illness a foolish fear?' asked Gill.

'No,' replied the Welshman. 'It was a blow to us but we've endured far worse.'

'Can you not see any significance in what happened?' said Quilter. 'Edmund was struck down during the play. That means this tragedy is tainted.'

'This tragedy will *end* in tragedy,' moaned Ingram.

'Not if we bend our back and give of our best,' argued Elias, bunching a fist. 'Everyone knows that I do not care for Michael Grammaticus – he is too much the university man for me – but I think he has written a wonderful play that deserves to be played to the hilt. Put aside your worries. Dear God! You sound like three old ladies, too frightened to step out into the street in case it rains.'

'And that's the other thing, Owen,' said Gill, wagging a finger at him. 'Have you seen the clouds? The sky will open this afternoon and we'll all be drowned by the rain.'

Elias was sarcastic. 'Do you feel water in your water as well, Barnaby?'

'Look to the heavens, man.'

'I prefer to look to our reputation and it will be sorely damaged if you step out on to that stage like three virgins tiptoeing into a bawdy house. Think of the *good* tidings we have had. Our melancholy landlord has left the city. We can revel in his absence.'

But even that reminder did not cheer his fellows. They were in the room that they used as their tiring-house, putting on their costumes for the afternoon performance of the new play. Acutely aware of the growing audience in the yard outside, Gill, Ingram and Quilter were not pleased to hear the buzz of expectation from the spectators because they had genuine doubts about *Caesar's Fall*. Like others in the company, they felt that ruination lay in ambush. If the play were not washed off the stage by a torrential downpour, it would, they felt, surely be bedevilled by some other means. Owen Elias, the ebullient Welshman, clicked his tongue as he surveyed the other sharers.

'I am disappointed in you, James,' he said to Ingram, 'and in you as well, Frank. I expected Barnaby to be full of woe because it is his natural condition. Every time he empties his bladder, he foresees the end of the world. You two should know better.'

James Ingram and Frank Quilter, the two youngest and most handsome sharers, had the grace to look shamefaced. In listening to Gill, they had allowed themselves to be drawn into a bleak pessimism. Elias had tried to lift them out of it and, though they still had lingering anxieties, they were grateful to him. The Welshman was not merely a fine actor, he had a spirit and determination that burnt inside him like a flame. Ingram and Quilter were reassured by his confidence. Gill remained dejected.

'*Caesar's Fall* has already caused Edmund's fall. We are next to drop.'

Elias was defiant. 'Not while *I* have breath in my body.'

'Nor me,' said Lawrence Firethorn, coming to stand beside him, 'My back is broad. If I have to, I'll carry this entire play on my own. Listen to me,' he went on, raising his voice so that it reached everyone in the room. 'This is no time for doubt and hesitation. Forget this talk of ill omens. We owe it to our playwright to breathe life into his work so that it bewitches all who see it. Yes,' he conceded, 'we have lost dear Edmund but what would he think of us if we let a fellow author down? He sends love and best wishes to us in this venture. He looks to receive glad tidings from us.'

'Then he looks in vain,' said Gill. 'This play is tarnished with bad luck.'

'That can be ascribed to *your* presence,' said Firethorn, sharply. 'Bad luck, thy name is Barnaby Gill. You'd poison any enterprise, were it not for the fact that we have acted with you so often that we know how to subdue your malign influence. Let's have no more carping from you, Barnaby. We go forth to certain triumph.' He indicated the book holder. 'Nick craves a word with you.'

'Yes,' said Nicholas, stepping into the middle of the room. 'Two things will give you heart. As you know, I was a sailor for three long years and learnt to read the skies like a book. The day is cloudy, I grant you, and rain looks certain but I give you my word that it will not fall during the play. Shake that fear from your mind.'

There was a collective sigh of relief. Nicholas's ability to forecast the weather was almost uncanny. It came from having sailed with Drake on the circumnavigation of the earth, an experience that left its scars on Nicholas but which also taught him so much about the vagaries of wind and rain. The second piece of information he was about to impart had already been confided to Firethorn, who had agreed with the book holder that it should be deliberately kept from the others until just before the performance. Aware that their fellows would be shackled by superstition, Nicholas hoped to liberate them with his announcement.

'Our choleric landlord has departed,' he said, drawing a ragged cheer from the actors, 'and a more worthy host has taken his place. I can now tell you that Adam Crowmere has promised to honour us with a feast as a gesture of good will.' There was general jubilation. 'One condition only is attached to the invitation,' Nicholas continued, looking round the smiling faces. 'Our new and hospitable landlord insists that *Caesar's Fall* – the very first play to be staged here under his aegis – be yet another success for Westfield's Men so that we have something to celebrate.'

With Firethorn's connivance, Nicholas had invented the condition in order to spur the actors on and the device had worked. Instead of the pervading gloom, a buoyant optimism now filled the tiring house. Firethorn traded a knowing glance with his book holder. Nicholas had made the actors forget all about their trepidation. They were now positively straining on the leash to get out on stage.

They did not have long to wait. At a signal from Nicholas, the musicians began to play and Owen Elias stepped out in a black cloak to deliver the Prologue. Though his voice was appropriately firm, his mind was on the promised feast and he could almost smell the roast pig upon the spit. He raised a hand to silence the murmurs in the crowd.

> '*Good friends, all you that now are gathered here,*
> *Behold a tale of villainy and fear*
> *In which a mighty conqueror is killed*
> *By those with spite and naked envy filled*
> *Until it drives them on to heinous crime*
> *And offers us a lesson for all time.*
> *For, mark this well, all subtle minds that can,*
> *This Caesar's Fall is like the Fall of Man.*'

And on he went. The rhyming couplets were deceptively simple at first but they had grown more intricate by the time the Prologue ended. Acknowledging a round of applause with a bow, Elias withdrew from the stage until it was time for him to re-enter in the guise of Brutus. The play, meanwhile, opened with a lively scene between a group of gullible citizens and a comical soothsayer. No sooner did Barnaby Gill skip on to the boards in the latter roll than the laughter started. The recognised clown was there to make sure that tragedy was shot through with a dark and ironic humour and, whatever his earlier reservations about the performance, Gill acted as if his life depended on it. His energy and commitment set the tone for the rest of the play.

The story of Julius Caesar was a familiar one and other dramatists had explored it in various ways. What set this new version apart from other plays on the same subject was the emphasis placed on Caesar's earlier career, showing him as a fearless soldier and a brilliant administrator. It was only later that the martial hero was corrupted by over-ambition. To maintain sympathy for a man with such a glaring flaw in his character, the play offered insights into Caesar's domestic life and – in one of the most vivid scenes in the play – it anticipated the assassination with a fall of another kind.

Until that point, Firethorn had given a stirring account of Caesar, brave, proud, intelligent, adventurous and endlessly resourceful. By the sheer force of his acting, he had transformed Julius Caesar into a demi-god. Then, at the height of his power, when the audience believed they were looking at an indestructible human being, Firethorn suffered from an attack of falling sickness, dropping to the ground without warning and having such a frenzied epileptic fit that everyone in the yard thought that it was real. It was Brutus, later to conspire against Caesar, who came to his friend's aid by inserting the handle of a dagger into his mouth to keep his teeth apart in order to prevent him from biting off his tongue. The same dagger would later help to bring about his ultimate fall.

Seated in the lower gallery, Michael Grammaticus watched with teeth clenched and hands clasped tightly together. Though the spectators were engaged from the start, he could not relax, fearing that the piece would lose its grip on the audience or that rain would come to dampen their ardour. His admiration for Westfield's Men increased with every scene. The problems that had dogged them during rehearsals had miraculously disappeared. Led by Firethorn, the whole company was in tremendous form. Grammaticus was also impressed by the way that the loss of Edmund Hoode was covered. At the suggestion of Nicholas Bracewell, the part of Trebonius was cut out altogether and James Ingram, who had taken the role, instead became Casca. Nobody missed a lesser conspirator.

Enlivened by the antics of Barnaby Gill throughout, the play mixed tragedy and comedy in judicious proportions, moving towards its climax with gathering speed. When the assassination came, it was so vicious and dramatic that there were cries of horror from all corners of the yard. Julius Caesar then gave them all a death scene to remember, staggering around the stage with bloodied hands trying to stem the flow from his various wounds and reviling his enemies in a speech of defiance that showed his true nobility. While his corpse was finally borne away to solemn music, the audience was in a state of profound shock. They had witnessed a sublime tragedy.

As the emperor reappeared to lead his company on to the stage, dark clouds parted and a shaft of sunlight peeped through. It was like a heavenly benediction. Applause was slow at first but it quickly built to a crescendo. Those in the pit stamped and cheered, those in the balconies were on their feet to acknowledge a magnificent performance by Lawrence Firethorn and his company. The ovation seemed to go on forever. Nobody clapped louder than Michael Grammaticus. Released at last from the tension that had made the afternoon something of an ordeal, he was overcome with joy at having fulfilled his ambition. A play with his name on it had taken the stage by storm. A whole new life had suddenly opened out before him.

Chapter Two

While the actors discarded their costumes and adjourned to the taproom to celebrate, Nicholas Bracewell organised the dismantling of the stage and made sure that the scenery and properties were safely locked away. He and Owen Elias then permitted themselves only one tankard of ale with their fellows at the Queen's Head before they slipped away to visit a friend. Edmund Hoode was dozing when they arrived at his lodging but his eyelids soon fluttered open. He gave them a tired smile of welcome.

'Nick . . . Owen,' he murmured. 'What brings you here?'

'We came to see how you are,' said Nicholas.

Elias grinned. 'Speak for yourself,' he joked. 'I only came to catch a glimpse of the landlady's beautiful daughter. What a fetching young creature she is, Edmund! Were I lodged here, I'd never spend a night alone in that bed.'

'Both mother and daughter have been very good to me,' said Hoode.

'You've enjoyed the *two* of them?' said Elias with a cackle of delight. 'No wonder you look so weary, if you've been ravishing them in turn. Your chamber is a veritable leaping house.'

'This is no time for mockery, Owen,' warned Nicholas, distressed at the sight of Hoode's deathly pallor. 'It's cruel to tease him so.' He put a considerate hand on the patient's shoulder. 'How are you, Edmund?'

'All the better for seeing two friendly faces,' replied Hoode in a querulous voice. 'I just feel so fatigued, Nick. I've scarcely the strength to sit up in bed.'

'What does the doctor say?'

'That the only remedy is a long rest.'

'A long rest?' echoed Elias, anxiously. 'I can see that the doctor knows little of a theatre company. If our beloved playwright has a long rest, we suffer the consequences. Westfield's Men without Edmund Hoode is like a river without water.'

'I think that you exaggerate, Owen.'

'We miss you on and offstage. It's like losing a limb. Is it not so, Nick?'

'Edmund is certainly missed,' agreed Nicholas, 'but he must be fully recovered before he returns to the fray. What has the doctor given you?'

'A magic potion that took aware all my pain,' said Hoode, gratefully. 'I was in agony when you carried me back here and thought I was like to die. Then I took this potion that Doctor Zander mixed. It saved my life.'

Elias was suspicious. 'Zander? That sounds like a foreign name.'

'So does Owen Elias,' said Nicholas with a smile, 'for nobody is more foreign to us than the Welsh. What does it matter where the good doctor hails from as long as he can cure this strange disease? Do you have faith in him, Edmund?'

'I do. Emmanuel Zander is kind and gentle.'

'When will he call again?'

'Tomorrow, Nick. But enough of me,' he said, trying to bring himself fully awake. 'Tell me about the play. How did *Caesar's Fall* fare this afternoon?'

'Excellently well.'

'Apart from scenes involving Casca, that is,' said Elias, trying to rally him with praise. 'Strive as he might, James Ingram was but a poor shadow of you in the part. You were Casca to the life, Edmund.'

'Is this true, Nick?'

'True enough, you were indeed a fine Casca,' said Nicholas, 'but James was a capable deputy. He never faltered. Lawrence and Barnaby stole most of the plaudits, as is usual, but Owen here matched them for quality as Brutus, and Frank Quilter's scheming Cassius was his best performance yet. *Caesar's Fall* was a signal triumph.'

'That will have made Michael happy.'

'You'd never have thought it from his face,' complained Elias. 'He squinted at us as if he was trying to read scribble. Michael Grammaticus lives inside his head. That's the failing of these university men. They do not know how to enjoy life.'

Nicholas grinned. 'That's not what I hear, Owen. The cry against most who study at Oxford or Cambridge is that they enjoy life far too much. They are forever being swinged for their indulgences. Michael is the exception to the rule,' he said. 'He's a true scholar, wedded to his studies.'

'Is that why he is so disdainful?'

'I've not seen that particular fault in him.'

'Nor me,' said Hoode. 'Michael Grammaticus has been politeness itself to me and, as you well know, I'm no university wit whose brain is crammed with Greek and Latin sayings. Compared to him, I'm raw and untutored.'

'But a far better playwright, for all that,' said Elias, loyally.

'Be fair,' urged Nicholas. 'Michael has great promise.'

'But he lacks Edmund's humanity. He's a dry stick, and I've never met a young man who carries such an old head on his stooping shoulders. Still,' he went on, 'let's forget our creeping playwright. We've news for you that will make you jump out of your sick bed with delight.'

'What news is that, Owen?' asked Hoode, stifling a yawn.

'Our landlord has quit London.'

'Only for a matter of weeks,' explained Nicholas. 'He has gone to Dunstable. His elder brother is ill and he means to keep vigil. For a while, it seems, we'll have no more black looks and stern reproaches from Alexander Marwood and his wife.'

'And the best of it is,' said Elias, 'that the new landlord

34

admires our work. He watched the play this afternoon and cheered us to the echo. Do you see what this means? In place of an arch enemy, we have gained a dear friend, one Adam Crowmere by name.'

Hoode yawned again. 'Fortune has smiled on us at last.'

'We deserve some consolation for the loss of Edmund Hoode.'

'What is the inn like without that melancholy landlord?'

'A place of mirth and merriment. But you shall judge for yourself.'

'Yes,' said Nicholas. 'Adam Crowmere wants to atone for the shabby treatment meted out to us at the inn. He also wishes to get to know us better. With that in mind, he is laying on a feast for the whole company on Sunday next, inviting Lord Westfield to join us in the festivities.'

Elias grimaced. 'Can you imagine Alexander Marwood doing such a thing?'

'He'd sooner turn us out into the street, Owen.'

'Adam Crowmere is a breath of fresh air, blowing through the Queen's Head. He understands the trade. His cordiality will double the profits of the inn. Our fellows cannot believe the changes he has wrought in a single day.'

'But you'll meet this paragon for yourself, Edmund,' insisted Nicholas. 'When Sunday comes, you'll feast alongside us. And if you are not well enough to walk to the inn, Owen and I will gladly carry you there.'

'Aye,' said Elias. 'Being with the company will be a medicine in itself.'

'What do you say, Edmund? Are these not glad tidings?'

There was no reply. The effort of staying awake to greet his friends had exhausted Hoode's limited strength. His eyes rolled, his lids closed and he went off into a deep slumber. A gentle snore soon rose from the bed. Nicholas looked down at him with mingled affection and sadness.

'Come, Owen,' he said, quietly. 'He needs his rest.'

The lane was long, narrow and twisting. Because it linked two main thoroughfares, it was always busy as people hurried to and fro about their affairs. Suddenly, the traffic came to a halt. Dressed in mud-covered rags, a young man promptly dropped to the ground as if he had been shot and went into a series of violent convulsions. There was blood on his face and he was foaming at the mouth. His female companion immediately went down on her knees and cradled him in her arms as she tried to stay his fit. The convulsions slowly died away but he lay unconscious in the dirt. Everyone crowded around to see what had happened to the unfortunate young man

'It's the falling sickness,' sighed the girl, looking up in despair at the faces that encircled her. 'My brother is too ill to work and too weak to fend for me. Spare a coin or two to help us, dear friends,' she pleaded, holding out a hand. 'If I had enough money, I could take him to a doctor.'

The young man twitched uncontrollably a few times and more white foam came bubbling from his mouth. It was a sight that played on the sympathy of the passers-by. A decrepit old woman in faded attire was the first to reach into her purse.

'Hold on, kind soul,' said a voice behind her. 'Do not part with money that you clearly need yourself. You are being tricked.'

'That is not so,' argued the girl, bursting into tears. 'You all saw what happened to my brother. He is grievous sick.'

'I think not.'

Nicholas Bracewell came forward to bend over the fallen man and grab him by the collar. With a firm heave, he pulled him upright then smacked him hard in the middle of the back. The young man spat out a piece of soap. Nicholas retrieved it from the ground and held it up for all to see.

'You have been gulled by a counterfeit crank,' he declared. 'This young man is as healthy as any of us here but he feigns the falling sickness to lure money from your purses. That is why he wears these rags and rolls in the mud. As for the blood,' he went on, using a hand to wipe it from the man's face, 'it comes from no wound, as you see. This fellow keeps a bladder of animal's blood to daub himself for effect.'

'The rogue!' cried the old woman. 'Send for an officer.'

'They should be whipped at the cart's-arse!' said a thickset man. 'Both of them.'

'Spare us,' implored the girl. 'We meant no harm. We are starving.'

'Beat the pair of them!' demanded the man, pushing forward.

'There is no need for that,' said Nicholas, standing in front of the couple to protect them. 'Their cunning has been duly exposed and your purses spared. That is enough.

Go your way, friends, and do not be fooled again by a counterfeit crank.'

The crowd slowly dispersed in a flurry of mutters and imprecations. Danger was over. Nicholas and Owen Elias had been on their way back to the Queen's Head when they chanced upon the two beggars. Taking care not to impede those who walked past, the book holder took a closer look at them. The man was in his early twenties, slim, dark and angular. Matted hair and a ragged beard covered what had once been handsome features. There was a scar on the side of his nose. His companion was younger, no more than sixteen or seventeen, with a trim figure and a pretty face that was masked by apprehension. Nicholas could detect no family likeness between the two of them.

'You are no brother and sister,' he remarked.

'Yes, we are,' lied the girl. 'We came to London when our parents died.'

'What are your names?'

'Why should we tell you?' retorted the young man, defensively.

'Because you might find we have something in common,' said Elias with a chuckle. 'That's a Welsh voice I hear, as clear and melodious as my own. *Noswaith da.*'

The beggar was tentative. '*Noswaith da.*'

Elias turned to the girl. 'I have two sisters back home in Wales and they both have my lilt. So should you, if you were raised across the border. Let's have no more of this nonsense about being brother and sister.' He smiled at them. 'I am Owen Elias and this is Nick Bracewell. We are not here to harry you.'

'No,' said Nicholas, adopting a softer tone. 'But I could not bear to see that poor old woman giving you what might have been her last groat. You are new to the city, I see, and picked the wrong place to beg.'

'Yes,' advised Elias. 'Always choose somewhere in the open so that you can take to your heels, if you are found out. Here, in this lane, you were trapped. Nick may have laid bare your device, but he also saved you from a sound beating.'

The young man gave a grudging nod. 'Thank you for that, at least.'

'So tell us your names.'

'I am Hywel Rees and this is Dorothea.'

'Dorothea Tate,' she admitted. 'And, no, we are not brother and sister. We met in St Albans, where Hywel rescued me from much worse than a beating.' She pulled back a sleeve to reveal ugly bruises all the way up her arm. 'There were two of the devils and they'd not be denied. Hywel took them on alone.'

'And sent them on their way,' said Hywel, proudly. 'I look after Dorothea now.'

'Then do it with more care,' suggested Nicholas. 'Do you have any money?'

'None at all. But we met this man on the road who told us that beggars could prosper, if they were guileful enough. He talked of a counterfeit crank he knew who could make six shillings a day with the falling sickness.'

'Six shillings a day!' exclaimed Elias. 'Hell's teeth! That's far more than I could earn, Hywel, and yet we are in the same trade.'

'Are we?'

'I am an actor with Westfield's Men. Nick here is our book holder.'

'Yes,' added Nicholas. 'This afternoon, we performed the tragedy of Julius Caesar and our manager, Lawrence Firethorn, in the role of the emperor, was called upon to do exactly what you did and feign the falling sickness.'

'We'll tell him about the soap to make him foam at the mouth. A clever touch.'

'It tastes foul,' said Hywel. 'The first time I tried it, I swallowed a piece.'

'It made him sick,' remembered Dorothea.

'There must be easier ways to earn a living.'

'There are, Hywel,' said Nicholas. 'You can do it by honest toil. Have you better clothing than these filthy rags?' Hywel nodded. 'Then we might be able to find you employment at the Queen's Head in Gracechurch Street. Our company performs there. We have a new landlord and he was looking to hire some more labour. If Dorothea was taken on as a kitchen wench, would you work as a serving man?'

Hywel was doubtful. 'I do not know.'

'It might be worth it,' said Dorothea. 'At least, we'd not go hungry.'

'Would you like me to speak to the landlord on your behalf?' asked Nicholas.

'Not yet,' said Hywel. 'Let us think it over. The Queen's Head, you say?'

'In Gracechurch Street. You'll always find us there.'

Elias reached into his purse. 'For a penny apiece, you can stand in the yard and watch us perform,' he said, pulling out some coins. 'Here's enough to buy you a good meal and take you to a wondrous play tomorrow afternoon.'

'Thank you, sir,' said Dorothea, grasping the money. 'You are very kind.'

'I hate to see a fellow Welshman having to beg.' He winked at her. 'And the same goes for his sister. I dare swear you are pretty enough to come from Wales.'

'*Diolch*,' said Hywel, squeezing his arm. '*Diolch yn fawr*.'

'*Cymru am byth*.'

Hywel gave his first smile and it lit up his face. '*Cymru am byth*.'

'What does that mean?' said Nicholas.

'What else?' returned Elias. 'Wales forever!'

Dorothea, too, now felt secure enough to smile, disappointed that Hywel's performance as a counterfeit crank had failed but sensing that they had made some good friends as a result. London had given them slim pickings since their arrival. On the previous night, they had slept beside the Thames and felt the cold wind of poverty. Thanks to their new acquaintances, she now had some money warming the palm of her hand. Hope began to flicker.

'We are not afraid of hard work, sirs,' she volunteered.

Hywel stuck out his jaw. 'We are not afraid of *anything*.'

'You know where to find us,' said Nicholas.

'Look for me when you come,' insisted Elias, 'and you shall have free drink.'

'And after that, you'll meet the landlord, Adam Crowmere.'

The young couple thanked them profusely, then stole away. In their tattered clothing, they were sorry figures. Dorothea was eager to look into the offer of possible employment at the Queen's Head but Hywel was obviously undecided. They were still discussing the subject when they vanished around the corner.

Elias sighed. 'Do you think we'll ever see them again, Nick?'

'I fear not. My guess is that your money will be spent within the hour.'

'Will not Hywel wish to see a fellow Welshman on the stage?'

'He's far more interested in eating food than watching plays,' said Nicholas. 'Besides, there's nothing that you can teach him, Owen.'

'What say you?'

'The fellow's such a fine actor himself.'

'Yes, that falling sickness of his took me in at first. It was every bit as persuasive as the bout that struck down Lawrence in *Caesar's Fall*. Indeed,' he added after reflection, 'in some ways, it was far better.'

'Are you going to say that to Lawrence?'

Elias laughed. 'I'd not dare, Nick. I value my life far too much!'

* * *

42

Margery Firethorn loved to watch her husband on the stage but domestic concerns kept her well away from the Queen's Head. As well as raising two lively children, she had to look after the company's apprentices and ensure that the ten people who slept under her roof were fed, clothed and cared for with maternal diligence. Even with the help of two servants, she had to work long and taxing hours at their home in Shoreditch. There were, however, compensations and they were not limited to the pleasures of seeing her sons enjoy a happy and healthy boyhood. While she knew her husband's defects all to well, she never ceased to love him nor did she forget how privileged she was to be married to the most celebrated actor in London. Whenever a new play achieved success, Margery was able to revel in her unique position.

Returning to the house in Old Street early that evening, Richard Honeydew, the most talented of the apprentices, had enthused about the performance and told Margery how well-received it had been. Modest by nature, he said little about his own role as Portia, wife to Julius Caesar, and instead praised the way that Firethorn had brought the Roman emperor back to life on the boards. Margery knew that the audience would not be the only beneficiaries. When her husband returned home that night, she was waiting in the bedchamber with a glass of Canary wine set out for him. Downing it in one gulp, he plucked at his doublet and gave a throaty chuckle.

'I have imperial longings, my love,' he said, eyes blazing with desire.

'Then take me like the conqueror you are.'

'You'll always be my most favoured prize.'

She held out her arms. 'And you are mine, great Caesar.'

Tearing off his clothes, he flung himself onto the bed and pleasured his wife until she moaned with ecstasy. Firethorn was at his most virile. Exhilarated by his triumph at the Queen's Head, and by the heady celebrations that followed, he was in the perfect mood to show his wife just how much he loved her. Margery responded with urgent sensuality. Neither of them minded that the rhythmical creaking of their bed could be heard by the apprentices in the room above, or, judging by the girlish giggles from next door, by the servants as well. At that moment, they were the only two people alive in the whole world and they could do whatever they pleased.

'You are an angel, Margery,' said Firethorn, rolling off her at last.

'A fallen angel, perhaps.'

'They are the best kind.' He kissed her on the lips. 'What a day we have had!'

'Dick Honeydew told me that you were beyond compare.'

'I always am.'

'Between these sheets, you are. I can vouch for that.'

He glared at her. 'With whom have you been comparing me?'

'With no man,' she said, pulling him to her, 'for it would be a waste of time. You are the king of your profession and a monarch of the bedchamber. I am doubly blessed.'

'Why, so am I,' he said, fondling her ample breasts in turn.

'They are always here for you,' she promised. 'When Dick told me how well you fared this afternoon, I knew that you'd not be late. Had the play failed badly, as some have done in the past, you'd not have come home at all.'

'I'd have been too ashamed to do so, Margery. My judgement would have been judged unsound, for it was I who chose the piece and took the leading part. But I had no fears with *Caesar's Fall*,' he confided. 'Nor did Nick Bracewell and he rarely makes a mistake about a new play. Michael Grammaticus is a true discovery.'

'With a mouth-filling name.'

'That mouth-filling name will fill the inn yard again. If *Caesar's Fall* is not revived, and soon, we'll all be deafened by the clamour. In the space of a couple of hours, I've made Michael Grammaticus famous throughout London.'

'What manner of man is he?'

'To tell the truth,' said Firethorn, 'not one that I could ever like. Michael is too cold, lifeless and scholarly. I doubt that he has any red blood in his veins at all. While the rest of us were toasting his play at the Queen's Head, he sat alone in a corner with his head in a Latin text. What kind of fellow is that?'

'Does he have no wife to share his success?'

'I doubt that he's ever touched female flesh.'

'He must have had a mother once.'

'No, my love. I think not. Michael Grammaticus was not born by any natural means. Some Cambridge professor opened

45

a tome in the library one day and Michael fell out full-grown.' He gave a lewd grin. 'Except for a certain part of his anatomy that grows not an inch beyond what he deems respectable. The fellow's a monk. A squinting, sour-faced, celibate monk.'

'How can such a man as you describe write such a moving tragedy?'

'How can Edmund Hoode, who had no schooling beyond the age of fifteen, give the world a string of plays that are touched with magic and awash with learning?' He hunched his naked shoulders. 'Who can fathom the mystery of the creative mind, Margery?' he asked. 'Not me, I know.'

'Is there any word of Edmund?' she wondered.

'Nick and Owen called on him earlier. They found him so tired that he could hardly keep his eyes open. Yet he's no longer in pain. That's one good sign.'

'I'll visit him myself, when I have the time.'

'Please do,' he said. 'I worry about him greatly. Edmund has never been robust yet he always manages to keep disease at bay somehow. I've never known him this unwell before.'

'When is he like to recover?'

'The doctor can give us no hope there, it seems. He is talking of a long rest.'

Margery was alarmed. 'How will you manage without Edmund Hoode?'

'I'm not sure that we will. There could be dark days ahead. All the more reason to make the most of present joys,' he decided, pulling her close to kiss her on the lips again. 'Come here, my fallen angel.'

She giggled. 'Your beard tickles me so.'

'Is that a complaint, my dove?'

'No, no,' she replied. 'I adore the feeling.'

'Then you shall have as much adoration as you wish.'

And with an upsurge of lust, he mounted her again and rode his wife with renewed energy until the bed threatened to collapse beneath the weight of their exertions.

They both slept soundly that night.

Adam Crowmere was as good as his word. On his first Sunday as landlord of the Queen's Head, he set aside a private room at the inn for Westfield's Men, and filled it with as much food, ale and wine as they could reasonably consume. The company's sharers were there and even the hired men were bidden to the feast. The one notable absentee was Edmund Hoode, who, though showing a slight improvement, was still too poorly to attend a public event. With great regret, he had declined the kind offer from his friends to carry him to the feast.

Unlike the companies who played at the two Shoreditch theatres, or at The Rose in Bankside, Lawrence Firethorn and his troupe were subject to city jurisdiction and thus unable to perform on the Sabbath. While their rivals drew large audiences to their plays, therefore, they were forced to lay idle and it always vexed them. This Sunday, it was quite different. Jollity was on display. From midday until mid-afternoon, they were the guests of Adam Crowmere and he did his best to make them feel at home.

'Eat and drink to your heart's content, my friends,' he said. 'You deserve it.'

'Are we like to have this every Sunday?' asked Owen Elias, hopefully.

Crowmere chortled. 'Not unless you wish to see me imprisoned for debt, Owen. No, this is my way of thanking you for all the pleasure you have given me, and for the money you've put into my coffers by attracting such thirsty customers to the Queen's Head. My first day here was a revelation. We had such a busy time after *Caesar's Fall* that I had to order fresh barrels from the brewery.'

'You'll need to order some more before we've finished this afternoon.'

'So be it,' said Crowmere, happily. 'I'll not stint my friends.'

He sauntered around the room to exchange remarks with each and every one of them. Nicholas Bracewell watched him, amazed at the way that he had learnt so many of their names in so short a time. Crowmere was a popular host, able to lapse into easy familiarity with his various guests while somehow retaining the authority of his position as landlord. What convinced Nicholas of the man's excellence was the effect he had had on his staff. Serving men, who had scurried about in fear of their master when Alexander Marwood was in charge, now moved with the brisk eagerness of people who were happy in their work. Adam Crowmere had created a joyous atmosphere at the Queen's Head.

'What do you play tomorrow, Lawrence?' he enquired of the actor-manager.

'*Love's Sacrifice*,' said Firethorn.

Crowmere grinned. 'We've all made *that* in our time.'

'And hope to do so again, Adam.'

'They say that desire fades with age.'

'I've not found it so. It seems to increase with each year that passes.'

'Then you are even more remarkable than I imagined,' said Crowmere, giving him a playful nudge. 'You can count on one spectator for *Love's Sacrifice*.'

Firethorn was astonished. 'But you've already seen three plays of ours.'

'I mean to see several more before I've done. What is the point of taking over the Queen's Head if I do not avail myself of its prime benefit? I'll turn spectator again and be seated in the gallery tomorrow.'

'We never got that death's head of a landlord to sit through a single play.'

'Alexander was blind to the delights of theatre.'

'Delight never entered his being,' said Firethorn with rancour. 'Nor that of the gorgon to whom he was married. How could two hideous creatures like them produce such a lovely daughter as Rose Marwood? It's unnatural.'

'It is surprising, I agree,' said Crowmere. 'Sybil is my cousin and I must love her for that, but she was never known for her good looks. Wedded bliss can put a bloom on the most ill-favoured woman. Alas, that is not the case with her. Marriage to Alexander has only served to harden my dear cousin.'

'The woman is pure flint from top till toe.'

'Make the most of her absence, Lawrence. One day, I fear, Sybil will return.'

'Is there no way that you could take over the inn?'

'Not unless they were willing to surrender it,' said Crowmere, wistfully, 'and that is unlikely to happen. When they return, I go back to Rochester. Meanwhile, however, I intend to make hay while the sun shines.'

'Then so shall we, Adam!'

Firethorn clapped him on the shoulder then reached for his wine. The landlord moved on to talk to Barnaby Gill, plying him with flattering remarks about his various performances. Gill basked in the praise. Nicholas was pleased when the landlord finally reached him and he stood up to speak to Crowmere.

'You have done us proud, Adam,' he observed.

'It was the least that I could do, Nick. Westfield's Men have graced this inn for too long without being given their due reward.' He looked around. 'It does me good to see you all in such good humour. The pity of it is that your esteemed patron could not be here to taste my pork and sip my wine.'

'Lord Westfield sends his apologies,' said Nicholas, 'but he is dining in the country with friends today. He hopes to trespass on your generosity another time.'

'Then so he shall.'

'We are truly in your debt, Adam. See how everyone is enjoying themselves.'

'All bar the spectre at the feast.'

'Who?'

'Our budding author, dressed in black.'

'Ah, yes,' said Nicholas, glancing across the room. 'In such a gathering as this, Michael is a fish out of water. He has my sympathy.'

Bent over the table, Michael Grammaticus was nibbling at a chicken leg without any real appetite. A tankard of ale remained untouched in front of him. While the rest of Westfield's Men were delighting in the convivial atmosphere, the playwright was finding it a positive trial. He was not helped by the fact that George Dart, the lowliest and least educated member of the company, was seated opposite him. Nobody in the room was more willing or more desperate to be liked than Dart, and he made several attempts to strike up a conversation with Grammaticus. They failed dismally. In his sober garb, the playwright chose to remain aloof and eat in grim silence.

'What's wrong with the fellow?' wondered Crowmere. 'If he did not relish the notion of a feast, why force himself to join us here?'

'Because he wishes to be one of us,' said Nicholas, thoughtfully. 'He'll never mix as easily with the players as you contrive to do, Adam, but that does not matter. In one sense, Michael may be suffering. That's plain for all to see. In another sense, I fancy, he may be taking a quiet satisfaction from the occasion.'

Crowmere gaped. 'Satisfaction! It's not the kind of satisfaction for which I yearn, Nick. Give me banter and merriment. Give me something that sets my blood on fire.'

'Michael has another source of pleasure. I think. But let us leave him to his own devices,' he went on, recalling his encounter with the two beggars. 'There's something I've been meaning to raise with you. You spoke of needing fresh hands to help you here.'

'Why, yes. If trade increases the way that I hope, serving men, cooks and kitchen wenches will be in demand. Aye,' he continued, 'and a chambermaid or two as well. I mean to offer more rooms to weary travellers. Why do you ask?'

'I may be able to guide two people in your direction.'

'Men or women?'

'One of each, both sound in wind and limb.'

'Seasoned in the work of a busy inn?'

'I'll not claim that,' said Nicholas, 'but they are quick to learn and ready to work every hour of the day. Might there be a place for them here, do you think?'

'If they come on your recommendation, there's every chance.'

'With luck, they may soon cross your threshold.'

'What are their names?'

'Hywel Rees and Dorothea Tate. Young, fit and able.'

'Where are they now?'

Nicholas was honest. 'Now, that is one thing that I'm unable to tell you.'

They eventually found a place not far from St Paul's. Those who streamed out of the cathedral precincts on that side had to pass the spot. Hywel Rees bided his time until he saw three men approaching in clerical attire. If he could not find compassion in the Church, he decided, he would find it nowhere. When the trio was almost upon him, Hywel let out a cry and hurled himself to the ground before twitching convulsively. It was a piteous sight. Dorothea knelt to hold him in her arms and looked up with desperation in her gaze. She did not even need to speak. Most of the people in the small crowd that formed around them tried to assuage their consciences by offering charity. Coins fell quickly in Dorothea's hands.

After thanking their benefactors, she helped Hywel to his feet and supported him as they moved to the shelter of an alleyway. Once out of sight, they embraced happily. In a matter of minutes, they had made enough money to last them for days.

'I'll be a true counterfeit crank yet,' boasted Hywel.

Dorothea smiled. 'Do not forget my part in the deceit.'

'Without you, I'd be lost. Together, we can do anything.'

'That Welshman helped us,' she reminded him. 'Owen Elias told us that we had to pick the right place. We could not have chosen more wisely.'

'Yes, you could!' snarled a voice behind them. 'Give me that money.'

They turned to see a burly man, standing over them with a cudgel in his hand. Like Hywel, he was dressed in rags that were sodden with mud and spattered with blood.

'I work here,' warned the man. 'Hand over what you stole from me.'

Hywel squared up to him. 'We stole nothing,' he said, defiantly.

The blow from the cudgel was so quick and hard that he had no time to avoid it. Catching him on the temple, it sent Hywel to the ground with blood oozing from the wound. He was too dazed even to speak. Letting out a cry, Dorothea knelt to help her wounded friend, but the man had no respect for the fairer sex. It took only a sharp flick with the cudgel to knock her out. As her hand opened, the coins were scattered on the ground. Their attacker collected them in a flash before he fled down the alleyway.

Chapter Three

Breakfast was always eaten early at Anne Hendrik's house in Bankside. Ever since the death of her Dutch husband, Anne, an attractive Englishwoman who had kept her good looks into her thirties, had taken over the running of his business in the adjoining property. Though she knew little about the making of hats when she first married, she turned out to have a natural talent for design and, when she was put in charge of the enterprise, Anne revealed herself as a person with administrative skills as well. Like many immigrants from abroad – so often reviled as 'strangers' – her husband had been refused admittance to the appropriate guild and was therefore compelled to work outside the city boundaries. Thanks to his application, the business slowly developed. Under the care of his widow, it had really prospered.

As she sat down for breakfast that morning, she glanced through the window.

'We are blessed with another fine day, Nick,' she said.

'Except for some rain later this morning.'

'But there's not a cloud to be seen.'

'There will be,' promised Nicholas. 'Mark my words. We'll have a light shower towards noon, then it will be sunshine for the rest of the day.'

Anne did not dispute his prediction. Ever since he had come to lodge with her, she, like Westfield's Men, had benefited from his ability to read the skies. It was only one of the talents that made him such a remarkable and wholly reliable man. Having rented out a room because she felt the need for companionship, Anne had been slowly drawn to Nicholas Bracewell and she soon discovered that the affection was mutual. By the time it had matured into love, they were sharing more than breakfast.

'What do you play this afternoon, Nick?' she asked.

'*Caesar's Fall*.'

'So soon?'

'The public demands it, Anne.'

'That must be music to your ears.'

'It is,' said Nicholas. 'There's always an element of danger when we stage a new play, for so many things can go awry. In this case – thank heaven – they did not.'

'Except that you lost poor Edmund,' she noted.

'That was not the fault of the play or the playwright.'

'No, but it must have hindered you.'

'Oh, it did. We had to make hurried changes at the eleventh hour.'

'Are you still worried about Edmund?'

'Very much so,' he confessed, reaching for some bread. 'It's almost a week now and he is still not back on his feet. Edmund tells me that he feels better, but there are no clear signs of it. His landlady says that he sleeps half the day. That alarms me, Anne.'

'Have you spoken with the doctor?'

'I expect to do so today. Doctor Zander is due to call on him again.'

Anne sipped her cup of whey. 'I can see why you fret so,' she said. 'Edmund is more than a fine playwright and a good actor. He's your dear friend.'

'I love him like a brother, Anne. To see him in this woeful condition stabs me in the heart. His illness could not have come at a worse time,' he said, soulfully. 'We have a large stock of plays – many by Edmund Hoode – but novelty is always in request or our work grows stale. It's the reason that Edmund has laboured so hard on his latest comedy. It was promised to us by the end of the month.'

'Is there no chance that he may complete it in time?'

'None at all. He can barely raise his head, leave alone lift a pen to write a play. That's the worst of it, Anne,' he went on, eyes filled with disquiet. 'Edmund tells me that he can no longer think straight. His brain is addled. Do you see what that portends?'

She gave a nod. 'It could be a disease of the mind.'

'And we may have lost that wonderful imagination forever.'

'That's a frightening notion. Who could replace a man like Edmund Hoode?'

'No such person exists, Anne.'

An idea struck her. 'I have a customer who dwells not far from his lodging,' she said. 'Preben has all but finished work on the lady's hat. When we deliver it to her, I could call in to see Edmund. Do you think that he would welcome a visitor?'

'As many as he can get,' said Nicholas, 'so that he knows how much we care for him. Owen and I have been there every day. Lawrence, too, has been regular in his visits and Margery has promised to go as well.'

'What of Barnaby?'

'He sends his best wishes but refuses to enter the house himself.'

'Why? Does he fear infection?'

'There's no danger of that or we'd all be struck down. No, Anne, he says that he hates to look on sickness for it distresses him so.' Nicholas swallowed another piece of bread and washed it down with a sip of his drink. 'Barnaby Gill is too selfish a man to spare much thought for others.'

'Does he not remember all the roles that Edmund has created for him?'

'He sees them as no more than so many new suits, commissioned from his tailor. Barnaby is such a slave to outward show,' said Nicholas. 'Yet he'll miss Edmund as much as any of us, if indeed we've seen the last of him.'

Anne was disturbed. 'You make him sound as if he's close to death.'

'As a playwright, I fear, he may well be. This malady has crippled him in every way. If his mind is crumbling, then his art has truly expired.'

Chastened by the grim thought, they finished their breakfast in silence.

After a farewell kiss, Nicholas soon set out on the long walk to the Queen's Head. There was much to occupy his mind but he did not let himself become distracted. Even in daylight, Bankside was a hazardous place, its narrow streets and twisting lanes haunted by pickpockets, drunkards, beggars, discharged soldiers and masterless men. Nicholas's sturdy frame and brisk movement deterred most people from even considering an attack but he had been accosted by thieves on more than one occasion. All of them had been repelled. When he heard heavy footsteps behind him, therefore, he was instinctively on guard. Someone was making an effort to catch him up. Sensing trouble, Nicholas went around a corner and stopped, hand on his dagger in case an assailant came into view.

His caution was unnecessary. The person who followed him around the corner was, in fact, a friend and colleague. Nathan Curtis, the troupe's carpenter, was striding along with his bag of tools slung from his shoulder. He grinned at Nicholas.

'I thought I'd never catch you,' he said, panting slightly. 'You walk so fast.'

'How long have you been on my trail?'

'Since you first set out.'

'But you had no need to come that way.'

'Yes, I did,' said Curtis. 'Walk on and I'll explain.'

Nicholas was surprised. Curtis lived in a tenement, several streets away. His route to London Bridge should not have taken him anywhere near Anne Hendrik's house. The carpenter was a big man with the wide shoulders and thick forearms of his trade. Strong, industrious and dependable, he was a true craftsman who made the scenery and the properties for all of the company's plays. Nathan Curtis was constantly employed to build new items of furniture or to repair old ones. He enjoyed an easy friendship with the book holder and the two men had often travelled back together to Bankside at night, either by foot or, from time to time, by boat across the Thames.

Distance seemed to shrink miraculously when they talked on their journeys and, as a rule, Curtis had much to say for himself. Today, however, he was unusually reticent. They had gone a hundred yards before he ventured his first remark.

'What work do you have for me today, Nick?' he asked.

'Repairs are needed to the throne for *The Corrupt Bargain*. When he carried it from the stage yesterday, George tripped and threw it to the ground. Two legs snapped off. There's more besides, Nathan. It will be a busy morning for you.'

'George Dart will always keep me in work. The lad is so clumsy.'

'Only when he is shouted at,' said Nicholas. 'Left to himself, he'd break nothing at all.' He glanced at his companion. 'But you did not lie in wait for me in order to berate George Dart. What brought you out of your way like this?'

Curtis licked his dry lips. 'I've a favour to ask.'

'Could it not have waited until I saw you at the Queen's Head?'

'That's too public a place, Nick. I sought a word in private.'

'As many as you wish.'

The carpenter obviously felt embarrassed. It was another hundred yards before he finally broached the subject. Having found the right words, he gabbled them.

'I-need-to-borrow-some-money-Nick-please-say-that-you'll-help-me.'

'Slow down, slow down,' counselled Nicholas. 'What's this about a loan?'

'I must have money.'

'Everyone will be paid at the end of the week.'

'I cannot wait until then,' said Curtis with an edge of desperation. 'I need the money now. Believe me, Nick, I'd not ask, except under compulsion.'

'Compulsion?'

'I've debts to settle.'

'We all have those, Nathan.'

'Mine are most pressing.'

Nicholas was the victim of his own competence. Because he discharged his duties as the book holder so well, he was always being given additional responsibilities by Lawrence Firethorn. One of them was to act as the company's paymaster, to keep an account book that related to the wages of the hired men. If an actor was engaged by Westfield's Men for the first time, Nicholas was even empowered to negotiate his rate of pay. The largest amounts went to the sharers, who were given an appropriate slice of the company's profits, but the hired men, including actors, musicians, stagekeepers, tiremen, gatherers, who took entrance money for performances, and people like Nathan Curtis, had a fixed weekly wage. With a family to support, the carpenter had always been careful with his money before. It was the only time he had ever asked for a loan and he was very upset at having to do so. Nicholas was sympathetic.

'Do you have troubles at home, Nathan?' he asked.

'I will have, if you spurn my request.'

'Why should I do that?'

'Master Firethorn would never lend a penny in advance. When others tried to borrow from him in the past, they were sent away with a curse or two. And I know that it's your strict rule to pay wages at the end of the week.'

'Except in particular circumstances.'

Curtis was rueful. 'These are very particular.'

'May I know what they are?' The carpenter hung his head. 'If it's a personal matter, I'll not pry. And I'll tell you this, Nathan. If most people came to me with the same plea, I'd turn them down at once because I know that they'd drink the money away that same night. You, however, can be trusted.'

'Thank you, Nick. How much will you let me have?'

'Three shillings. Will that suffice?'

'I was hoping for more,' said Curtis.

'Then you'll have the full amount. Does that relieve your mind?'

'Mightily.'

'It's heartening to know that I've done one good deed this day,' said Nicholas, happily. 'I'll pay you when we reach Gracechurch Street, then you can settle your debts.'

'God bless you, Nick! I knew that I could count on you for help.'

'Do not make a habit of this,' warned the other.

'I'd never do that,' vowed Curtis. 'I've learnt my lesson, I promise you.'

Propped up in bed at his lodging, Edmund Hoode spent most of the day vainly trying to remember favourite speeches from his plays. It was a pointless exercise. His mind was so befuddled that he could not even recall the names of the plays themselves. His landlady, a considerate woman with a real affection for her lodger, brought him food and drink, yet when her buxom daughter bathed his face tenderly with cold water, Hoode could not feel even the faintest stirrings of lust. That mortified him. His mind and body seemed to have surrendered the power to react. Sleep was his only escape.

It was late afternoon when the doctor eventually called. Emmanuel Zander was a short, round, fussy man in his forties with a black beard that reached to his chest and eyebrows so thick that he had to look at the world through curling strands of hair. When he opened his satchel, he revealed a collection of surgical instruments that made Hoode gurgle with fright but the doctor only extracted a tiny bottle of medicine. He spoke with a guttural accent.

'I've brought something new,' he said, putting the bottle on the table.

'Will it cure me?' asked Hoode.

'It may or it may not. That remains to be seen, Master Hoode. What I do know is that it will not make your condition any worse.' He bent over the patient to scrutinise his face. 'How do you feel this morning?'

'Much the same, Doctor Zander.'

'Have you recovered your appetite?'

'Not yet.'

'What of your memory?'

'Far too uncertain. That worries me most, doctor.'

'It worries me as well,' confessed Zander, clicking his tongue. 'In all my years in medicine, I've not seen a condition like this. You've lost weight and remain in a state of fatigue. Have you suffered any pain?'

'None at all,' said Hoode. 'There are times when I feel quite numb.'

Zander scratched his head. 'Why should that be?'

He pulled back the sheets to examine Hoode in more detail, feeling his body and limbs for any sign of swelling before producing an instrument from his satchel to listen to the patient's heart. When he had finished, he put the instrument away.

'I'll need another sample of your water.'

'You'll find it in a jar under that cloth,' said Hoode, pointing to the table. 'It was darker than ever this morning. Is that good or bad?'

'It's disappointing.'

They heard a knock on the front door below. The landlady opened it to admit someone and there was a brief conversation. Feet then ascended the stairs. There was a tap on Hoode's door and it swung back for Nicholas Bracewell to step into the room. Tears welled up in Hoode's eyes at the sight of his friend.

'Nick, dear heart!' he cried. 'It's so good to see you again.'

'I'm glad that I came in time to meet Doctor Zander.'

Nicholas introduced himself and shook hands with the doctor.

'How does he fare?'

'Not well, not well,' said Zander, peering at Hoode with a frown. 'If I knew the exact nature of his malady, I could treat it accordingly but I've not seen a case like this before. I've been through every book that I possess, but none describe a disease such as the one we have before us.'

'How, then, can he be cured?'

'By trial and error.' He indicated the potion on the table. 'He is to have two drops of that, three times a day. If nothing else, it will stop the spread of the infection.'

'It's already spread too far,' wailed Hoode.

'Be brave, be patient. We'll find the remedy in due course.'

'How much longer must I suffer, Doctor Zander?'

The doctor clasped his hands across his stomach. 'We've

conquered the pain,' he said, defensively. 'Do not forget that. And we've brought some colour back to your cheeks. That, too, is encouraging. Rest is still your best medicine, Master Hoode.' He closed his satchel, collected the jar from the table and made to leave. 'I'll come again in two days.' He gave Nicholas a glance. 'Do not stay too long, sir. Company tires him.'

Nicholas opened the door then closed it behind him. He crossed to sit beside the bed so that he could hold his friend's hand. There was no strength in Hoode's grip. The playwright managed a pale smile.

'Thank you for coming, Nick,' he said. 'The very sight of you revives me.'

'How do you feel, Edmund?'

'As if I'm beyond feeling. It's strange and worrying. I'm in another world.'

'Come back to ours, for we miss you dreadfully.'

'I'm no use to you like this, Nick. My mind is a ball of wool. No sooner do I try to think than it unravels.' He looked balefully around the room. 'I've lost count of the number of plays written in here for Westfield's Men. I've penned hundreds of scenes and thousands of lines. Yet I struggle to recall a single speech. All those wondrous words have gone as if they were never there. I shake with terror. What's happening to me, Nick?' he implored, grabbing his friend with both hands. 'Has my brain grown dull? Am I to end my days as a gibbering idiot in Bedlam?'

'No, Edmund,' said Nicholas, firmly. 'Put away that thought.'

'I fear that I may wake up one day and not know who I am.'

'*We* know who you are, and we'll not rest until you're restored to us in rude health. The truth may be that *we* are to blame,' suggested Nicholas. 'The company asks you to carry too burdensome a load and you've cracked under the weight. As well as writing new plays for us, you keep old ones, by other hands, in a goodly state of repair. Yet you still manage to tread the boards as often as anyone else.'

'The theatre is my home,' said Hoode, simply. 'At least, it was until now.'

'It shall be so again.'

'Tell me what you played this afternoon. Rekindle my spirit, Nick.'

'I'll try.'

Nicholas told him about the second successful performance of *Caesar's Fall* and made him laugh at some of the antics that took place behind the scenes. Hoode began to show some animation at last. He was even able to quote a few lines that he had learnt as Casca in the play. It brought a cry of joy to his lips. Nicholas crossed to the table to pick up the bottle left by Doctor Zander. Uncorking it, he sniffed the contents. A sweet odour invaded his nostrils. He corked the bottle and put it back.

'The doctor will not treat you out of charity, Edmund,' he said. 'Let me know how much we owe him and I'll gladly pay the amount. I'll not have you worrying about such things as that.'

'But I've no need to worry. Doctor Zander's services are frcc.'

'Free?'

'They come at no cost to me,' explained Hoode. 'That was made clear at the start of my illness. The doctor told me that my bills would be paid by a friend of mine, who insists on bearing all the expenses.'

Nicholas was puzzled. 'A friend of yours? Who can that be?'

'The author of *Caesar's Fall* – one Michael Grammaticus.'

The cottage in Cornhill had stood for over a hundred and fifty years, long enough for the beams to settle and to distort the original shape of the half-timbered structure. Light was partially restricted to the upper rooms because the thatched roof overhung the windows, and the problem was compounded by the property on the opposite side of the street. Built and owned by a wealthy merchant, it rose to four storeys and left the thatched cottage in permanent shadow. Michael Grammaticus had particular cause to complain. Since the room in which he lodged was at the front of the cottage, it enjoyed very little natural light. Even on a fine summer's evening, therefore, he was obliged to work with the aid of a candle. It made him squint more than ever.

Grammaticus was slow and methodical. Dipping his quill in the ink, he wrote with great care and with frequent pauses for meditation. Every line of the Epilogue was subjected to scrutiny and revision. It would be the last memory of the play that an audience would carry away with them and he wished it to have a lasting impact. Since it was in the form of a sonnet, each word had to earn its keep and dovetail neatly with its fellows. Grammaticus was tired and his eyes were burning slightly but he pressed on. Buoyed up by the second performance of *Caesar's Fall* that afternoon, he longed to hear the ringing cheers of acclaim once more. London had accepted him as a playwright of rare promise. His position now had to be confirmed.

Hunched over the table in the window, he cudgelled his brain for a telling rhyme.

As he turned into the yard of the Queen's Head, the first person that Nicholas Bracewell saw was a giant of a man, who was wheeling an empty barrel along before standing it beside two others. Wiping his hands on his leather apron, he was about to go back into the building when he noticed the book holder. A broad grin ignited his face.

'Nick!' he said. 'I wondered where you had gone after the play.'

'I promised to call on Edmund,' explained Nicholas.

'How is he?'

'Much the same, alas. I saw no change on him, Leonard.'

'Be sure to give him my best wishes when you see him next. Edmund Hoode has always been kind to me. I look upon him as a friend.'

Leonard was a shambling man with slow speech and limited intelligence but Nicholas was very fond of him. They had met by chance in the Counter, one of the city's most notorious jails, where the book holder had been wrongly imprisoned for a short time. Fortunate to be absolved of his own crime, Leonard was unable to resume his former occupation as a brewer's drayman. It was Nicholas who found him work at the Queen's Head and the latter was eternally grateful to him, even though he was at the mercy of Alexander Marwood's strictures.

'Do you miss your old landlord, Leonard?' asked Nicholas.

'Yes, Nick. As a dray horse misses the whip.'

'You have a kinder master now, I think.'

'It's a joy to work for such a man,' said Leonard, folding his arms. 'He treats us with respect and knows how to get the best out of us. Everyone will tell you the same. Adam Crowmere is a saint. I've not met a better landlord, and I met dozens when I was working for the brewery. He's even talked of putting up our wages.'

'He recognises your true worth.'

'It's wonderful, Nick. We'll make the most of it while we can, for it will all change when he leaves. Summer will be over then,' he sighed, 'and the cold winter will return in the shape of our landlord and his wife.'

'They left the Queen's Head in excellent hands.'

Leonard nodded sadly. 'There'll be tears when he goes back to Rochester.'

Nicholas was glad to have his own impression confirmed. Adam Crowmere had not merely made the inn more congenial to those who visited it. He put new spirit into those employed there so that even someone like Leonard, who did menial chores, felt the benefit of his arrival. The Queen's Head was a different place under Crowmere.

'It grieves me that Edmund is not here to witness the transformation,' said Nicholas. 'He was struck down at the very moment when your landlord took his leave.'

'We are all praying that our master is away for a very long time.'

'Westfield's Men will join you in those prayers.'

He waved farewell to Leonard and headed for the taproom. The place was full and the atmosphere boisterous, but Nicholas was surprised to see that a number of people were missing. There was no sign of Owen Elias or Frank Quilter, and some of the hired men who invariably congregated there of an evening had somehow vanished as well, Nathan Curtis among them. Given the improvements under the new landlord, it seemed strange that so many of Westfield's Men had chosen to leave. Nicholas crossed to a table where Lawrence Firethorn and Barnaby Gill were sitting.

'Well, Nick,' said Firethorn. 'How is he?'

'As weary as before,' replied Nicholas, taking the empty chair. 'Edmund has no fever, no pain and no evident sickness. Yet he is so listless that he needs help to walk across the room. Doctor Zander is perplexed beyond measure.'

'So are we,' said Gill, gloomily. 'A new comedy was promised to us.'

'Yes,' said Firethorn, ruffling his beard. 'That's our other concern. Edmund was contracted to deliver it within ten days.'

'Then you must release him from the contract,' advised Nicholas. 'There is no way that he'll be able to fulfil its terms. Edmund is not even able to *read* a play, let alone write one. You'll have to wait.'

Gill was tetchy. 'I cannot bear to wait,' he said, 'nor can my host of admirers. They have not seen me in a new comedy for months. Instead of creating fresh wonders to dazzle them, I am forced to rescue dark tragedies like *Caesar's Fall* from the boredom into which they would otherwise sink.'

'There's nothing boring about my Julius Caesar,' boomed Firethorn, striking his barrel chest with a palm. 'Distraction only sets in when the soothsayer is onstage.'

'Yes, Lawrence. I distract the audience from the misery, carnage and tedium that you inflict upon them. Tragedy needs the saving grace of a clown.'

'Then it's a pity we do not have one worthy of the title.'

Gill was outraged. 'That's unforgivable!'

'And quite unjust,' said Nicholas, bringing the exchange to an end before the insults really began to flow. 'Everyone knows that in Barnaby we have the finest clown in London. Since we also have the greatest actor, the company will always outshine its rivals. Together – and only together – you help to make us what we are.'

'Only if I am given the opportunity to shine in a comedy,' said Gill.

Firethorn flicked a hand. 'Comedy, tragedy or history,' he said, airily. 'Give me any of them you wish and I'll turn it to gold with my Midas touch.'

'Midas touch! Your touch is like a leper's handshake.'

'You are the one whose performances are always diseased, Barnaby.'

'Need we bicker so?' asked Nicholas, looking from one to the other. 'We'll not solve our problem by calling each other names. Edmund must be allowed to rest. If we want a new play, we must look elsewhere.'

'Only Edmund can show me at my best,' said Gill, haughtily. 'Is there not someone else we can employ to finish the piece while the author languishes in bed? Lucius Kindell, perhaps?'

Firethorn shook his head. 'He'd not be equal to the task.'

'He and Edmund have worked together before.'

'Lucius has his strengths,' argued Nicholas, 'and he will grow as a dramatist, but he's no counterfeit Edmund Hoode. Ask him to finish the play and you'd see a glaring join between what each of them wrote. It could not be concealed. And there is the question of Edmund's pride. He might not wish another hand to meddle with his play.'

'Yet we must offer some novelty for our audience,' said Firethorn. 'Look how well they respond to *Caesar's Fall*. It allows us to display our skills in new ways. And there is nothing to match the challenge of performing a work for the first time. It keeps us on our toes.'

'As a dancer,' boasted Gill, 'I am always on my toes.'

'Your fault, dear Barnaby, is that you keep treading on everyone else's.'

'There is one hope,' said Nicholas, rubbing his chin. 'Michael Grammaticus may be able to furnish us with what we need. He told me that he was working on something clsc, though I've no idea how far he has advanced, or if the piece would be suitable.'

Gill was dismissive. 'It would be another tragedy. You only have to look at the fellow to know that he has no humour in his soul. Michael is too saturnine. He inhabits the murky underworld of drama, creating tragic heroes with besetting faults that lead to their destruction.'

'That may be so,' said Firethorn, 'but his tale of Ancient Rome had spectators queuing halfway down Gracechurch Street this afternoon. Speak to him, Nick. I'd be interested to read anything that comes from his fertile brain.' He pulled a face. 'I just wish that I could bring myself to like Michael a little more.'

'He has many good qualities,' said Nicholas, 'and is generous to a fault. Did you know that he's been paying Doctor Zander's bills?'

Firethorn was taken aback. 'Why should he do that?'

'Because he worships Edmund and draws his inspiration from him. He also feels guilty that it was during the rehearsal of *Caesar's Fall* that Edmund suffered his own collapse. It seems that Michael insisted on paying for any treatment needed.'

'That could be costly if the illness drags on.'

'It makes no difference to Michael,' said Nicholas. 'He told Edmund that nothing was more important to him than finding a cure for this mysterious ailment.'

'I begin to admire this Michael Grammaticus, after all,' said Firethorn.

Gill was more critical. 'He's too arid a companion for me.'

'He'll be relieved to hear that, Barnaby. He's shown no interest in women but, by the same token, he'd not wish to become one of your pretty boys either. I think the fellow's taken a vow of chastity.'

'What's this about chastity?' asked the landlord, cheerfully, coming to stand beside their table. 'If you seek it here, my friends, you are in the wrong place. Chastity's the one thing that's not on our bill of fare. Some have lost it here,' he added with a chortle, 'but none, I dare swear, have ever managed to find it.'

Firethorn laughed. 'I cannot even remember what chastity is, Adam.'

'You were born a rampant satyr,' taunted Gill.

'It's the secret of a happy life.'

'Happiness comes from having an occupation that you love,' said Adam Crowmere, complacently. 'The stage is your kingdom, Lawrence, and I hold court here. As you see,' he went on, using an arm to take in the whole room, 'my happiness consists in spreading happiness. Listen to that laughter and merriment.'

'We had precious little of that under our last landlord. What news of him?'

'A letter came from Dunstable today. Alexander complains that his brother's hanging on to life by his fingernails, but will not have the grace to go. It may be weeks before he's ready for his coffin.'

'If only they would bury that rogue, Marwood, alongside him.'

75

'He'll not know the Queen's Head when he returns,' said Crowmere. 'We've more trade and livelier company in here. Oh, and that reminds me, Nick,' he added, turning to the book holder. 'You spoke of two friends in need of work. If they care to come here tomorrow, I've places for them now.'

'You may need to fill them with someone else,' said Nicholas, accepting the truth of the situation. 'I fancy that Hywel and Dorothea changed their minds about coming here. They must have found employment elsewhere.'

London was not the ready source of money that they had imagined. Until they arrived in the capital, Hywel Rees and Dorothea Tate had not realised how many beggars were already there. They were competing with a whole army of vagrants, wounded soldiers, disabled children, vagabonds, tricksters and rogues, many of whom had staked out their territory and who were prepared to defend it with brutal force. The newcomers had been repeatedly beaten, cursed, chased, harried and, in one street, had even suffered the indignity of having the contents of a chamber pot emptied over them from an upper window. It left them in low spirits.

'We should have gone to that inn they told us of,' argued Dorothea.

'No,' said Hywel.

'Any work is better than this.'

'Who would employ us, Dorothea? We have neither passport nor licence. We are strangers in the city, with no fixed abode. What innkeeper would look at us?'

'The one at the Queen's Head might do so. Those friends

offered to speak up for us and I judge them to be as good as their word. That Welshmen liked you, I could see. What was his name?'

'Owen Elias.'

'Let's seek him out and ask for his help.'

'We'll manage on our own,' he said, stubbornly. 'We are still learning the trade.'

She was sorrowful. 'Must we spend the rest of our lives like this?'

'We have each other, Dorothea. I'd endure anything to be with you.'

'And I with you,' she said, brightening. 'I never knew such love until we met.'

Hywel took her in his arms and hugged her. After giving her a kiss, he released her so that he could get himself ready. They were standing in a quiet lane where nobody bothered them except an occasional scavenging dog. Before they began the day's begging, Hywel required her assistance. When he tucked one leg up behind his buttocks, Dorothea used a piece of rope to tie it into position, pulling his tattered clothing over the leg so that it was concealed. Hywel reached for the crutch that he had fashioned out of a piece of driftwood rescued from the Thames. Dorothea, meanwhile, tied a bloodstained bandage around her head then tucked one arm inside her dress so that it looked as if she had also lost the limb. They were a sorry sight. Composing their features into expressions of great suffering, they went off to take up their position.

The Raven was a small tavern in Eastcheap and it had

proved a wise choice on their previous visit. Customers going into the place hardly noticed the two beggars who lurked outside because such people were all too familiar on the streets of London. When they had been drinking, however, some customers became more benevolent, and, as they tumbled out of the tavern in a joyful mood, spared a few coins for the sad-faced girl with one arm and the young man forced to hop through life on a single leg.

While Dorothea collected the money, Hywel always raised his cap in gratitude. If anyone hesitated to give them alms, she told them that her brother had lost his leg while fighting abroad for his country. An appeal to patriotic spirit seemed to loosen the strings on a purse. In the first hour, they had garnered almost a shilling and felt that their luck had changed at last. Hywel was more watchful now. After violent encounters with other beggars, he made sure that he kept an eye out for any rivals who might resent their presence outside the Raven. Fortunately, none appeared.

'Dorothea,' he said at length. 'I need to rest.'

'Is the leg hurting you?'

'It does not like being strapped up like this.'

'Let me help you,' she offered.

With the crutch under one arm, he put a hand on her shoulder and limped back to their refuge. As soon as they left the main thoroughfare, Dorothea undid the rope so that he could lower the leg that had been tied out of sight. Cramp had set in and he was wincing with pain. He rubbed his leg with both hands.

'I hate to see you suffer so,' she said.

'It was in a good cause, Dorothea. How much did we get?'

'I'll need two hands to count it.'

While she struggled to pull out the arm that was hidden beneath her dress, two figures came around the corner with purposeful strides. Hywel saw the constables first and he yelled a warning but, when he tried to run, his weakened leg would not hold him and he fell to the ground. Dorothea bent to help him up but a pair of firm hands pulled her away. The other constable seized Hywel and hauled him to his feet.

'Ah!' he said with heavy sarcasm. 'You've grown another leg since you left the Raven, have you? And the little lady now has a second arm. Out of kindness, God has seen fit to restore your missing limbs. It means that there's more of you to arrest.'

Chapter Four

The first sign of trouble came the following morning. When the rehearsal was over in the yard of the Queen's Head, and the company was beginning to disperse, Hugh Wegges seized the opportunity for a minute alone with the book holder. Nicholas Bracewell had just finished giving some instructions to George Dart about the position of the stage properties in the opening scene of the play. When he saw his friend approaching, he assumed that it was to discuss some aspect of the costumes. Hugh Wegges was the tireman, the person responsible for making, altering, repairing and looking after the large stock of costumes used by Westfield's Men.

'A word in your ear, Nick,' said Wegges.

'I think I know what it will be, Hugh.'

'I doubt that.'

'You wish me to speak sharply to Barnaby Gill,' said

Nicholas. 'He has torn three different costumes during this morning's rehearsal and needs to take more care when he cavorts around the stage.'

'I told him that myself. If he tears anything else, then he can repair it. No,' said Wegges, glancing round to make sure that they were not overheard. 'I wanted to talk about something else.'

'Speak on.'

'In brief, Nick, I'm sorely pressed for money.'

Nicholas smiled. 'That's a common complaint.'

'My need is greater than most,' insisted Wegges, 'or I'd not trouble you. To get to the heart of the matter, I must ask for my wages before they are due.'

'But you've only a few days to wait before you are paid, Hugh.'

'One day more would be too long.'

'Is the situation so dire?'

'I fear so.'

Nicholas was surprised. Wegges had a wife and four children to support and, as a consequence, worked hard and spent little on himself. A dyer by trade, he used his skills to good effect as the tireman, giving dull, old, faded cloth new colour and life. He also used needle and thread expertly and took great pride in the high standard of his work. To help the family's finances, his wife took in washing and, Nicholas knew, she sometimes helped to repair and clean the troupe's costumes without charge. Wegges was a short, solid, ginger-haired man in his late thirties with a tendency to grumble, but he was dedicated to Westfield's Men and bereft when they went on tour and left him in London.

What puzzled Nicholas was that the tireman was the second person in two days who had asked for his wages in advance. Like Nathan Curtis before him, Wegges was in a predicament of some sort. It was too much of a coincidence.

'May I know the reason for this favour?' asked Nicholas.

'I'd prefer that you did not.'

'That only makes me more curious, Hugh. Yours is not the only request of this kind. Someone else petitioned me for his wages and, like you, he has never done so before. It makes me think there may be a connection between the two of you.'

'That may be so, Nick. All I know is that I need the money.'

'Why?'

'To put food on the table for my wife and children.'

'That's an honourable enough reason, but I still wish to know what lies behind it.'

Wegges shifted his feet. 'I did something unwise. It will not happen again.'

'You lost money? Is that what you are telling me?'

'Yes, Nick.'

'When others in the company do that, it always means they have been roistering in a bawdy house or had their purses taken by a subtle hand. I do not believe that Hugh Wegges would be guilty of either folly.'

'No,' affirmed Wegges. 'I love my wife too much to need the one and guard my purse too carefully to fall victim to the other. My folly was of another kind.'

'Tell me what it is and it will go no further than here.'

'It already has, Nick. Others were there when it happened.'

'Members of the company?'

'Owen Elias, for one. And Frank Quilter. They witnessed my misfortune.'

'Misfortune?'

'That's what it was, alas. The first time I went there, I won handsomely and that encouraged me to go back, only to lose all that I had gained and more besides.'

Nicholas understood. 'So you have been gambling. Dice or cards?'

'Cards. I had such a run of luck.'

'It always ends, Hugh. Where did the game take place?'

'Why, here at the Queen's Head.'

'But our landlord hates gambling. He says that it attracts the wrong custom. In any case, he does not have a licence to turn this inn into a gaming house. Nor would he ever seek one from the Groom-Porter's office.'

'It may have been so with our old landlord,' said Wegges, 'but our new one is more tolerant. He's rented a room to one Philomen Lavery, who sits behind a table and plays cards all night. I am not the only one to lose to him.'

'No,' said Nicholas, thinking of Nathan Curtis, 'and my worry is that you'll not be the last. How many more will come in search of their wages ahead of time? I'll not hand out money so that it can be thrown away at the card table again.'

'I swear that I'll not go near the fellow again, Nick.'

'How do I know that?'

Wegges put a hand to his chest. 'I give you my word of honour.'

'Then I'll hold you to it. Think of your family.'

'I did,' said Wegges. 'I sought to improve their lot by winning some money.'

'We are all prey to such temptation, Hugh, but it must be resisted. Did it not occur to you that, if this Philomen Lavery plays cards every night, he might be a more skilful practitioner than you? Such men make their living by deceiving gulls.'

Wegges was dejected. 'I own that I'm one of them. The more I lost, the more I played on in the hope of regaining those losses. It was a madness that drove me on. I've no excuse and you've every right to turn me away.' He gave a hopeless shrug. 'But I do need that money or I shall have to borrow elsewhere.'

'There's no call for that,' said Nicholas. 'If you were led astray at the card table, do not add to your woes by seeking out a moneylender. They charge such high rates of interest that you'll require an eternity to pay them off. You shall have your wages.'

'A thousand thanks!' Wegges embraced him. 'My pain is eased. I knew that I could count on you, Nick.'

'Try to remember that your wife and family count on *you*.'

'That thought is ever in my mind.'

'As for this card player, I'll mention him to Adam

Crowmere. If there's cozenage taking place under his roof, our new landlord will not be pleased. He'll want this Philomen Lavery to ply his trade elsewhere.'

'Oh, I think not.'

'Why do you say that?'

'It was Adam Crowmere who first enticed me into the game.'

Edmund Hoode did not know whether to be pleased or alarmed when his landlady showed in his latest visitor. Margery Firethorn seemed to fill the room, less with her physical presence than with her voice and personality. As soon as she saw the playwright, sitting up in bed with a glazed look in his eye, she swooped on him to embrace him warmly and to place a kiss on each of his pallid cheeks. Fond as he was of her, and grateful when anyone came to enquire after his health, Hoode was also rather frightened. Against her gushing affection, he was quite defenceless. He also feared her abrasive honesty.

'You are no Edmund Hoode,' she accused, standing back to appraise him. 'You are mere shadow of the man I know and love. Why do you dare to counterfeit him?'

'It is me, Margery,' he said, faintly. 'I do assure you of that.'

She looked closer. 'Heavens! I do believe it is my Edmund.' She shook her head in disbelief. 'You have shrunk to *this*?'

'For my sins.'

'What sins?' she snorted. 'I've never met a less sinful man than you. I've always held that you are too good for this world. If virtue brought any reward, you would be the healthiest man in London.'

'I feel as if I am the sickest.'

'Looks do not lie. When we buried him last month, my uncle was in far better condition than you. It is almost as if you are wasting away before my eyes. Yet Lawrence told me you were improving.'

'Slowly,' said Hoode. 'Very slowly.'

'Too slow for my liking. Are you in any kind of pain?'

'No, Margery.'

'Can you pass water? Empty your bowels?'

'From time to time.'

She felt his forehead. 'There's no fever,' she pronounced. 'That is good but your head is as cold as stone, Edmund, and you lack any colour. Are you able to sleep?'

'I can do little else,' he wailed. 'That's what vexes me. I am as weak as a kitten.'

'Kittens are playful. You have no spark of life in you.'

'Doctor Zander is sure that I will recover in time.'

'Lawrence tells me that the doctor does not even know what is wrong with you.'

'He cannot put a name to the malady, it is true,' admitted Hoode, 'but he brought a colleague with him yesterday, a Doctor Rime, older and more learned. He has seen the disease before and commended a herbal remedy. I started on it this morning.'

'It has made no visible difference,' she observed.

'I *feel* better, Margery, that's the main thing. The fog has cleared slightly.'

'Fog? What are you talking about? The sun is shining brightly today.'

'Not inside my head,' he explained. 'My mind has been shrouded in mist for days. I could neither reason nor remember. I feared I would sink into idiocy.'

'Perish the thought! Your imagination is your greatest asset.'

'Until today, that imagination had deserted me, Margery.'

'No wonder you were afraid,' she said, perching on the edge of the bed and taking his hand between her palms. 'You poor thing! It must have been an agony for you. What can I do to comfort you, Edmund? Shall I fetch food or water?'

'Neither, neither. Your presence is a comfort in itself.'

Hoode had finally come round to the view that she was, after all, welcome. Margery Firethorn was a formidable woman when roused and he had always taken great care not to provoke her scorn or anger. As a result, they had become firm friends. In one sense, her forthrightness was a blessing. She was a clear mirror in which he could view himself. Others, out of sympathy, pretended to notice signs of progress that were not really there. Through Margery's keen eyes, he saw himself as he really was.

For her part, compassion was now oozing out of Margery. She gazed down at him as if he were one of her own children, fighting a mysterious illness and needing a mother's love and support. Hoode felt cared for and reassured.

'Is your landlady looking after you?' she asked.

'Very well. She and her daughter have been angels of mercy.'

'They'll answer to me if they let you down, Edmund.'

'It's I who have let them down,' he confessed, sadly. 'All that my rent buys me is the use of this lodging yet they have treated me like one of the family. Their tenderness has been a solace to me. I said as much to Adele when she brought my breakfast.'

'Adele? Is that the daughter?'

'Yes.'

'I think she would be a solace to any man,' said Margery with a grin. 'I begin to see why Lawrence has been such a regular caller here. He comes to feast his eyes on her as well as to see you. Adele is a girl of rare beauty. If *she* does not make your heart lift up, then you are truly stricken.'

'Oh, I know, I know!'

'Apart from my husband, who else has been to see you?'

'Nick Bracewell, of course. He comes every day. Owen Elias, too. And most of the other sharers have looked in at some time. The only one to avoid me is Barnaby.'

'Would he desert you in your hour of need?'

'He has always been squeamish about disease.'

'Squeamish or selfish?' she asked, sharply. 'Barnaby is inclined to be both. He ought to be here out of simple friendship, if nothing else. I'll tax him about it.'

'No, no,' he pleaded. 'Let him be. I have visitors enough without him. He is likely to bring more reproach than sympathy, and I would rather avoid that.'

'What on earth could he reproach you for, Edmund?'

'Being unable to finish a play that I was contracted to write.'

'Illness delays you. That is not your fault.'

'Barnaby would make me feel that it was. He has badgered me for a new comedy and, when I am on the point of completing it, I am struck down. He feels robbed.'

'I'll rob him of something else if he dares to chide you,' vowed Margery, 'and his voice will be much higher as a result. I think it barbarous that he ignores you when you have taken to your sick bed. Has he no Christian charity?'

'Barnaby is a law unto himself.'

'I think his treatment of you is shameful, and I'll say so to his face. As for this new comedy,' she went on, 'it can surely wait. Lawrence says that they look for another in its stead. Michael Grammaticus is writing a second play.'

'Nick told me as much,' said Hoode, 'and I was heartened by the news. If we have something new to offer, I'll not feel that I have failed the company.'

'You could never do that, Edmund.'

'I pray that Michael can come to our rescue.'

'Oh, what a sweet creature you are!' she said, bending forward to kiss him on the head. 'Most authors are green with envy when they hear of the success of others, yet you seek to help your rivals.'

'Michael is no rival. He is a burgeoning playwright. It's my bounden duty to nurture his talent so that Westfield's Men can benefit. *Caesar's Fall*, as I hear, carried all before it.' He smiled up at her. 'Is it possible that Michael Grammaticus can write something as accomplished as that again?'

* * *

Nicholas Bracewell could see the transformation that success had wrought in him. On the eve of its performance, Michael Grammaticus was as taut as a lute string, fearing that the play was inadequate or that it would somehow founder before an audience. The applause that had greeted *Caesar's Fall* had put a deep satisfaction in his eyes. He had passed a crucial test and the relief was immense. Although he was still not at ease with most of the company, he somehow felt that he was at last part of them. Nicholas did his best to encourage that feeling.

'Come whenever you wish, Michael,' he said. 'We are always pleased to see you at the Queen's Head. You have earned the right to rub shoulders with Westfield's Men.'

'Thank you, Nick. I regard it as an honour.'

'Then you are a rare author indeed.'

'Am I?'

'Others who live by the pen often believe that it is the actors who should honour them. They demand respect. Some even want veneration.'

'Vanity is nought but weakness of character,' said Grammaticus.

Nicholas chuckled. 'Do not let Lawrence Firethorn hear you say that,' he advised. 'Or Barnaby Gill, for that matter. Their vanity is a real source of strength.'

'Long may it flourish!'

They were sitting alone at a table in a corner of the taproom. It was early evening and some of the actors, having celebrated the afternoon performance of *Marriage and Mischief* with a tankard of ale, had drifted off. Nicholas was pleased to note that Nathan Curtis and Hugh Wegges were among those who had left, chastened men returning to their families, deeply grateful to the book holder for helping them to discharge their debts by paying them their wages in advance. Michael Grammaticus, by contrast, was patently not a family man, nor did he have any interest in becoming one. There was an aura of loneliness about him that made Nicholas feel sorry for the playwright.

'When can we see this new play of yours, Michael?' he asked.

'I am not sure that it is ready for performance yet.'

'Let us be the judges of that. Is it finished?'

'More or less,' said Grammaticus, squinting at him. 'Strictly speaking, it is not a new play. I worked on it for months before setting it aside to write *Caesar's Fall*. When I went back to it, I was able to improve it out of all recognition.'

'I like the sound of that. What is its title?'

'*The Siege of Troy*.'

'Ah,' said Nicholas. 'You are deserting Rome for ancient Greece.'

'Both are rich with possibilities for an author,' said Grammaticus with a flash of enthusiasm. 'It is of a different order to *Caesar's Fall*. It is as much about the tragedy of Troy itself as about the suffering of individuals. And it has much more comedy in it.'

'That will appeal to Barnaby.'

'The part of the clown was written with him in mind. The role of Ulysses is the one that I tailored to meet

Lawrence Firethorn's talents. I hope that he will be tempted.'

'Show us the play and we will find out.'

'Let me complete the Epilogue first. I have struggled with it for days.'

'Struggle on while we read the rest,' suggested Nicholas. 'An epilogue is only an afterthought to the drama itself. Give us the five acts already written and it will be plenty on which to base a decision. Come, Michael,' he said, seeing the hesitation in the other man's face. 'Do you not wish us to present another of your plays?'

'Yes, yes. But only when it is worthy of the stage.'

'How can we know, if you will not let us see the piece?'

Grammaticus seemed to be wrestling with some inner demon. Desperate for more success, he had doubts about the quality of the other play and did not wish to lose the good opinion of Nicholas and the others by offering them an inferior work. At the same time, he could not let such an opportunity pass. Westfield's Men were soliciting him.

'Very well,' he said at length. 'You may read *The Siege of Troy*.'

'I'll bear you company to your lodging and collect it.'

'No, no. I'll fetch it, Nick. I've no wish to take you so far out of your way.'

'I'd willingly go a hundred miles to find a play like *Caesar's Fall*.'

'You'll not need to walk a hundred yards for this one,' said Grammaticus, getting to his feet and moving to the door. 'Stay here with the others. I'll not be tardy.'

Nicholas let him go. He had no time to wonder why the playwright was so anxious to keep him away from his lodging. Out of the corner of his eye, he saw Adam Crowmere enter the taproom. The landlord was as full of exuberance as ever. After greeting many of the customers by name, he came across to Nicholas's table and stood beside it with arms akimbo.

'This hot weather is good for business, Nick,' he said, happily. 'We sold far more drink than usual during the play. My servingmen filled pitchers all afternoon.'

'It's not only the bright sunshine that makes them thirsty. Give some credit to *Marriage and Mischief*. I have noticed before that comedy seems to quicken the need for ale or wine more readily than any tragedy. Do not ask me why, Adam.'

'If this be so, let's have more comedies.'

'We need to offer a range of plays,' said Nicholas. 'Our audiences would soon tire of comedy if that is all that they could see at the Queen's Head. Tragedy and history also have their place.'

Crowmere beamed. 'Whatever you perform, it is always enchanting.'

'Thank you. That's a fine tribute. But I am glad you mention enchantment,' he went on. 'From what I've been told, it is not confined to the inn yard.'

'I do not follow you.'

Nicholas rose from his seat. 'Some of the actors, it seems, have been enchanted by one of your guests, a certain Philomen Lavery.'

'A gentleman of that name is staying here, it is true.'

'Did you know that he is playing cards in his room?'

'There is no law to prevent him doing that, Nick. As long as he pays for his lodging, he can do as he wishes. What harm is there in a game of cards?'

'Far too much, if you happen to lose.'

'That's a chance that every player must take,' said Crowmere, easily.

'Not so,' corrected Nicholas. 'There are some who use all manner of tricks to make sure that it is not a game of chance. Innocent victims are forced into debt, lured by the vain hope that they may win a fortune.'

The landlord frowned. 'I hope that you do not accuse Master Lavery of being a cony-catcher, Nick,' he said, seriously. 'Come and meet the fellow and you'll see what a false allegation that is. He is the real victim here, ensnared by a love for card games. Sometimes he wins but he loses just as often. Master Lavery plays for the sheer fun of it.'

'There is no fun is watching decent men being led astray, Adam. Yes,' he added, holding up a hand before Crowmere could interrupt. 'I know that they are old enough to make up their own minds. But this ale of yours is strong and it weakens their resistance. One of them told me it was you who pointed him in the direction of the game of cards.'

'I do not deny it. I enjoyed a game or two myself.'

'And was there no suspicion of cheating?'

'None at all,' asserted Crowmere. 'If he were a cheat, why would Master Lavery come to the Queen's Head when he could fleece far more gulls at a gaming house? He asked me to send up anyone who might be interested in a game and this I did. He satisfies a demand. From the moment that I came here,' he said, 'I heard complaints that Alexander will not allow dice or cards in the taproom. Master Lavery will not want for company at his table.'

'How long is he staying?'

'For a week or so.'

Nicholas was worried. 'He could empty many more purses in that time.'

'And fill a few in return. I won ten times what I wagered.'

'Others have not be so lucky, Adam.'

'Nobody is forced to sit at that table,' said Crowmere, reasonably. 'They do so because they are ready to take the risk. Actors are grown men, Nick. You cannot watch over them all the time like a mother hen.'

It was a fair comment and Nicholas accepted it as such. He took comfort from Crowmere's judgement of the character of Philomen Lavery. The landlord's instincts had been sharpened by many years in a trade where an ability to weigh strangers up was a necessity. It might be that the man who was staying at the Queen's Head was not the cunning cheat he imagined him to be, but Nicholas nevertheless resolved to take a closer look at him in due course. He did not want other friends getting into debt.

'Alexander is too much the puritan,' said Crowmere, looking around. 'Customers should be allowed to revel in any way that they choose. There'd be many more of them, if he was to loosen the reins a little. Dice, cards and bowling are pleasures that every Englishman loves. Why frown on them so?'

'You will have to ask him that.'

'It may be some time before I can do so, Nick.'

'You've heard from him again?'

'A letter came this very afternoon,' explained Crowmere. 'His brother has rallied a touch and is clinging to life with a tenacious grip. Alexander is annoyed that he lingers so and fears the wait may go on for weeks.'

'Nobody here will wish for his speedy return.'

Crowmere laughed. 'Then I must be getting something right at last. Custom has increased and I've had to take on new labour. Oh,' he went on, 'and that reminds me, Nick. There's been no sign of those two young friends of yours. I've had perforce to look elsewhere.'

'It was good of you to think of them, Adam,' said Nicholas. 'I am sorry that they have let you down. Hywel and Dorothea must have found work on their own account.'

Bridewell Palace was a large, rambling structure that was built around three courtyards. It stood on a site west of Ludgate Hill, bounded by the Fleet River to the north and by the Thames to the south. Originally a royal home for Henry VIII, it had been presented to the city by his only legitimate son, Edward, so that it could become a workhouse for the poor and idle who thronged the streets of London. In the intervening years, Bridewell had lost much of its regal charm but there was still a faded magnificence about its exterior. It was not something that those inside the building appreciated. They felt that they were locked in a kind of prison.

'Keep working,' warned the old woman, 'or you'll be whipped again.'

'But we did nothing wrong,' complained Dorothea Tate.

'You are poor, my girl. That's your crime.'

'Are we prisoners, then?'

'Of a sort.'

Dorothea was still in a daze. After their arrest in Eastcheap, she and Hywel Rees had been dragged before a Justice of the Peace, convicted of vagrancy and taken to Bridewell where they each received twelve harsh strokes of the whip on their bare backs. As she sat at the rough wooden table, carding wool with the others, Dorothea's pain was still intense and it was matched by the embarrassment of having to strip to the waist in order to receive her punishment. Bridewell was no palace for her. It was a species of Hell in which she was forced to labour throughout the day while being kept apart from Hywel.

'Where might he be?' she wondered.

'Forget about your friend,' said the old woman.

'Have they hurt him? I keep hearing cries of agony.'

'Enemies of the state. They torture them.'

Dorothea gasped. 'They will not torture Hywel, will they?'

'If he is slack, he'll feel the whip again but that is all. Carding wool and winding silk is woman's work,' declared the other. 'Your friend will be put to wire-drawing or, if he rebels against that, to nail-making among the more stubborn souls. It's foul work.'

'Can they keep us here against our will?'

'They can do as they wish.'

'How long have you been here?'

'Years.'

'Do you look for an early release?'

'Where would I go?'

'Back to your family.'

The old woman grimaced. 'What family? They all starved to death.'

Dorothea was one of nine women in the room, all wearing the same blue dress and slaving away at a task that she found both tedious and tiring. Her hands and shoulders were already beginning to ache. Yet she dared not stop. One of the keepers, a burly man with an arrogant strut, walked through the room at regular intervals to make sure that they did their allotted work properly. Dorothea glanced around. As well as being the youngest person there, she was by far the healthiest. The old woman beside her had a face that was pitted with disease and a body that was hooped by age. Weak eyesight meant that she could barely see to thread the wool with her skeletal fingers.

It was the same with the others. All were disfigured by a lifetime of poverty and deprived of any spirit. Dorothea was horrified to think that she belonged in such a hideous place alongside such broken women. The high hopes with which she and Hywel had set out for London had now turned sour. Her greatest fear was that she might never see him again. Hywel had rescued her and changed her life.

As fond thoughts of him came flooding back, Dorothea let her hands fall to her lap. She soon came out of her reverie when the old woman's elbow jabbed her in the ribs.

Striding down the room was the keeper. Before his gaze fell on her, Dorothea quickly resumed her work but he nevertheless stopped beside her. He was not alone. His companion was a tall, wiry, gaunt individual in his thirties. The flamboyant colours of his doublet and hose were in stark contrast to the bleakness of the surroundings for the room, high and vaulted, had only the meanest furniture in it. As she worked on, Dorothea could feel the newcomer's eyes upon her but she dared not look up. The wounds on her back still smarted and she did not wish to invite another whipping.

'What is your name, child?' asked the stranger.

'Dorothea Tate, sir,' she whimpered.

'How old are you?'

'Seventeen, sir.'

'Let me see you properly.'

With a finger under her chin, her turned her head towards him and stared at her with an intensity that unnerved her. The frankness of his scrutiny brought a blush to her cheeks. Pulling his hand away, the man let out a soft laugh.

'We will see more of you, Dorothea,' he said. 'I look forward to it.'

One of the many things that Anne Hendrik admired about him was his ability to stick to any task that he set himself. After a full day at the Queen's Head, he had come back to the house in Bankside that evening with a new play under his arm, determined to read it before he went to bed. She did not disturb him. Seated opposite Nicholas at the table, she studied her designs for new hats while he applied himself to *The Siege of Troy*. His expression gave nothing away and she could not tell whether the play that Michael Grammaticus had given him was good, bad or a mixture of both. All that she could hear was the crisp rustle of parchment as he turned over each page.

Nicholas was so involved in what he was doing that he did not even notice when the shutters were closed and the candles lighted. Oblivious to all else, he read on by their dancing glow. When he eventually came to the final speech, he studied it for a moment before closing his eyes. Anne thought at first that he had gone to sleep but his lids soon opened once more. He gave her a smile of apology.

'I did not mean to keep you up so late, Anne,' he said.

'I was happy to keep you company.'

'You must have thought it selfish of me to lose myself in a play like that.'

'I am interested to hear what you thought about it,' she said. 'Do you agree with Lawrence's opinion of the work?'

'He has no opinion of it for he has not yet seen it. Lawrence wanted me to be the first to read the play and so did Michael Grammaticus. They value my judgement.'

'And so they should, Nick. You have an eye for quality.'

'Indeed, I have,' he said with a fond smile, 'and you are the clearest proof that my judgement is sound. I could not have chosen better, Anne. Had you been a play, you would hold an audience spellbound for hours on end. Like me, they would never tire of watching you.'

'But I would very soon tire of being watched.'

'Then you will never be an actor. They thrive on attention.'

'Women are not allowed on the stage,' she observed. 'It is a man's preserve. We have to see ourselves portrayed by the likes of Dick Honeydew and the other apprentices. That is no reproach. We marvel at their skills. But, even if we were invited to play our part, I'd decline the offer. The very thought of it would make me tremble.'

'Read *The Siege of Troy* and you might change your mind.'

'Why?'

'Because it would make anyone eager to clamber up on stage.'

'Including you?'

'I was on fire while I read it.'

'There was no sign of the flames in your face.'

'They were crackling within, Anne,' he explained. 'I do not know why Michael was so reluctant to let us read this. It's a stirring piece of work and I've no doubt that Lawrence will think the same.'

'How does it compare with *Caesar's Fall*?'

'Favourably.'

'That's high praise.'

'I'd go further in my commendation,' he said, gazing down at the sheets of parchment. 'We hoped to have a new comedy from Edmund Hoode but we are offered a tragedy by Michael Grammaticus in its stead. There is no loss here. I love Edmund dearly and admire his work as much as anyone, but truth must out.' He looked up at her. 'I think that *The Siege of Troy* is a better play than any he could write.'

Chapter Five

Owen Elias was among the last to arrive at the Queen's Head on the following morning. He was clearly in some kind of distress. His normally jaunty stride was now no more than a gentle shuffle, and he kept putting a weary hand to his head. Instead of greeting the others with his usual affability, he could manage no more than a forced smile of acknowledgment. As soon as he had entered the inn yard, he leant against a wall for support. Nicholas Bracewell noticed the difference in him at once. He hurried anxiously across to the Welshman.

'What is wrong with you, Owen?' he asked.

'Please!' said the other, recoiling slightly. 'Not so loud, Nick. Your voice is like a cannon in my ear. It makes my head pound.'

'Are you ill?'

'I'm all but ready for my coffin. Place an order for it now.'

'How do you feel?'

'Even worse than I must look.'

'Be more precise,' said Nicholas. 'I pray to God that you are not stricken by the same disease as poor Edmund. Where is the pain? Do you have a fever? Why are you so unsteady on your feet today?'

'It is all my own fault, Nick.'

'What ails you?'

'Too much ale ails me most,' confessed Elias. 'Add greed and revelry to that and you have the truth about my sorry condition. I went too far.'

'In what direction?'

'Pleasure.' He peered uncertainly at Nicholas through bleary eyes. 'That's what you see before you. I suffer the searing pain that follows too much pleasure. It was naked greed that took me to his room again. I had such a lust to win.'

'Ah,' said Nicholas, relaxing. 'I begin to understand. This is no malady. You went to play cards with Master Lavery.'

'No, Nick. I had a darker ambition. I went to take his money from him.'

'And did you succeed?'

'Oh, yes. I got back every penny I'd lost the night before and won another seven shillings. What else could I do but celebrate with friends? We drank until it was late, then I called on a certain lady to share my good news with her.' He gave a tired grin. 'You may guess the rest. We revelled the night away in each other's arms. Had she not shaken

104

me awake this morning, I'd have slept for a week.'

Nicholas was relieved to hear that he was suffering from no disease, but he was disappointed in his friend. He had never seen him in such a state before. As a rule, Elias thrived on long nights with demanding lovers. A single man with a determination to live life to the full, he had the constitution that allowed him to indulge himself. Evidently, on this occasion, even his remarkable vigour had been exhausted.

'Lawrence will take you to task for this,' warned Nicholas.

Elias blenched. 'Keep him away from me, Nick,' he begged. 'If Lawrence bellows at me as he is like to do, my eardrums will burst and my head will split asunder.'

'It's no more than you deserve, Owen. We play *Vincentio's Revenge* today, and you take one of the leading parts. You'll need to be at your best to carry it.'

'I look to have recovered my zest by then.'

'You should not have lost it in the first place.'

'Blame that on the ale.'

'I'd sooner blame it on the itch that took you to the card table,' said Nicholas. 'That is where this all started. You were so elated by your win that you had to spend the money at once. It was gained too easily to stay in your purse.'

'Good fortune sat beside me.'

'Well, it did not do the same for Nathan Curtis or Hugh Wegges. Both of them lost heavily at cards. Others, no doubt, will do the same.'

'Do not ask me to weep for them,' said Elias with a hint of truculence. 'Everyone knows the risk. Like me, they take their chance. Master Lavery makes that clear.'

'What manner of man is he?'

'A marvellous strange one, Nick.'

'In what way?'

'Look at him and you would not believe that Philomen Lavery had ever seen a pack of cards. You would be more likely to take him for a lawyer, if not a priest. There is a weird innocence about the fellow.'

'Does he dissemble?' wondered Nicholas.

'I think not,' replied Elias. 'I have been in many gaming houses and know how to smell out a cony-catcher. Master Lavery is not one of them. The first thing he did was to let me inspect his cards to see for myself that they were not marked in any way. How many would do that?'

'Very few, Owen. Unless they work by the quickness of their hand.'

'I take him for an honest man. How else could I have won?'

'I see that I will have to talk to Master Lavery myself,' said Nicholas, curiosity sparked by what he had heard. 'But leaving him aside, have you had any sight of those young beggars we met the other day?'

'The counterfeit crank and his girl?'

'Yes, Owen.'

'No, I've not spied them. What about you?'

'I've seen neither hide nor hair of them. The pity of it is that I found them both a place here at the Queen's Head. As a favour to me, Adam Crowmere would have given them work, food, and shelter. They would have been rescued from the street.' Nicholas thought about them for a moment and felt a surge of compassion. 'I fear for them, Owen. They are strangers here. They do not know the perils of the city.'

'You forget something,' said Elias airily. 'Hywel Rees is Welsh. He has the same unquenchable spirit I do. That will see him through.'

'I do not descry any of that unquenchable spirit in you now,' said Nicholas with amusement.

Elias mustered some defiance. 'It is still there, I promise you,' he said, thrusting out his jaw. 'But have no qualms about Hywel and his pretty Dorothea. They will survive. Whatever troubles they meet in London, I am sure they will overcome them.'

Though he could neither read nor write, Hywel Rees had a great capacity for learning. His ears were sharp, and what they did not pick up, his other senses somehow gleaned. In his short time in Bridewell, he had gathered a deal of information about the place, much of it profoundly troubling. It was both a house of correction and a workhouse, an institution that took in children of the poor, capable of nothing more than manual labour, invalids who were sufficiently recovered to undertake light employment, and vagrants. It was a severe blow to Hywel's pride that he and Dorothea were considered to belong to the group of sturdy rogues and loose women who had been convicted by a court.

Bridewell was also the home of captives from the Spanish Armada as well as those who were persecuted for their religion. Like Dorothea, he had heard the anguished cries of nameless Roman Catholics and the occasional Puritan as they were put to the torture in order to extract confessions from them. It disturbed him that he was under the same roof as these unfortunate prisoners and therefore might be subject to the same punishment. Yet the keeper who stood over him while he toiled with the other men told Hywel that he was there to be cured. Hard labour seemed to him a cruel medicine.

'How many of us are there?' he asked.

'Less than there used to be.'

'They let people out, then?'

'Dozens of them, Hywel. My brother was one of them.'

'Why did they discharge him?'

'Less mouths to feed,' said the boy.

Hywel's companion was no more than twelve, a scrawny lad with a habit of glancing nervously over his shoulder as if expecting to be hit at any moment. The bruises on his face and bare arms suggested that his apprehension was well founded. His name was Ned Griddle, and he had been in Bridewell for almost three years. He and Hywel were unloading a cart in one of the courtyards, carrying heavy wooden boxes between them to the kitchens. The smell of fresh fish in one box was so strong and appetising that it brought an involuntary smile to Hywel's face.

'Not for the likes of us,' warned Griddle. 'They'd sooner see us starve.'

'Who?'

'Those that have taken over the place. Master Beechcroft is the worst of them.'

'Why?'

'He treats us like dirt.'

They left the box of fish in the kitchen and went back out into the courtyard. Hywel kept scanning the windows all around him, hoping for a glimpse of Dorothea. He was desperate to get in touch with her but did not even know where she was. They reached the cart and manoeuvred another box off it. Hywel glanced at the casks of wine.

'What is all this food and drink for, Ned?' he wondered.

'Master Beechcroft and the others will have another feast.'

'There is enough here to feed dozens of people.'

'There always is.'

'Who are the guests?'

'Not you and me, Hywel.'

'Will anyone in Bridewell be invited to the feast?'

'Only if they are pretty enough'

'What do you mean?'

Griddle was about to reply when he suddenly received one of the blows he had feared. A stocky man hit him across the back with a stick and ordered him to get on with his work. The boy was too frightened to speak after that, and Hywel was left to speculate on what he had meant by his remark about the feast. The Welshman was deeply alarmed. His resolve to get to Dorothea was stiffened.

* * *

Lawrence Firethorn had played the leading role so often that it was lodged forever in his mind. While others checked their lines or rehearsed their moves, he was able to relax before the performance, certain that the blank verse would spring to his lips when required. Firethorn's memory was truly phenomenal. Since he knew well above two dozen plays by heart, he could offer a wide range of choice to spectators when he was on tour. His role in *Vincentio's Revenge* was one that he could recall instantly. Nicholas Bracewell sought to add another to the actor-manager's repertoire.

'The tragedy is called *The Siege of Troy*,' he explained.

Firethorn was blunt. 'Is there a part worthy of me?'

'Ulysses will be very much to your taste.'

'Then why is he not in the title? Did Michael tell you that? Why did he not name his play *Ulysses and the Siege of Troy*? As you know, Nick,' he said, adjusting his costume, 'I have a fondness for title roles.'

'You would enjoy this play if it had no title at all.'

'It comes with your approval, then?'

'It does,' said Nicholas. 'It has all the virtues of *Caesar's Fall* and others unique to itself. Its only fault, if fault it be, is that it is at times too clever.'

'Too clever?'

'Aimed more at the trained scholar than the ordinary spectator. For instance, there are five or six hidden sonnets in the play. Most of our audience will hear them without even recognising what they are. They will be lost on the common herd.'

'So is much that we play,' said Firethorn. 'As long as we have fights, arguments, deaths, dances, and comic antics, the vulgar souls in the yard will be satisfied. When the performance is over this afternoon, give me Michael's tragedy. I'll devote the whole evening to it.'

'Your time will not be wasted.'

'Thanks to you, Nick. Had the play been feeble, you'd not foist it upon me. That's the reason I gave it first to you.' He stroked his beard and struck a pose. 'Did I incur Anne's displeasure?'

'How could you do that?' asked Nicholas.

'By making you read five acts of a drama. You must have been a dull companion for her last night. Margery will not stomach my presence if I dare to study a play while I'm abed.' He gave a bountiful smile. 'Beg Anne's forgiveness for me.'

'None is needed. Work of her own kept her occupied.'

'I wish that it were always so with my wife,' said Firethorn enviously.

They were in the tiring house, and other members of the company were starting to come in. Nicholas had no real worries about the performance. *Vincentio's Revenge* was a blood-soaked tragedy that never failed to work on stage, and the troupe always acted it with surpassing confidence. Now that Owen Elias seemed to have recovered his customary vitality, everything pointed toward another success. It was Firethorn who voiced a slight concern.

'I took the liberty of inspecting your account book today, Nick' he said.

'You've every right to do so.'

'I have to keep a wary eye on the company's purse.'

'Then you'll want to know why two of the hired men were given their wages in advance,' said Nicholas, anticipating his question. 'I know that it is something on which you frown, but there were pressing needs in both cases.'

'A house burnt down? A death in the family?'

'Thankfully, nothing of that degree.'

'Then the wages should not have been paid,' argued Firethorn, 'for those are the only reasons that would soften my heart. You establish a foolish precedent here, Nick.'

'I acted in the best interests of the company.'

'Did you?'

'Would you rather that Nathan Curtis and Hugh Wegges were imprisoned for debt?' asked Nicholas. 'For that is what their creditors threatened them with. Where would we find such a willing carpenter and such a reliable tireman again?'

'They would be a loss to us, I grant you.'

'Then hear my tale.'

As quickly and succinctly as he could, Nicholas told him about their bad luck at the card table set up by Philomen Lavery. He also mentioned that Owen Elias's win the previous night had led indirectly to his sluggishness that morning. Firethorn began to roll his eyes and gnash his teeth. He looked like Vincentio on the point of getting his revenge.

'A pox on this card table!' he declared. 'Why did you not tell me of this before?'

'I thought the landlord might have mentioned it to you.'

'I wish he had, for I'd have forbidden most of the company from going anywhere near it. Some of the sharers may have money to lose – though I am certainly not one of them – but hired men cannot afford to hazard all on such low wages.'

'I think that Nathan and Hugh both understand that now.'

'So must the others. I'll speak to them all later and issue a warning. As for Owen,' he said, looking vengefully around the room but unable to see the Welshman, 'I wondered why he was half asleep today. He should set an example to the others, not throw his money away at a card table.'

'But he made a profit there. That was his downfall.'

Firethorn was quivering with anger. 'If he turns up like that again,' he said, *'I'll* be his downfall. Death and damnation! We are beset by enough problems as it is. Has he forgotten what's happened to Edmund, one of the pillars of this company? Take him away and Westfield's Men begin to totter. Owen must help to support us.'

'He knows that, and he has called on Edmund every day.'

'Well, I hope that he did not turn up in that state, or Edmund, kind-hearted man that he is, would have climbed out of bed and put Owen into it instead. When he arrived this morning, that Welsh satyr might have clambered out of his grave.'

'Owen is duly repentant.'

'Let him rest his wagging pizzle for a while and we'd need no repentance.'

'He accepts that,' said Nicholas, wanting to protect his

friend from Firethorn's ire. 'Owen will make amends on stage this afternoon. He is much better now. I wish that Edmund could recover just as quickly.'

'I wish only that he will recover, Nick '

'There's no question but that he will.'

'That's not Margery's opinion,' said Firethorn uneasily. 'My wife is no mean physician. She's nursed grandparents and parents through their last hours on earth, and she knows the signs. When she called on him yesterday, Margery was shocked to see him. She believes we may have lost Edmund forever.'

'Why does he not come into the house?' asked Hoode. 'You cannot leave him outside.'

'Preben would prefer it that way,' said Anne.

'It makes me feel a poor host.'

'You are in no fit state to welcome anyone, Edmund. He only came with me to deliver a hat that he made. Preben van Loew is very shy. He would be nervous company. Let him cool his heels at your door.'

Hoode was touched when Anne Hendrik came to his lodging but embarrassed that she should see him in such a weak condition. He had more colour in his face now and more animation in his body, but he was still troubled by fatigue. Like his other visitors, she was worried by what she saw. Slim by nature, Hoode had nevertheless lost weight. Anne had never seen his cheeks so hollowed, but she concealed her anxiety behind a warm smile. In every way, she was a much gentler presence than Margery

Firethorn, and he was grateful. Anne helped to soothe him.

'Nick tells me that you are sorely missed at the Queen's Head,' she said.

'I miss them all in return.'

'You'll soon be able to take your place among them, Edmund.'

'I begin to lose hope of that,' he confided with a deep sigh. 'This new herbal compound has cleared my head but done little to restore my strength. Look at me, Anne. I struggle to sit upright in my bed.'

'I thought this second doctor had seen the disease before.'

'He has. Doctor Rime called it by a Latin name that only he and Doctor Zander understood. They think it may be months before I regain my health. Months!' he said in despair. 'I cannot be away from Westfield's Men for that long. It's a betrayal of them.'

'Do not even think that,' said Anne. 'To have you back with them, your fellows would gladly wait a year without complaint. You forget what you have already done for the company. While you lie here, the plays of Edmund Hoode still delight the audiences at the Queen's Head.'

'Old plays, Anne. Tired heroes. They cry out for something new to cheer.'

'And you will give it to them in the fullness of time. Meanwhile, enjoy the rest that you have deserved. Nick will say the same when he calls here later on.'

'Has he talked perchance of another play by Michael Grammaticus?'

'He has done more than talk of it, Edmund,' she said. 'Last night, he brought it home to read it through. It's called *The Siege of Troy*.'

Hoode brightened. 'A subject I have always wanted to explore,' he said. 'It offers so much to any dramatist. Michael is steeped in Greek history and will sound deeper chords than I could manage. What did Nick say of it?'

'Oh, he liked the play.'

'Come, Anne. Do not think you will injure my feelings by heaping praise on another. I have no jealousy here. Why should I?' he asked. 'I admire Michael Grammaticus and his work. If this new tragedy of his can fill the gap that was left by me, it will bring me such pleasure and relief. Nick liked the play, you say?'

'Very much. But the decision does not lie with him.'

'To all intents, it does. Lawrence will lean heavily on his advice.'

'Then I think the play will be bought.'

'These tidings warm my heart,' said Hoode with a smile. 'Many authors have only one play of merit in them, and I feared it might be so with Michael. But he has the skill to build on his early triumph. *Caesar's Fall* will have raised expectations. I delight in the knowledge that he has fulfilled them.'

His sincerity was apparent. Anne was struck once again by his readiness to praise the work of others. In a profession where pride and arrogance flourished, Hoode remained untouched by either and was refreshingly modest about his own achievements. Out of consideration for his feelings, she did not tell him what Nicholas had said about *The Siege of Troy* being superior to anything that he could write, but she sensed that even that judgment might not upset him. Eager to assist the career of another playwright, Hoode was more likely to pass on the comment to Michael Grammaticus in order to inspire him. She recalled something about the new author.

'Is it true that he pays the doctor's bills?' she said.

'Michael does more than that, Anne.'

'Does he?'

'He comes here every day to see how I am and to run any errands for me. I think that it is his way of thanking me for the encouragement I have been able to give.'

'Nick says that he's a lonely man who does not make friends easily.'

'He certainly has my friendship,' said Hoode. 'Michael will do anything for me. Had you come an hour earlier, you'd have met him yourself. He'd just come back from the market.' He indicated a bowl of fruit. 'That is what he bought for me.'

'How kind!'

'Doctor Zander prescribed fresh fruit, so Michael brings whatever I need. At the doctor's behest, he has even made and fed me a broth. Oh, yes,' he went on, 'Michael Grammaticus is much more than a gifted playwright. He's been friend, nurse, and cook to me as well.'

At the rear of the Queen's Head was a small garden, tended by Leonard, that produced a few vegetables as well as a variety of flowers. It was there that Nicholas Bracewell finally tracked down the card player. Philomen Lavery cut an odd figure as he strolled around, gait slow and head down in contemplation. He could be no more than thirty, but the grey hair and pinched face added at least another twenty years to his appearance. What struck Nicholas was the paleness of the man's skin. Blue veins ran in tributaries all over his forehead, and his eyebrows were no more than wisps of white hair. Lavery was a small man with an almost feminine daintiness about him. Owen Elias had said that he might pass as a priest, and Nicholas could see why. There was a faintly spiritual air about Philomen Lavery.

When Nicholas introduced himself, the other man gave a self-effacing smile.

'Your reputation goes before you, sir,' he said.

'What reputation?'

'The landlord tells me that you are the prop that holds up Westfield's Men. Actors are a breed apart. They live by different rules than the rest of us. It must be difficult to work with such capricious and quicksilver characters.'

'We have our awkward moments,' admitted Nicholas.

'Yet, from what I hear, you take them in your stride.'

'I try, Master Lavery. I try. But what brings you to London?'

'I came to do some business,' replied the other. 'Most of my day is spent at the Royal Exchange with other merchants. My evenings, as you know, are dedicated to business of another kind.'

'Yes,' said Nicholas. 'I wished to speak to you about that.'

'I am all ears, my friend.'

Lavery seemed so friendly and looked so innocuous that Nicholas found it hard to believe he was involved in deception at the card table. His doublet and hose were of good quality but muted colours, and he wore no hat while enjoying the evening sunshine in the garden. His grey locks were ruffled by a light breeze.

'I gather that some of my fellows visit you in your room,' Nicholas began.

'That is so. You are welcome to join them.'

'I've no love for games of chance.'

'Then why do you work in the theatre?' asked Lavery. 'Is that not the biggest game of chance of all? Think what risks you run every day. You are at the mercy of the weather, the city authorities, and the fickleness of your audiences.'

'Do not forget the plague, Master Lavery. That closes down every playhouse.'

'In short, you live by putting yourself in jeopardy.'

'There's every likelihood of it,' conceded Nicholas. 'That is true.'

'Then you are a brave man, Master Bracewell. You and your fellows tempt fate in your occupation. It requires a lot less courage to play a game of cards.'

'Courage or folly?'

Lavery smiled. 'That depends on whether you win or lose.'

'My concern is with those who lost,' said Nicholas. 'Two of the hired men came to grief so badly at your table that they were forced to ask for their wages in advance. Both were married men who lacked the money to feed and clothe their families.'

'Then they were unwise to play cards. Each did so of his own free will.'

'Only because the game was here to tempt them.'

'They'd find cards or dice in many taverns, if they knew where to look. And I did not sit down with my pack in the taproom. I simply asked the landlord if he knew of anyone who might enjoy a game or two.' He gave a hollow laugh. 'I lived to rue the day I made that request.'

'Why?'

'Because he was the first through my door. Adam Crowmere is the luckiest man I have ever played against,' he complained. 'I thought myself hard done by when I lost seven shillings to a laughing Welshman last night.'

'That was Owen Elias.'

'No sooner had he quit my room than the landlord steps in and wins almost twice that much from me. If I do not recoup my losses tonight,' he said jokingly, 'I may not be able to pay the rent.' He looked up at Nicholas. 'Why not come to my room?'

'I told you. I've no interest in cards.'

'You'll take an interest in these, I believe.'

'Will I?' asked Nicholas.

'Yes, my friend. I can see in your face that you think me a cheat. I do not blame you for that,' he said, holding up a hand. 'When a stranger like me arrives here without warning and coaxes money out of the purses of your fellows, you are bound to think me a cony-catcher. Examine my pack of cards and you'll find them clean and unmarked.'

'I do not accuse you of deception, Master Lavery.'

'Then why did you accost me out here?'

'To see you for myself and to tell you of my worries.'

'I am pleased to meet you,' said Lavery, 'but you bear your anxiety to the wrong person. If some of the actors cannot afford to lose, keep them away from my room. I've no wish to deprive any wife or child of sustenance.'

'Master Firethorn has already given a stern warning. After the performance this afternoon, he told the whole company about the danger of playing cards.'

Lavery's eyes gleamed. 'But therein lies its excitement.'

'There's no excitement in losing all your wages.'

'Oh, but there is, there is. As soon as you turn over the first card, your heart begins to beat much faster. Win or lose, you feel the blood pulsing through your veins. And do not tell me you've not courted danger in your time,' he went on, head to one side as he grinned at Nicholas. 'I talk to a man who once sailed with Drake around the world. What terrors and tempests you must have endured! And yet you are afraid of a harmless game of cards. Shame on you, my friend!'

Philomen Lavery gave a nod of farewell before heading back toward the inn. He was a mild-mannered man whose voice was soft and educated, yet Nicholas had found the conversation rather unsettling. He was convinced that Lavery was no cheat, preying on gullible fools who were enticed to play cards with him, but he was still uneasy. He sensed that he was at a disadvantage. Nicholas had learnt very little about the man. Lavery, on the other hand, seemed to know far too much about him.

The high ideals that inspired those who first set up Bridewell as a workhouse had long been abandoned. It was a house of pain now. Hywel Rees hated everything about it. Its constraints irked him; its regimen was strict and its atmosphere oppressive. Boys like Ned Griddle endured it all with quiet resignation, but Hywel could not do that. He was a natural rebel who was ready to question, challenge, and, if necessary, resist. It earned him a few beatings from the keepers, but his spirit was not broken. After five long days in Bridewell, he was as defiant as ever.

'Have you never tried to escape, Ned?' he asked

'Never.'

'Why not?'

'Where would I go?'

'Back home to your family.'

'I have no family,' said the boy. 'My mother died years ago, and I've no idea who my father was. We lived on the streets. When they let my brother out, that was his only home. He'll sleep in the open till the bad weather comes.'

'And then?'

'He'll have to find cover.' Griddle looked gloomily around the room. 'At least we have a roof over our heads.'

'Yes,' said Hywel resentfully, 'and four thick walls to keep us in.'

'We get our meals.'

'Do you call that *food*? It makes my stomach turn. When I worked on a farm in Wales, we gave better fare to the pigs.' His lip curled in disgust. 'I thought they were meant to cure us here. With food like that, we are more likely to catch a foul disease.'

'It's better than starving, Hywel.'

'I'd rather take my chances on the streets.'

'Look where it got you.'

'They'd not catch us again.'

Hywel gazed wistfully out of the window. Along with a handful of others, they were locked in a room on the second floor of a building that overlooked one of the courtyards. In former days, the palace had echoed to the footsteps of royalty and of visiting ambassadors, but it had a decided air of neglect now. The courtyard was deserted. It was evening, and work had finally ceased. Having been given their meal, the inmates were all under lock and key. Ned Griddle had settled into the routine without complaint, but his companion was restless.

'I must get out of here,' said Hywel.

'We all think that at first.'

'I have a friend, Dorothea. She needs me to look after her.'

'You'll forget her in time.'

'Never!' retorted Hywel. 'I love her.'

Griddle shrugged. 'You may never see her again,' he said. 'They let us out and keep the women here. There's far more work for them to do. The lucky ones eat good food and wear fine clothes.'

'Lucky ones?'

'Stay here a while. You'll see.'

Hywel did not have long to wait. Ten minutes later, a carriage appeared and the clatter of hooves reverberated around the courtyard. When the vehicle stopped outside the door to the main hall, five men in rich apparel hauled themselves out and exchanged noisy banter. It was clear from their laughter and unsteady movements that drink had been taken. A tall figure in ostentatious attire emerged from the door to greet them.

'Master Beechcroft,' said Griddle.

'Is this the night of the feast?'

'Yes, Hywel. The women will be here soon.'

But it was a second carriage that next swept into the yard, bringing with it another bevy of loud and mirthful guests. The four men who alighted were all middle-aged, and they embraced Beechcroft in turn before going into the hall. Hywel watched with growing discomfort as other guests arrived on horseback. They were all men, and, judging by their hilarity, they were intent on enjoying themselves. When they had dismounted and tethered their horses, they followed Beechcroft through the doorway.

When the women finally came into view, Hywel was revolted by what he saw. They were denizens of Bridewell, convicted harlots, let out to play and to provide entertainment for the guests. Dressed in gaudy taffeta and wearing cheap trinkets, they tripped across the courtyard. Some were young, but most were older women, experienced members of the trade, painted and powdered to make them look more appealing. From the sound of their happy chatter, it was evident that they, too, were looking forward to the festivities in the main hall.

There was one exception. She was the youngest and prettiest of them all, but she wore her dress of red taffeta with great reluctance. While the other women hurried across the courtyard like a gaggle of geese, she was struggling to get away from the keeper, who was dragging her along by the wrist. When she emitted a cry of pain, Hywel leant right out of the window to call to her.

'Dorothea!' he yelled.

Chapter Six

The meeting took place in a private room at the Queen's Head because it gave them both quiet and privacy. Since the advent of Adam Crowmere, the inn had become much more popular and the taproom was in a state of happy tumult every evening. It was not just the quality of his ale, the standard of service or the charms of the buxom tavern wenches that brought in more custom. By a combination of hard work and warmth of personality, the new landlord had created a more joyous atmosphere at the inn. Everyone noticed it.

'The taproom has truly come alive tonight,' said Owen Elias. 'It was never like this when our old landlord was here.'

'No,' agreed Lawrence Firethorn, pouring a glass of Canary wine for all four of them. 'Under that ghoul, Marwood, it was more like a morgue. That fearful wife of his used to send shivers down my spine.'

'Can you imagine sharing a bed with that old crone, Lawrence?'

'She'd turn my prick to ice!'

'Can we begin?' asked Barnaby Gill, impatiently. 'You may all have time on your hands but I have somewhere important to go.'

'What's his name?' teased Firethorn.

'There's much to debate,' said Nicholas Bracewell. 'Shall we make a start?'

'Aye, Nick. We must not detain Barnaby from the pleasures of the night.'

They were seated around a table on which a candle had been lighted to stave off the evening shadows. Its flickering flame threw a halo around *The Siege of Troy,* the play they had now all read. There were a number of sharers in the company but its policy was determined, for the most part, by Firethorn, Gill and Edmund Hoode. In the absence of the playwright, Elias had been invited to the table. Though not of equivalent status, Nicholas was always included in such discussions because of his wise counsel.

Firethorn was decisive. 'I like the play,' he said, slapping it with the palm of his hand. 'Nick and Owen are of like opinion. I urge that we accept it.'

'You are too hasty, Lawrence,' said Gill, raising a finger. 'We should not be so rash to part with our money until *The Siege of Troy* meets all our demands. Changes must be made.'

'Of what kind? I call for no changes.'

'Nor me,' said Elias. 'The only change that I would

gladly make is the name of the author. A fine play it is, I know, but I wish that it had been penned by anyone but Michael Grammaticus.'

'Yet he's the only author who *could* have written it,' argued Nicholas. 'Even our own dear Edmund does not have that great a knowledge of history.'

'I agree, Nick. My quarrel is not with *The Siege of Troy*. I take it to wrest the laurel wreath from *Caesar's Fall*. No,' he went on, 'what troubles me is that we will have that mournful face watching us rehearse it. Michael is such lugubrious company.'

'Ignore his presence. Think only of your role.'

'That's what I have done,' said Gill, tasting his wine, 'and my role falls short of perfection. It needs at least two more songs to give it body, and a jig in the last act.'

Firethorn bridled. 'The last act belongs to Ulysses,' he declared. 'I'll not have the audience distracted by your antics, Barnaby. You only follow where I lead.'

'You will lead us into boredom if there's no comedy in Act Five.'

'What of the scene between the three servingmen? That must earn laughs.'

'But I do not happen to be in it,' said Gill, tapping his chest. 'Why have a clown if he is not allowed to clown his way to the end of the play?'

'Why have an author if you do not obey his dictates?'

Gill sneered. 'Since when did *you* ever obey the dictates of an author, Lawrence? If it serves your purpose, you carve his work to shreds without a scruple.'

'I make improvements, Barnaby, that is all.'

'Then let me do the same.'

'A fair point,' said Nicholas, searching for a compromise. 'Barnaby's complaint is easily answered. Ask our playwright to amend the scene with the servingmen so that it involves the clown and all objections vanish. Is that not so?'

Elias congratulated him on having found the solution and Gill was mollified. With a little persuasion from the book holder, Firethorn was eventually reconciled to the idea. There were other scenes that aroused discussion but none that required any major alteration. They were soon able to move on to the scenery and the costumes. An hour later, it was all settled.

'Good!' said Firethorn, rubbing his hands together. 'We can come to composition with Michael Grammaticus. I'll have our lawyer draw up the contract.'

'May I suggest one of its terms?' asked Nicholas.

'No,' said Gill, flatly. 'You have no voting power here.'

'He ought to have,' attested Elias, loyally.

'Let's hear him out,' said Firethorn. 'Nick talks more sense than any of us.'

'Then listen to my device,' resumed Nicholas, picking up the play from the table. '*The Siege of Troy* is more than a work of high quality. Were we to turn it down, one of our rivals would surely take it up and use it to their advantage. What it proves is that Michael Grammaticus is an author we must nurture.'

'Edmund said as much from the very start,' recalled Firethorn.

'Then he would approve what I advise. When you draw up a contract for this play,' said Nicholas, 'write into it that Westfield's Men have first refusal on the next play that comes from the same pen. That way, we safeguard ourselves from poachers.'

'Why stop at one more play, Nick? We'll bind the fellow to us in perpetuity. Let it be set down that everything written by Michael Grammaticus is first offered to us.' He patted Nicholas on the arm. 'As always, you point us in the right direction.'

'Nick gives us sage advice,' said Elias. 'Is it not so, Barnaby?'

Gill rose to his feet. 'I was about to advocate it myself,' he lied, 'even though it is less like sage advice than common sense. If we are to lose Edmund, we need a playwright who can match his steady flow of work.'

'Edmund will be back,' insisted Nicholas. 'He is not lost forever. He begins to show hopeful signs, Barnaby, as you would know if you deigned to visit him.'

'I never sit beside a sick bed. It always upsets me.'

'He would be well pleased to see you.'

'And that is more than any of us would dare to say,' remarked Firethorn. 'Think of someone else for once, Barnaby. Go and call on Edmund.'

'I'd not wish to look upon him in that parlous condition,' said Gill, crossing to open the door. 'I prefer to remember Edmund as he was, in his prime. To watch him dwindle away before my eyes is more than I can bear.'

He left the room and the others exchanged a knowing

glance. Elias was the next to depart, anxious to join his friends in the taproom. Nicholas and Firethorn got up from the table. The actor-manager was pleased with the way their deliberations had gone.

'Michael will still be here,' he said. 'Acquaint him with our decision and ride over any objections he may have to what we propose. If he wishes to ally himself with Westfield's Men, he'll do so on our terms.'

'I'll mention the changes that you require,' said Nicholas, snuffing out the candle between a finger and thumb. 'When they are made, I'll take *The Siege of Troy* to the scrivener and set him to work.'

Firethorn sighed. 'We lose one author but gain another. Is it a fair exchange?'

'Nobody could replace Edmund Hoode. He brings so much more to the company than Michael ever will. And he'll do so again,' said Nicholas, hopefully. 'This malady of his cannot last forever.'

Edmund Hoode was dozing when his visitor arrived but he soon awoke. Not expecting anyone to call that late in the evening, he was delighted to see his friend and to share in his good news. Michael Grammaticus had come from the Queen's Head in a state of suppressed excitement, believing that only another playwright could understand how he felt. Hoode was thrilled for him.

'These tidings are the best medicine yet, Michael.'

'Nick Bracewell said that all who read *The Siege of Troy* enjoyed it greatly.'

'If it reads well, it will play even better,' said Hoode. 'And Lawrence wants more work from that teeming brain of yours. That shows the faith he has in you.'

'I hope I have the means to justify it, Edmund.'

'No more of this modesty. A man who can write *Caesar's Fall* is destined for the highest rewards. Take what is due to you.'

'I will,' said Grammaticus, a tear in his eye. 'But enough of me,' he added, briskly. 'I am still a novice where you are a master. Nobody in London has written as many plays as you.'

'If only I could remember how I did it!'

'What mean you?'

'That I have to take your word,' said Hoode, 'and that of my other friends. Since all of you praise my achievements, I must accept that they were mine to praise. Yet I've neither the memory to recall them nor the will to add to them. I'm done for, Michael,' he confided. 'Behold a posthumous playwright.'

'Away with such thoughts! You are but resting between plays.'

'If only I could believe that.'

'You must,' said Grammaticus. 'Two doctors have attended you and both foretell your recovery. Time and patience must be your nurses, Edmund. When your health returns, as surely it must, your mind will be as fruitful as ever. Why,' he went on, 'I can see an improvement in you since this very morning.'

'True,' said Hoode, sitting up in bed. 'This afternoon,

I was able at last to walk around the room. I sat in the window for an hour to watch people walk by. That cheered me more than I can say.' His face crumpled. 'But the feeling did not last.'

'Why not?'

'I tried to read my new play, Michael. I've three acts finished and a fourth begun. If I picked it up again, I thought, the juices of creation would run inside me again.' He shook his head in dismay. 'I was asking for a miracle.'

'What happened?'

'I could not read a line, let alone write one. *A Way To Content All Women*, that is the title. How cruel it now seems!' exclaimed Hoode, looking down at himself. 'I've not the strength to give *one* woman contentment. My manhood is but an empty husk.'

Grammaticus was curious. 'You've three acts written, you say?'

'And almost half of the fourth.'

'There may be one way to get your new comedy finished, Edmund.'

'I despair of ever seeing it upon a stage. The play is stillborn, Michael.'

'Not if someone else were to give it life,' said the other, thoughtfully. 'I confess that I know little of how to content women but, it seems, I am entitled to call myself a playwright now. Let me put my meagre talents at your service,' he offered, leaning over the patient. 'I'll be your co-author, if you wish, and finish the play with you.'

* * *

Rain fell throughout the night but it had eased by morning. When he left the house in Bankside, all that Nicholas had to contend with was light drizzle. The streets were glistening and he had to step around the frequent puddles that had formed. He had just crossed London Bridge when he caught up with another resident of Bankside.

'Good morrow, Nathan!' he called, quickening his stride.

Curtis turned round. 'Well met, Nick!' he said, adjusting the bag of tools over his shoulder. 'I thought to make an early start today. There's much to do.'

'And even more when our new play goes into rehearsal.'

'Is this the comedy promised by Edmund Hoode?'

'Alas, no.'

Nicholas told him about the purchase of *The Siege of Troy* and explained what scenery and properties it would require. Curtis grumbled at the prospect of additional work until the book holder pointed out that extra hours would increase his wages. The carpenter nodded soulfully.

'Give me all the work you can, Nick,' he said. 'I need the money.'

'Not to lose to Master Lavery, I trust?'

'No, I've told that particular Satan to get behind me.'

'He does not look like Satan,' observed Nicholas. 'I found him to be a reasonable man. And he does not win at his table all the time. Master Lavery told me of his losses.'

'All that I think of are my own losses,' said Curtis, balefully.

'When you asked for your wages, why did you not tell me how you went astray?'

'I was too ashamed, Nick. It was a grievous fault. When I picked up those cards, I betrayed my family. All that I look for now is a chance to redeem myself.'

'You are not the only one to say that. Hugh Wegges has made the same vow.'

'There'll be others who'll suffer at the hands of Philomen Lavery.'

'Then they must accept the blame,' said Nicholas. 'They've been warned. When he addressed the whole company about the danger, Lawrence did not mince his words.'

Curtis grinned. 'He does not know how to mince his words.'

In spite of the drizzle, the market in Gracechurch Street was as busy as ever and the two men had to shoulder their way through the crowd. Amid the deafening noise, conversation was almost impossible so they did not even attempt it. They walked on and let the rich compound of smells invade their nostrils. Eventually, they turned into the yard of the Queen's Head. George Dart came trotting obediently towards Nicholas.

'I'm glad to see you here so early, George,' said the book holder.

'I know how much there is to do today.' He looked at Curtis. 'I'm sorry that I broke that stool yesterday, Nathan. It was an accident.'

'It always is,' moaned the carpenter. 'Try to be less clumsy.'

'I will. Oh, Nicholas,' he went on, turning back to him. 'You have a visitor.'

'Do I?'

Dart pointed to a figure curled up in a corner of the yard. Nicholas did not at first recognise her. Dressed in rags and soaked to the skin, Dorothea Tate got up nervously and came across to him. When she brushed the hair back from her face, Nicholas could see that she had been crying.

'Please!' she begged. 'I need your help.'

By the time that Owen Elias arrived, Nicholas had calmed the girl down, taken her inside to dry off and bought her some breakfast. Dorothea consumed it hungrily. While she ate, Nicholas was able to take a closer look at her. She was not simply bedraggled. She was heavily bruised. Her temples were discoloured, her lip swollen and both her wrists had telltale marks of violence on them. Alerted by the message from the book holder, Elias came hurrying into the taproom.

'George Dart said that you wanted me post haste, Nick.' He saw the girl. '*Iesu Mawr*!' he exclaimed. 'Is that you, Dorothea?'

'Yes,' she murmured.

'What's happened to you?'

'She was out in that rain all night,' said Nicholas.

'Where's Hywel?'

'That's what she was just about to tell me, Owen. Sit down and we'll hear the tale together.' Elias lowered himself onto a stool. 'Dorothea knows nobody else in

London. We are the only people she can turn to for help.'

'We're not people, Nick,' said the Welshman, grinning at the girl. 'We're friends. We'll do all we can for her and Hywel. He's a fellow countryman of mine.'

They waited for Dorothea to speak but she was hesitant, unsure if she could trust two men whom she had only met briefly, and not certain if she had the courage to put into words the horrors that had befallen her. She looked from one to the other.

'Bear with her, Owen,' said Nicholas, softly. 'She has suffered, as you see.' He gave her a reassuring smile. 'Do not speak until you are ready, Dorothea. Feel free to take your time.'

'Thank you,' she said. 'You are very kind.'

'Ask anything you will.'

'Yes,' said Elias. 'Where have you been since last we saw you?'

'In Bridewell.'

'God's mercy! No wonder you are cowed. What brought you there?'

'We were arrested for begging in Eastcheap. We had no papers.'

Shivering as she recalled the experience, Dorothea told them about the arrest, the appearance in court, the whipping administered at Bridewell and the laborious work she was forced to do there. What made the place so intolerable was that she was kept apart from Hywel Rees. She could not sleep for thinking about him.

'Did nobody tell you where he was?' asked Nicholas.

'No,' she replied. 'I might never have seen him again if they had not made me go to that feast. I fought as hard as I could but it was no use. The keeper was too strong.'

'What's this about a feast?' wondered Elias.

The words came out haltingly. 'Some guests were invited to a feast in the main hall,' she said, averting her eyes. 'Gentleman from the city. I was told to please them or I'd be whipped again. The other women were set onto me. They tried to persuade me.'

Elias was disgusted. 'Bridewell whores, eh? You do not belong with them.'

'That's what I kept saying,' she explained. 'But the women dressed me to look like them and I was dragged to the hall, protesting all the way. As we crossed a courtyard, Hywel saw me from his window. He was shocked.'

'What did he do?' asked Nicholas.

'He tried to rescue me.' Her face lit up for second. 'How he escaped from his room I cannot tell you but I knew that Hywel would somehow come to my aid. I was in the hall, arguing still and being chastised by Master Beechcroft, when he burst in. As soon as Hywel saw what they were doing to me, he flung himself at Master Beechcroft and beat him to the ground. It took three men to pull him off.'

'Who is this Master Beechcroft?'

'One of the people who runs Bridewell.'

'What did he do when Hywel was overpowered?'

'He wanted revenge,' said Dorothea, wringing her hands. 'There was blood streaming from his nose and he was shaking with anger. If he'd had a weapon on him, I

think he'd have drawn it against Hywel. As it was . . .'
The words tailed off. Dorothea needed a moment to gather
herself. 'As it was,' she continued, 'he swore an oath then
said something that made me catch my breath.'

'What was it?' asked Elias.

Her lips trembled. 'Master Beechcroft said Hywel had
caused enough trouble at Bridewell and that he'd not get
the chance to cause any more.' She shivered violently. 'Then
they took Hywel out and I never saw him again.'

'What happened to you?' said Nicholas. 'Were you
forced to stay at this feast?'

'No, I was taken away and beaten. A couple of days
later, they discharged me.'

'So soon? But you'd been sent there by a court.'

'They do as they wish at Bridewell,' she said, bitterly.
'Master Beechcroft boasts about it. People come and go all
the time. They had no need of me so I was thrown out.'

'Yet they kept Hywel in there?'

'No. He's not at Bridewell. They told me so.'

'Then where is he?'

'I do not know,' she cried. 'That's why I came to you.
Something terrible has happened to Hywel. I sense it. He
tried to save me and they punished him for it in some way.
He was my only real friend in the world. I must find out
what happened.'

'Hywel was brave,' Elias said, admiringly. 'He tried to
save you.'

'But at what cost?' asked Nicholas. 'I do not like the
sound of what we heard.'

'No more do I, Nick.'

'I think this Master Beechcroft will bear close inspection. If he's empowered to run Bridewell, there are rules that must be obeyed. It's a place where the poor are put to work, not a house for revelry and licence.'

Dorothea was pathetically grateful. 'You'll help me, then?' she said.

'Do not doubt it.'

'We'll find Hywel for you,' vowed Elias. 'You may rely on us, Dorothea. Apart from anything else, I want him to teach me the trick of counterfeiting the falling sickness. It may come in useful one day.'

But the girl was not listening. Overcome with relief, she burst into tears.

The spectators who stood in the yard that afternoon had their numbers reduced and their spirits dampened by the weather. Overhanging eaves gave those who sat in the galleries a degree of protection that was not shared by those below. Undeterred by the persistent drizzle, Westfield's Men put their hearts and souls into a performance of *The Maid of the Mill*, a rustic comedy that drew much incidental humour from its many references to blazing sunshine. When the actors pretended to wipe sweat from their brow, they were merely brushing away the moisture that coated every face. The drizzle gave them other problems. It not only made the stage slippery, it soaked into their costumes and made them much heavier to wear.

The irony was that the weather finally improved as the

play neared its end. When the maid of the mill was duly married in the final scene, the drizzle abated and the clouds began to drift away. The audience signalled its thanks by applauding the company with enthusiasm. Wet and weary, the actors trudged off to the tiring house. They were glad to have survived intact. Their troubles, however, were not over.

'Where was he found, Adam?'

'In a passageway at the back of the inn,' said Crowmere.

'Who did this to him?'

'Nobody knows.'

'Was all the money taken?'

'Every last penny, Nick.'

Nicholas was disconcerted. At the end of each performance, one of his tasks was to collect the takings for the day. Gatherers had been positioned at the doors to take the admission fee and to charge extra, from those in the galleries, for a cushion to set on the hard benches. When the play began, one man, Luke Peebles, took charge of all the money so that he could hand it over to the book holder afterwards. Peebles was now seated in the taproom with his head swathed in a piece of blood-stained linen. He was still too dazed to remember much.

'He was hit from behind,' said Crowmere, regarding the man with sympathy. 'The wound is on the back of his head. I bound it as well as I could.'

'Thank you,' said Nicholas. 'How do you feel now, Luke?'

'My head still aches so,' said Peebles, weakly.

'Do you have any idea who attacked you?'

'None at all, Nick.'

'Was it one man? Two, perhaps?'

'It happened so quickly,' recalled Peebles, raising a hand to his skull. 'I heard some footsteps then I felt this pain at the back of my head. The next thing I remember, the landlord was helping me up.'

Crowmere was angry. 'I feel so guilty about this, Nick.'

'Why?' asked Nicholas. 'It was not your fault.'

'But it happened on my premises. I've a responsibility.'

'It's our responsibility to guard our takings, Adam. We do not look to you.'

'Nevertheless,' said Crowmere, 'I would like to offer remuneration. When Luke is well enough to tell us how much money was in his satchel, I'll meet that amount out of my own pocket.'

'Master Firethorn would not hear of such a thing.'

The landlord grinned. 'He'd not hear of it from Alexander, I know that. He's the meanest man in Christendom. But you'll not say that of me,' he went on, solemnly. 'This crime took place on my property. I've a duty here.'

'The only duty you have is to serve your customers,' said Nicholas, 'and you do that very well. Look at the terms of our contract with the Queen's Head and you'll see that it absolves the landlord of any liability for losses that we incur. I am the one who feels guilty. I should have instructed Luke to have a guard with him when he collects up all the money.'

'It's never been needed before, Nick,' said Peebles.

'It will be in future. We'll not put you in danger again.'

Nicholas was sorry to see the man in such evident pain. Peebles was short, slight and unarmed. Though still quite young, he was not robust. A blow that might only have stunned a tougher man had knocked him senseless. It was cruel to press him for details that were still too hazy in his mind.

'Wait here, Luke,' he advised. 'I'll find someone to take you home.'

'Thank you, Nick.'

Nicholas turned to the landlord. 'I'm sorry that this has happened, Adam. I can see how much it's upset you. But talk no more of offering us money. We'll bear the loss.'

'Can I give you no compensation?' asked Crowmere.

'None. The matter is closed.' He looked around. 'Where is the girl I asked you to keep an eye on while we performed this afternoon?'

'Dorothea is still in the kitchen.'

'I warned her not to be a nuisance to you.'

'The poor creature is too tired for that. She slept for hours.'

'Good,' said Nicholas. 'She needed the rest.'

'She'll not be able to stay, I fear,' said Crowmere. 'I have hands enough to help in the kitchen and she's not fit to serve in the taproom. Dorothea is far too timid for that.'

'The girl will not be staying, Adam.'

'What will become of her?'

'I'll find somewhere for her to spend the night,' said Nicholas. 'First, I must report this crime to Lawrence. He'll not be pleased. We lacked numbers in the yard but the galleries were full and they bring in more money. We've lost a tidy sum.'

Crowmere was livid. 'Find me the villain who did this and I'll tear him in two.'

'If I get my hands on him,' said Nicholas, 'there won't be any of him left.'

Following his orders, Owen Elias went straight to Bridewell. Instead of sharing a drink with the others after the play, he thought only of a young man in jeopardy. The fact that Hywel Rees came from Wales put an extra urgency in his step. Nicholas had schooled him to curb his aggression, telling him that he would learn little by making intemperate demands. Elias had to be more devious. The notion appealed to him.

When he reached the building, he stopped to look up at its waning grandeur. Impelled by the best of motives, King Edward VI had granted the palace to the city of London to be used as a workhouse for the poor and idle. It was a handsome gift and, as he studied the looming proportions, Elias wondered at this example of royal benevolence. The irony was self-evident. Constructed for the mightiest person in the realm, Bridewell was now the home of the lowliest members of society. He went in search of one of them.

'I am looking for a cousin of mine,' he said. 'Hywel Rees, by name.'

'We allow no visitors here, sir.'

'At least, tell me if he's still held in Bridewell.'

'Are you certain that he came here in the first place?'

'Yes,' said Elias. 'About a week ago.'

'Then he is like to be still with us.'

The keeper who manned the gatehouse was a plump, officious man in his thirties with a face that might have been hewn from granite. It seemed incapable of expression.

'Do you not keep records?' pressed Elias, glancing at the ledger on the desk.

'We do,' said the man.

'Then it's but a simple matter to see if my cousin still resides here.'

'This is no residence, sir. Bridewell is here to correct.'

'Then open your ledger and find out if Hywel is being corrected.'

The man was stubborn. 'I lack the authority to do that.'

'Is it authority that you lack or the simple urge to help me?'

'Go your way, sir. There's no more I can do for you.'

'But there is,' said Elias with excessive politeness. 'You can tell me your name. If, that is, your parents gave you the authority to do that. I'll need to know who you are when I report to Master Beechcroft how obstructive you have been.'

'I do what I am paid to do. Nothing more.'

'Master Beechcroft may have other ideas. I am not here out of idle curiosity.'

'No, sir?'

'A place this size must be expensive to run,' said Elias, 'and I know that charity is solicited. If my cousin Hywel is still here – and if I can find someone with the authority to verify that – I'll make a donation out of my own purse. Will you turn me away and lose all hope of my money?'

The keeper stared at him blankly. Elias was smartly dressed and he had a faint air of distinction about him. His request could be easily met even though the keeper was forbidden to volunteer information to strangers. If the Welshman's enquiry were spurned, there could be awkward repercussions. The man's resolve weakened.

'What was the name again, sir?' he asked, opening his ledger.

'Hywel Rees, convicted of vagrancy.'

'Was he alone when he was brought here?'

'No,' said Elias, 'a friend was with him. A young girl called Dorothea Tate.'

'I think I may remember them.' He used a finger to run down a list of names. 'Here's one of them. Dorothea Tate. She was discharged yesterday.'

'What of my cousin?'

'No longer here, sir. According to this, he left Bridewell days ago.'

'Then why is there no sign of him? He'd surely have come first to me.'

'Would he?' said the man, suspiciously 'If you are so concerned for his welfare, you could have saved him from being arrested in the first place. What sort of man are you to let a cousin of yours beg for a living on the streets?'

'A repentant one,' replied Elias, conjuring up a look of contrition. 'You are right to chide me, my friend. When he came to me for money, I turned Hywel away and I've been overcome with remorse ever since. It's such a shameful thing that a member of my family should end up in Bridewell.' He glanced at the ledger. 'Why was he discharged?'

The book was slammed shut. 'Never mind, sir. He has gone.'

Dorothea Tate was so unaccustomed to generosity that she could not believe that it was happening. Since she had turned up at the Queen's Head, she had been fed, comforted and treated with a respect she had never known before. Two men with whom she had only a fleeting acquaintance had immediately come to her aid, and the landlord had shown her indulgence as well. Suddenly, she glimpsed a different world. Dorothea feared that her good fortune could not last and, when Nicholas Bracewell invited her to return to his lodging, she resisted the idea strongly. In the past, most men had only sought her company for one vile purpose. What had made Hywel Rees so different was his kindness and consideration. Where others tried to molest her, he offered her protection.

It took Nicholas some time to persuade her and she set out with misgivings. She felt excited at being rowed across the Thames for the first time, though the foul language of the waterman made her cheeks burn. It was when they plunged into Bankside that her apprehension grew. It was a haunt of desperate men and the kind of shameless women she had met in Bridewell, standing brazenly in tavern doorways to beckon custom. Nicholas hustled her on until they turned into a quiet street. The houses were much bigger here and thatch had been replaced by tile. They stopped outside a door.

Dorothea drew back. 'I'll not go in alone with you,' she said.

'I do not expect you to,' he replied. 'Wait here a minute. I'll not be long.'

Nicholas let himself into the house and closed the door behind him. Left alone in the street, she mastered the impulse to run, telling herself that he had shown her nothing but kindness. Though he had exposed Hywel's deception at their first encounter, Nicholas had also saved them from a beating in the street. She had to trust him. If he had designs upon her, they would have been made clear by now yet he had treated her throughout with paternal concern. There was something else that influenced her. Everyone who spoke to Nicholas Bracewell at the Queen's Head did so with fondness and respect. That was the clearest indication of his upright character.

When the front door opened, she expected him to come out again but it was an attractive woman who appeared. She took the girl gently by the shoulders.

'Come in, Dorothea,' she said with a welcoming smile. 'My name is Anne. Nick has told me all about you. There's shelter for you here until we find your friend.'

'Something has happened to Hywel. I fear for him.'

'He may yet be safe. Do not torment yourself with anxious thoughts,' said Anne, leading her into the house. 'God willing, your friend is still alive and well.'

* * *

148

It was the hand that gave him away. Looped around a piece of driftwood, the arm seemed to be clinging on desperately. As the piece of timber bobbed in the dark water of the Thames, the white hand broke the surface time and again to wave farewell to life.

Chapter Seven

The next day being the Sabbath, it began as usual with a visit to church. Nicholas Bracewell accompanied Anne Hendrik and Dorothea Tate through the streets of Bankside to the sound of a medley of bells. Washed, well fed and restored by a good night's sleep, Dorothea was wearing one of the servants' dresses and a borrowed hat that had been designed by Anne. When the girl knelt in prayer at the church, Nicholas had no doubt who was in her thoughts. Racked with anguish, she was pleading for the safe return of her friend and protector. After the service, Nicholas escorted the women back to the house, then left them alone in the hope that, if Anne could spend some time alone with Dorothea, she would win her confidence and draw out details that the girl had been too embarrassed to divulge to a man.

Nicholas, meanwhile, had to meet a friend on the other side of the river.

'What did you learn, Owen?' he asked.

'Precious little from the gatekeeper at Bridewell,' grumbled Elias. 'He'd have told me nothing at all had I not wheedled the facts out of him.'

'How did you do that?'

'By posing as Hywel's cousin.'

'You have the looks and accent to carry it off.'

'It was like getting blood from a grain of sand.'

He told Nicholas what had transpired. The two of them were in the Welshman's lodging, a long, low room that was filled with amiable clutter. On the bed in the corner, the sheets were still rumpled from a night of passion, and from the sudden departure to church of the woman with whom Elias had been sleeping. There was a faint aroma of tobacco from the pipe that had been smoked earlier. Nicholas was disappointed that such scanty information had been gained at Bridewell. Elias added a telling detail.

'I peeped into his ledger as he checked it,' he explained. 'Beside the name of Dorothea Tate was a scribble that I took to be a record of her discharge. But there was nothing beside Hywel's name. Instead, it was scratched through with a line of ink.'

'Scratched through?'

'It was almost as if they were pretending that Hywel Rees did not even exist.'

'That's worrying news.'

'I did not give up there, Nick. Since I got such short shrift at Bridewell, I decided to look elsewhere for help. I reasoned that, if anyone could tell me how that workhouse was run, it had to be a lawyer.'

'Which one did you choose?'

'The only one that I could trust. That friend of Frank Quilter's. The jovial man who gave us so much assistance when Frank's father was unjustly accused.'

'I remember him well,' said Nicholas. 'Henry Cleaton.'

'He told me things that bear out what Dorothea was saying.'

'You surely did not doubt her word?'

'No, no,' replied Elias, 'but she's a young girl, wounded by her experience at Bridewell and still confused about what really happened there. Master Cleaton was able to throw more light on how the institution is administered.'

'What did he say?'

Elias took a deep breath. 'Bridewell has been dogged by corruption for years,' he said. 'One treasurer was dismissed for letting it flourish under his nose, another convicted for taking money that should have gone to the poor souls inside the place. A third, I discovered, was so incompetent that he paid several bills twice by mistake thus losing any profit that might have been made. Like the prisons,' he continued, 'the management and victualling of Bridewell is leased out to the highest bidder.'

'Is that how this Master Beechcroft became involved?'

'Joseph Beechcroft has a partner in the enterprise,' said Elias. 'A man named Ralph Olgrave. They somehow persuaded the good aldermen of this city to pay them no less than £300 a year to take over Bridewell.'

Nicholas was astonished. 'As much as that?'

'Master Beechcroft is a weaver, as I hear, and Master Olgrave a tailor. They wove a clever deal and tailored it to fit their needs. You can see why the two of them took an interest in the workhouse.'

'Yes,' said Nicholas. 'They can watch their trades practised there. According to Dorothea, wool is carded, cloth woven, suits made up. Dorothea said that hides are tanned there as well – and not only those belonging to the inmates. Joseph Beechcroft and his partner have found a means of using cheap labour.'

'The cheapest kind of all, Nick. They get no wages.'

'Only bed and board.'

'You heard Dorothea. The beds are hard and the food is dreadful.'

'So even more money is saved.'

'Henry Cleaton said that rumours have been coming out of Bridewell for some time, but they are only rumours. No clear proof of mismanagement has been found. In fact, the place is at last being run with some efficiency. What shook me,' said Elias, 'was how much power those men have. Our merry lawyer claims that the terms of their contract make them positive kings inside Bridewell.'

'Kings or tyrants?'

'Whichever they choose to be.'

'Joseph Beechcroft does not sound like a benevolent monarch.'

'Dorothea dubbed him a monster.'

'And she got close enough to him to make that judgement.'

'Why release her when she could make allegations against him?'

'To whom could she complain?' asked Nicholas. 'What strength does the word of a convicted vagrant carry? She was no threat to Master Beechcroft. No, Owen,' he concluded, 'I believe that she was discharged to get her out of the way. Dorothea knew too much. As long as she was inside Bridewell, she'd have been trying to find out what happened to her friend. That would irritate them.'

'And, to her credit, she refused to turn punk at Master Beechcroft's request.'

'So she could not serve her purpose in that respect. As far as he knew, she was alone and friendless in the city. When he had her turned out, Joseph Beechcroft believed that he was throwing Dorothea to the wolves and would never hear from her again.'

'He reckoned without us, Nick.'

There was a long pause. 'Let us suppose,' said Nicholas, trying to think it through, 'that the gatekeeper was telling the truth. Imagine that Hywel Rees was indeed discharged a few days ago. What would he have done?'

'Banged on the door until they let Dorothea out as well.'

'And if he'd been chased away?'

'He'd have done as she did, Nick,' decided Elias. 'Hywel would have turned to the two people in London who showed him any friendship. I fancy that we'd have seen him at the Queen's Head, asking for our help.'

'That's my belief. Yet there's been no sign of him. As I know to my cost,' said Nicholas with a wry smile, 'the Welsh are nothing if not tenacious. Hywel is like you, Owen. He'd not give up without a fight. But, all of a sudden, he disappears from the city. Would he desert Dorothea like that?'

'Never!'

'Then there are only two explanations.'

'He has either been hounded out of London altogether.'

'Or he is no longer alive,' said Nicholas, solemnly. 'Master Beechcroft, we are told, swore that he'd not be allowed to cause any more trouble at Bridewell. How far would he go to shut Hywel up?'

Lawrence Firethorn's day also began with a visit to church, taking the entire household with him. When he had seen his wife, children, servants and the apprentices safely returned to the house in Old Street, he mounted his horse and headed for the city. His first port of call was Edmund Hoode's lodging and he was pleased with what he found.

'You are out of bed at last, Edmund,' he observed, approvingly.

'I have been on my feet for the best part of an hour,' said Hoode, embracing his friend. 'I am trying to build up my strength again.'

Firethorn nudged him. 'And I know why, you rogue. That comely girl, the daughter of the house, let me in. Adele looks even more fetching today. You'll need all your strength to board that pretty little carrack.'

'I'd not even think such thoughts on the Sabbath.'

'More fool you!'

Firethorn inspected him more closely. Simply by exchanging his nightshirt for his doublet and hose, Hoode looked markedly better. His cheeks were still hollow but there was a sparkle in his eye and more zest in his voice. He sat near the window and waved his visitor to the chair opposite him.

'What's this I hear of a theft at the Queen's Head?' he asked.

'Yes,' said Firethorn, angrily, 'some rogue beat Luke Peebles to the ground and stole our money. We lost pounds that we can ill afford.'

'Have you no idea who the culprit might be?'

'No. Adam Crowmere has questioned all his servants but none could help us.'

'Thank heaven this did not happen under our old landlord,' said Hoode. 'He'd have used it as an excuse to lever us out of the inn.'

'His substitute shows Marwood up for the miser that he is. We could not ask for more sympathy. Adam even offered to make good our losses.'

'A worthy benefactor!'

'Our contract ties us and we had to refuse. But we saw his true character.'

'Everyone has kind words to say of him. Michael Grammaticus told me that this generous landlord has been trying to help the company in other ways.'

'Yes,' said Firethorn. 'He's done things that would

156

never even cross the mind of that maltworm, Alexander Marwood. New benches have been added to the galleries so that we may seat another sixty buttocks, and a better range of food is being served in the yard. More people have been tempted in.'

'Michael spoke of playbills.'

'Yes, Adam Crowmere lets us put them on every wall we choose. Nobody can pass the Queen's Head without knowing what Westfield's Men offer next. It's such a joy to have a landlord who is on our side.'

'If only I were there to share the joy.'

'You will be, Edmund. I see a new man before me.'

'The old problem persists, Lawrence. I am still tired for most of the day.'

'That will pass in time,' said Firethorn. 'Before you know it, you'll be reaching for *A Way to Content All Women* again.' He gave a chuckle. 'Though *I* could tell you how to do that for I've devoted my life to the art.'

'My interest in the play has been rckindled,' confessed Hoode.

Firethorn was thrilled. 'You've started work on it again?'

'No, but I talked about it with Michael. He's offered to help me finish it.'

'How? He has no ear for comedy. Just *look* at the man!'

'Do not be misled by appearances,' said Hoode. 'Michael has a keen sense of humour. When he was at Cambridge, he acted in two comedies by Plautus. Admittedly, they were performed in Latin but they taught him much about how to provoke laughter.'

'He can more easily produce tears. That's where Michael's skill lies, in the realms of tragedy. Flashes of humour there may be in *The Siege of Troy*, but it's a play that will move an audience with its dark and mysterious power.'

'Do not forget that I, too, have written tragedies.'

'Yes, but you are Edmund Hoode, who can turn his hand to anything. How many authors are able to do that? Michael Grammaticus will never ape you in that respect.'

'Give him the chance to try, Lawrence.'

Firethorn was unconvinced. 'We'll see, we'll see.'

They talked for half an hour before Hoode began to weaken visibly. His visitor decided to take his leave. Getting to his feet, Firethorn clapped him on the shoulder.

'Welcome back, Edmund!' he said. 'You've risen from the dead.'

'Bear my fondest regards to all of our fellows.'

'To those that deserve them, I will. But not to Barnaby, the wretch, who cannot find the time to call on you when you need comfort. And there are one or two others who do not merit your affection.'

'Why not, Lawrence?'

'They have let the company down badly.'

'How?'

'By allowing themselves to be seduced,' said Firethorn, scornfully. 'If there was a woman in the case, I would not mind, but the seduction involves a card table.'

'At the Queen's Head? Our landlord detests both cards and dice.'

'Adam Crowmere does not share his objections. He

158

has a man, lodging at the inn, who plays in his room and conjures money out of our fellows' purses. Nathan Curtis and Hugh Wegges were the first to suffer. They had to beg Nick to give them their wages in advance. The latest victim is Frank Quilter.'

'That surprises me,' said Hoode. 'Frank is such a level-headed man.'

'Not when he gets ensnared in a card game. All common sense then vanishes. He lost a lot of money at the table. I mean to raise the matter with Master Lavery.'

'Who is he?'

'The cunning devil who deals out the cards,' replied Firethorn. 'The sermon this morning urged us all to confront Satan in his various guises. I mean to do just that.'

The naked body lay on a cold stone slab in the morgue, the stink of decay softened by the smell of herbs that had been scattered around. Nevertheless, both Nicholas Bracewell and Owen Elias coughed when the foul air first hit their throats. They took care not to inhale too deeply. Though there was blazing sunshine outside, the room was dank and chill. The coroner, an elderly man with a wispy beard, indicated the latest cadaver to join his grim collection.

'This is the only one who might meet your description,' he said.

'Where was he found?' asked Nicholas.

'He was pulled out of the Thames yesterday evening.'

Elias was doubtful. 'I'm not sure that it's him.'

159

'Water disfigures the face,' warned the coroner. 'As you see, the body's bloated well beyond its normal size. We cut his clothing off and burnt it. He was wearing nothing but rags.'

Nicholas ignored the body and stared at the face, trying to imagine what it would be like without the gashes on the temple where the head had been bludgeoned. It was the nose that caught his attention. He pointed to a long scar.

'Look at that, Owen,' he said. 'Do you remember that scar on Hywel?'

'I thought it was more to the left.'

'No, I fancy not. This young man – God rest his soul – is the right age and height and colouring. That mark on his nose tells me that it might well be Hywel Rees.'

Elias bit his lip. 'If only I could hear his voice! I'd know him then.'

'Who was he?' said the coroner.

'A counterfeit crank. He feigned the falling sickness better than those that suffer from it. Hywel was a natural actor.'

'Even he cannot counterfeit death,' said Nicholas. 'And this, I think, is him.'

'It pains me to agree with you, Nick, but I must.'

'What was the name again?' said the coroner, plucking at an ear lobe. 'Hywel Rees? I do not like to see any man go to his grave anonymously.'

'Hywel Rees, late of Wales. Would that the poor fellow had stayed there.'

'Which part of the river was he found in?' wondered Nicholas.

'Not far from Westminster.'

'Downstream from Bridewell, then.'

'The body would have been carried much farther by the current had it not been caught in a piece of driftwood that snagged on the bank.' He glanced at the two men. 'Would you like to be left alone with him for a while?'

Nicholas nodded and the coroner quietly withdrew. They were grateful for his consideration. It enabled both men to lose themselves in thought, to feel a mixture of pity and rage at the hideous sight before them, a young life brought to a premature end by a brutal and unknown hand. The more they looked, the more convinced they were that Hywel Rees was lying there before them. It was Elias who eventually broke the silence.

'How will you break the news to Dorothea?' he asked.

'Gently,' said Nicholas.

Dorothea Tate thought that she was dreaming. She had met with such compassion from a complete stranger that she did not know how to respond. Anne Hendrik had not only given her a soft bed and decent food, she had allowed the girl to settle in without exerting any pressure on her. Because Anne did not pry, Dorothea was drawn to her. They sat in the parlour of the house in Bankside and listened to the church bells as they began another booming round to remind people what day it was. Dorothea became inquisitive.

'Do you live alone here?' she asked.

'Apart from my servant and Nick, who lodges here.'

'You have no husband, then?'

'He died some years ago,' explained Anne, 'and left me with his business. What I did not know I soon learnt and I have some of the best hatmakers in London working for me. All Dutch, all outsiders.'

'That was Hywel's complaint. He was treated like a foreigner as well.'

'Why was he on the road?'

'He worked on his uncle's farm until the old man died. A cousin took over and he had no love for Hywel. He forced him off the land,' she said, bitterly. 'It was cruel. Hywel had no other family. He was driven to leave his native country.'

'What of you, Dorothea?'

'I, too, was orphaned when my parents died of plague. I'd lived in Bedford until then. Nobody would take me in so I set out for London.'

Anne was concerned. 'How did you live?'

'By stealing food and sleeping under hedges,' said Dorothea. 'Two men caught me in St Albans and took me to a field for sport. Hywel saw my plight. He risked his own neck in saving me.'

'Nick told me that he was a brave young man.'

'He was fearless, Anne. He proved that in Bridewell.'

'What was it like to be imprisoned in that place?'

Dorothea swallowed hard. 'Worse than I could tell,' she said. 'They made us work all day and never took their eyes off us. Most of the ones I met were old women or young girls, robbed of their childhood. It was frightening.'

'Nick mentioned a man by the name of Master Beechcroft.'

'He's not a man, he's fiend from hell and his partner was even worse.'

'His partner?'

'Master Olgrave,' said Dorothea with a shiver. 'The one only had me whipped for disobeying him but the other, Ralph Olgrave – he kept asking me to call him by his Christian name – did far worse than that.'

She went off into a reverie and Anne waited until the girl looked at her again.

'Are you able to talk about it, Dorothea?'

'No,' whispered the other. 'Not yet. It still troubles me so.'

'When you are ready, you've only to turn to me.'

'Thank you, Anne.'

'Do you wish to eat now or would you prefer to rest?'

'I'll not rest properly until I know what's happened to Hywel.'

'You love him, I can see.'

Dorothea's eyes moistened. 'He's the only person who ever let me love him.'

'Then he's a true friend.'

There was a tap on the door and the servant popped her head around it. Anne went across to give her instructions about the preparations for dinner. Dorothea looked around the room. It was not large but it was well furnished and very comfortable. The girl had never been in a house with such a friendly atmosphere. She studied Anne with mingled awe and bewilderment. When the servant left, Anne turned to smile at Dorothea.

'Why are you being so kind to me?' asked the girl. 'I do not deserve it.'

'I think that you do, Dorothea.'

'But you know nothing about me.'

'I know enough to see that you are in need of help.'

'But you – and Nicholas – have given me much more than help. You've taken me in off the streets and listened to my woes. How can I ever repay you?'

'We seek no payment,' said Anne. 'From what you tell us, a grave injustice has taken place. It's our Christian duty to look into that. I know that it causes pain but the more information you can give us, the easier that will be. You've been inside Bridewell: we've not. So we can never understand the real horrors that go on behind those high walls. You were whipped, you say?'

'That was not the only punishment I suffered.'

'What else?'

Dorothea looked down and played with her fingers. Anne could see the blend of anger and embarrassment in the girl's face, and she felt guilty for asking the question. There was a taut silence. After a few minutes, Dorothea found her voice again.

'They took me to Master Olgrave's room,' she murmured.

* * *

Lawrence Firethorn was taken aback when he first met the man. Philomen Lavery was not at all what he had expected. Having knocked hard on the door of the man's room at the Queen's Head, he was confronted by a sight that drained him instantly of the fury he had built up. Lavery did not only look meek and mild, he was holding a Bible in his hands. He gave his visitor a luminous smile.

'Master Firethorn,' he said. 'This is an honour.'

'You know who I am?'

'All London knows who you are, sir, and I have had the privilege of seeing you on the stage here. You are beyond compare as an actor. I humble myself before you.'

Firethorn was flattered. 'Which of my roles do you admire most?'

'All are played with equal skill,' said Lavery, opening the door wider. 'But do step inside. I knew that you would come to see me sooner or later.'

'You *knew*?'

'The landlord told me that you frowned upon my presence here.'

'Well, yes,' said Firethorn, stepping into the room and trying to assert himself. 'True it is, I have some qualms about you, Master Lavery. This is the first moment I've had to voice them.'

Lavery closed the door. 'Speak on, sir.' He put the Bible on the table. 'Unless you wish me first to remove my shoes.'

'Your shoes?'

'So that you may inspect my feet to see if I have cloven hooves.'

'There's no need for that.'

'You'll have to take my word that I lack a forked tail,' said Lavery, 'for it would be indecent of me to lower my breeches.'

Firethorn grinned. 'If Barnaby Gill were here, it would also be unwise.'

'I am no creature from Hell. As you see, I study Holy Writ on the Sabbath.'

'The Devil has been known to quote scripture, Master Lavery.'

'But he has never been known to lose at cards.'

'Lose?'

'That's the fate that befell me last night,' said Lavery. 'I won money from Frank Quilter and even from Adam Crowmere, then along comes a member of your company and I am suddenly out of pocket again.'

'One of the actors?' asked Firethorn in annoyance.

'James Ingram.'

'He *dared* to come here after I'd warned him against doing so?'

'With the greatest respect, Master Firethorn, you are not his keeper. You may warn but not coerce your fellows. Had he listened to you, James Ingram would not now be able to count his winnings.'

'I am worried about those who incur losses at your table.'

'Then you must extend your sympathy to me,' said Lavery with another smile. 'I fell in love with card games many years ago. I'd play for the sheer pleasure of it, without

166

a penny changing hands, but those who come to my room insist on placing a wager. What can I do, Master Firethorn?'

'Turn them away.'

'And deny myself the joy of a game?'

'If you wish to play cards, visit a gaming house. The city is full of them.'

'And the gaming houses are full of cony-catchers, men who play with marked cards that allow them to win at will. I want an honest game where chance is paramount.' Lavery became anxious. 'Has anyone complained that I cheat?'

'No, that charge has not been levelled against you.'

'Do they think me dishonest?'

'You are exonerated there as well, Master Lavery.'

'Then wherein lies my offence?'

'You are distracting my fellows,' said Firethorn.

'Every man needs distraction of some kind. Look around you. Some find their pleasure in ale, others in women, others again in bear baiting or cock fighting. London is brimming with such distractions,' Lavery pointed out, 'and the theatre is among the best of them. Those who come to the Queen's Head take the same risk as a card player. They pay money in the hope of gain. If the play is dull or the actors jaded, the spectators have lost all that they invested.'

'That never happens here,' said Firethorn, proudly. 'Our audiences always get far more than they pay for, Master Lavery. Do not insult us by comparing us to a game of cards. Westfield's Men offer drama and excitement.'

'Both of those are on display here, albeit in smaller measure.'

167

'I do not see them.'

'That is because you have not felt the surge of blood as you turn a card.' Lavery crossed to a shelf and took down a pack of cards. 'Allow me to show you, sir.'

Firethorn took a step back. 'Keep those away from me.'

'They'll not bite you, Master Firethorn. How can they? Look,' he said, putting the pack on the table and spreading it out. 'Are you afraid of a few pieces of card?'

'I've seen what they do to others.'

'Yes, they can fill a purse. Speak to James Ingram on that account.'

'I'll speak to him to chide him for his folly.'

'At least know what drew him to my table,' said Lavery. 'It is so simple and yet so pleasurable. Watch me.' He turned over a card. 'Now, Master Firethorn, choose one yourself and see if it is higher than mine.'

'Do you dare to trick *me* into a game?' roared Firethorn.

'This is no game, sir. I merely offer proof. Come now, I do not seek your money, only your understanding.' He indicated the cards. 'Turn one over then tell me if you did not feel a twinge of excitement.'

Firethorn was reluctant. 'I prefer to find excitement in other ways.'

'What can you lose? There's no trickery here. Chance determines all.'

'That's what you said to Nathan Curtis and Hugh Wegges.'

'They pressed me to play for money,' said Lavery. 'I could not refuse a wager. Here, there is no such risk. All that you forfeit is your suspicion of the game.'

'Do not rely on that,' said Firethorn, eyeing the cards. 'I choose one?'

'From anywhere in the pack.'

'How do I know they are not marked?'

'Examine them, if you wish.'

'No, no, I'll take your word for it.'

After a moment's hesitation, Firethorn selected a card and turned it over. The face of a red king stared up at him. He could not resist a smile at his good fortune.

'You see?' said Lavery. 'You are the winner. Had you wagered a groat on that card, you'd be walking away with two. Now, Master Firethorn,' he went on, collecting the cards up again, 'tell me the truth. Do you feel defiled for having played a game? Were you disappointed when you made your choice? What do you say?'

There was a considered pause. 'Let's try it again,' said Firethorn.

Nicholas arrived back at the house to discover that Dorothea Tate had retired to bed for the afternoon. He was very grateful. It gave him an opportunity to pass on the sad tidings to Anne Hendrik. She was aghast at what she heard.

'Her friend was *murdered*?' she said.

'Battered to death then tossed into the river.'

'Can you be certain that it was him?'

'No,' admitted Nicholas. 'We only met Hywel once and that was brief enough. But we recognised a scar upon his nose and it seems too great a coincidence that he should turn up where and when he did. Owen and I are persuaded that it is him, but only Dorothea would know for definite.'

'Must she, then, view the body?'

'I think not, Anne. It's the last thing she must do. It's a gruesome sight for anyone to look upon. No,' he decided, 'Dorothea must be allowed to remember him as he was. Were she to visit the morgue, that bloated image would haunt her forever.'

'Who could have done such a thing to him?'

'We have one suspect at least.'

'Master Beechcroft?'

'Yes,' said Nicholas. 'I had to restrain Owen from charging off to Bridewell to accuse the man to his face. We have no proof as yet. Besides, the man may be innocent of the charge. Hot words were spoken against Hywel but that does not mean they were acted upon. Joseph Beechcroft may not be involved at all.'

'Then who is?'

'I do not know, Anne. London is full of danger and we know that Hywel would not run away from a fight. He might have been attacked by a gang, who threw him in the Thames. Or fallen foul of a sailor who tumbled out of a tavern. Bodies are all too often hauled out of the water.'

'What will you tell Dorothea?'

'As little as possible.'

'She must be told that he's dead, Nick, and she's bound to ask the cause.'

'I want to spare her as much pain as I can.'

'Dorothea is stronger than you think,' said Anne. 'We talked for hours while you were away. She spoke about her childhood, such as it was. It's been a very hard life for her. Only someone with strength and courage could have come through it.'

'If she spoke so freely, she must have trusted you.'

'I think she does, Nick. Why?'

'It might be better if you were to tell her about Hywel.'

'Teach me what to say and I'll gladly take on the office.'

'Thank you,' said Nicholas, leaning forward to kiss her on the forehead. 'You'll do it better than I could manage. While you comfort Dorothea here, I can try to pick up a trail that leads us to the killer.' He glanced upwards. 'How long will she sleep?'

'Who knows? She said she'd not stir from this room until she knew what happened to Hywel, but she fell asleep in the chair so we put her to bed.'

'Did she tell you anything about Bridewell?'

'A great deal, Nick. Her time in that workhouse has marked her for life.'

Anne told him what she had learnt about the way that the institution was run and how Dorothea Tate had suffered at the hands of her keepers. Nicholas listened intently to the description of what had happened at the feast to which the girl had been unwillingly dragged. It was clear that she had given Anne a much more detailed account.

'She never mentioned Master Olgrave to us,' he said.

'He's a ruthless man, Nick, even more so than his partner.'

'We'll need to look at both of them in time.'

'Start with Ralph Olgrave,' advised Anne. 'He committed the greater crime against Dorothea. He had her brought to his room one night. Master Beechcroft only had the girl whipped. His partner robbed her of her virtue.'

Nicholas was shocked. 'Dorothea was raped?'

'It left her feeling so ashamed, Nick. She broke down when she told me.'

'Ralph Olgrave will be called to account for this,' he promised. 'Their contract with the city authorities gives them such wide powers inside Bridewell that they think that they can get away with anything. We'll have to show them otherwise.'

'Go carefully. They are dangerous men.'

'Dangerous but cowardly, Anne. It is easy to strike at people who are defenceless. Only cowards do that. We'll see how much courage they have when they meet someone on equal terms. Joseph Beechcroft and Ralph Olgrave have a shock awaiting them.' He rose from the chair. 'I'll back to Owen and acquaint him with what I've heard.'

'Shall I speak to Dorothea when she wakes?'

'If you would. All you need to say is this.'

Before he could instruct her, however, there was a tap on the door and Dorothea came into the room. She rushed across to Nicholas and looked up hopefully at him.

'Did you find Hywel?' she asked.

'Yes,' he replied, quietly. 'I fear that we did.'

Dorothea read his expression and tried to hold back tears. Anne immediately put a comforting arm around the girl's shoulders. Tightening her jaw and bunching her fists, Dorothea looked up at Nicholas.

'Tell me the truth,' she insisted. 'I can bear to hear it. How did he die?'

Chapter Eight

Most people would protest if they found themselves suddenly interrupted on the Day of Rest, but Henry Cleaton could not have been more welcoming. The visitors were invited into his parlour and given refreshment. Cleaton was a man who did not always conform to the rules of his profession. His appearance set him completely apart from his fellow lawyers. With his shock of red hair and his rubicund cheeks, he might have been a farmer and he had a stocky frame that hinted at long years of manual labour. There was also a genial quality about him that flew in the face of the lawyer's traditional caution. Meeting him again after a lapse of time, Nicholas Bracewell was reminded of the new landlord at the Queen's Head. Henry Cleaton had the same willingness to please.

'We are sorry to trouble you at home,' said Nicholas, 'but we need advice.'

'Then you were wise to call here,' said Cleaton, indicating the room. 'It is far tidier than my office and much more comfortable. As for disturbing me, think no more of it. I am glad of your company. Since my wife died and my children moved away, it can be very lonely on a Sunday afternoon.'

'We are not imposing, then?'

'Not at all, Nicholas. The case interests me. When Owen called on me yesterday, my ears pricked up at the mention of Bridewell. You are trying to find a young man who was recently imprisoned there, I believe.'

'We found him,' said Elias. 'On a slab at the morgue.'

'Dear me! How did that come to pass?'

'With your help, we mean to find out.'

'Did he die a natural death?'

'No,' said Nicholas. 'His skull had been cracked open. Thus it stands.'

He related the salient facts as swiftly and dispassionately as he could. Elias felt obliged to make comments from time to time but it was Nicholas who controlled the narrative. Cleaton was intrigued by all that he heard.

'Murder, rape, mismanagement,' he said. 'These are serious charges.'

'One can certainly be nailed to the door of Bridewell,' asserted Nicholas, 'and that's the violation of Dorothea Tate. The girl is not given to lies.'

'But she is, alas. Did you not tell me that she was the accomplice to a counterfeit crank? That's blatant dishonesty. The first thing she told you was that she and this Hywel Rees were brother and sister. Forgive me,

Nicholas,' said Cleaton, 'but this girl is plainly seasoned in deceit.'

'She would not deceive us about a thing like this.'

'How do you know?'

'I'd stake every penny I have on it, Master Cleaton.'

'Your loyalty is admirable and, since you've met Dorothea Tate, I'll have to trust your judgement. No court would do so, however. Ralph Olgrave is an upright citizen. For a vagrant like this girl to accuse him of rape would be a waste of breath.'

Elias was roused. 'Are you saying that he's allowed to get off scot-free?' he demanded. 'That he can deflower any maid at will and face no consequence? That's not justice, Master Cleaton.'

'It's the way the law functions and you must beware of that.'

'In short,' said Nicholas, 'we need more evidence.'

'Nothing less than a confession would satisfy a court, and I doubt that Master Olgrave will be minded to oblige you with one. Seek other ways to bring him down.'

'Will you give us some guidance in the matter?'

'I'll do more than that. I'll work with you to unmask these rogues.'

'We've no proof that either was involved in the murder,' Nicholas reminded him. 'And even if they were, I doubt that they would have struck the fatal blows themselves. Confederates would have been hired.'

'Yes,' said Elias. 'Alehouse ruffians that would kill their own mothers for a fee.'

Cleaton pondered. He had met both men when dealing with a case that concerned their friend, Frank Quilter. In the course of the investigation, the lawyer had got to know Nicholas particularly well and come to respect him highly. It was the reason he had admitted them to his home at such a time. Unless the matter was serious, Nicholas would never have ventured to disturb him like that.

'Why are you doing this?' he asked.

'Does a lawyer need to be told that?' said Nicholas with surprise. 'Crimes have been committed. Rank injustice has occurred. Prompt action is required, Master Cleaton.'

'Yes, but why do you have to instigate it? These young people have been cruelly abused, but it is not your duty to fight on their behalf. Until a week or so ago, they were total strangers to you.'

'Hywel is Welsh,' said Elias. 'That's enough for me.'

'What of the girl?'

'She turned to us for help,' replied Nicholas. 'We'll not disappoint her.'

'Then you must realise that obstacles will face you at every turn. You are up against cunning men who occupy positions that are well nigh impregnable. Do not think to storm Bridewell.'

'I could not even get through the door,' confessed Elias.

'Then work another way,' suggested Cleaton. 'Let me make enquiries. Joseph Beechcroft and Ralph Olgrave will both have apartments at the workhouse, but they will also have homes elsewhere. That's the place to stalk them.'

'Can you find out where they live?' said Nicholas.

'I think so.'

'We would be very grateful.'

'It might be safer if you accost them alone, Nicholas.'

Elias was piqued. 'Why? I can ask as straight a question as Nick.'

'But you'd do so in a voice that would remind them of Hywel Rees,' argued Cleaton. 'That would put them on their guard at once. If you wish to squeeze the truth out of them, they need to be treated with care. Accuse them of nothing. Simply make enquiries about the whereabouts of Hywel Rees.'

'I will,' said Nicholas. 'I know how to tread softly.'

'So do I,' insisted Elias with a hint of belligerence. 'I am softness itself.'

'There'll be work enough for you, Owen. Have no fear.'

'I want to meet this Ralph Olgrave.'

'So you shall, in the fullness of time. Let me talk to him first.'

'Marry,' said Cleaton, 'that's the eftest way. I'll furnish you with addresses. If such heinous crimes did take place inside Bridewell, then they must be exposed or others will be at the mercy of those two men.'

Elias put a hand on his dagger. 'I'd like to have the pair of them at *my* mercy!' he said. 'By the time that I'm done with him, Ralph Olgrave will never be able to force himself on a woman again.'

'Take the law into your own hands like that,' warned Nicholas, 'and you'll end up in prison. Leave these men to me, Owen. I'll move more stealthily. And as we've learnt this afternoon from Master Cleaton,' he continued, smiling at their host, 'people are more at ease in their own houses. They can be taken unawares.'

Doctor Zander stood over him as he drank the medicine. Edmund Hoode shuddered.

'It tastes foul,' he said, pulling a face. 'Can you not sweeten it in some way?'

'That would reduce its potency, Master Hoode. If you would recover, you must endure the bitter taste. Eat a slice of apple when I've gone and that will please your palate a little more.' He studied the patient, who was now back in bed again. 'You seem much better today.'

'This morning, I was able to get up and walk around. I even dressed myself for the first time. Lawrence noticed the difference in me at once.'

'Lawrence?'

'Lawrence Firethorn, the actor.'

'Ah, yes,' said the doctor. 'Master Grammaticus has mentioned the name to me. He reveres the fellow. But, then,' he added, 'he idolises you as well, Master Hoode.'

'How can anyone idolise a man in my condition?'

'You'll get well in time if you do not tax your strength.'

'I cannot stay in bed all day, Doctor Zander.'

'Oh, I agree. A little exercise is important. What worries me, however,' said Zander, scratching an itch somewhere on his thigh, 'is that you are too popular. You have too many friends who feel the need to call.'

'They wish to know how I am.'

'Then let your landlady tell them. Visitors tire you because you make such an effort while they are here. Ask them to come less often and your health will improve.'

'But I like to see them,' protested Hoode. 'If I'm left alone, I have to fight off boredom. My friends bring me such cheer, doctor.'

'And rightly so. All that I advise is moderation.'

'I'd not be able to stop Lawrence coming here, if I tried. The same goes for Owen Elias and Nick Bracewell. They visit me every day.'

Zander made a dismissive gesture. 'I'll say no more. If you would let them prolong your illness, be it on your own head. Do not blame me for a tardy recovery.' He picked up his satchel. 'I'll away, Master Hoode.'

'When will you call again?'

'In two or three days' time. I look to find you much improved.'

'You will, you will,' said Hoode. He raised a hand. 'Before you go, doctor, there is a matter I must discuss. It has bothered me from the start.'

'Oh? And what is that?'

'You never ask me for payment.'

'Master Grammaticus takes care of all the bills.'

'But it's wrong for him to do so. I put too much strain on his purse.'

'He hates to see you in such a state,' explained Zander,

'and will pay anything to find a cure. Do not worry about his purse, Master Hoode. He is never short of money and he tells me he has sold a new play.'

'Yes,' said Hoode with a grin. '*The Siege of Troy*. I hear wondrous reports of it. Michael has come of age as an author.' The grin faded. 'But I would not have him bear the cost of my doctoring. Send the next bill to me.'

'It has already been paid by Master Grammaticus.'

'He takes too much upon himself.'

'No, Master Hoode,' said Zander, moving to the door. 'He loves you for what you did to inspire him. No price can be set on that. Try as you may, you will not pay a penny for any treatment that I give you. I am contracted to work for Master Grammaticus alone in this matter.' He opened the door. 'Get some sleep, sir. Farewell.'

When he called in at the Queen's Head late that afternoon, Nicholas was just in time to intercept Lawrence Firethorn. The actor was about to mount his horse in the yard. When he saw the book holder, he removed his foot from the stirrup.

'Nick, dear heart!' he boomed. 'You come upon your cue.'

'I hoped to catch you here.'

'And I was equally hopeful of being caught. I've good news for you. Edmund is starting to rally at last. He'll soon be chasing the landlady's daughter around his room.'

'I rejoice at these tidings,' said Nicholas. 'I've been too

busy to call on him so far but mean to go there now. He's well, you say?'

'Well enough to walk around the room. Best of all,' said Firethorn, happily, 'that clouded mind of his begins to clear at last. He even talked of working on *A Way to Content All Women*.'

'His new comedy? Then he is truly recovered.'

'Not enough to complete it himself, alas. He needs help from a co-author.'

'Whom did he suggest?'

'That's the rub. It was Michael Grammaticus.'

Nicholas was amazed. 'But comedy requires lightness of touch,' he said, 'and Michael does not have that. At least, I've seen no evidence of it. There are scenes in his tragedies that have a comical edge to them, but they have nothing of Edmund's deftness. What made him name Michael as his co-author?'

'I had the feeling that the idea came from our new playwright himself.'

'He's certainly eager to please.'

'But will he please an audience?' asked Firethorn. 'If three mirthful acts by Edmund Hoode are followed by two solemn dirges by Michael Grammaticus, we'll content nobody, let alone the women in the title. The notion appals me.'

'Yet the offer would not have been made without due thought. Michael must believe that he *can* catch Edmund's voice, or he'd not put himself forward. There's an easy solution here,' said Nicholas. 'Let him read what there is of the play and write two or three new scenes for us. We'll soon know if he has a comic gift.'

'Set it in motion, Nick. Though I still think his ambition outruns his talent.'

'He deserves the chance to prove us both wrong.' He glanced at the inn. 'Did you manage to speak to Master Lavery? I know that it was in your mind to do so.'

'Yes,' said Firethorn, 'I bearded him in his den. What a peculiar fellow he is! Have you ever known a card player who reads the Bible on a Sunday? That's what he was doing when I called upon him. He looked more like a saint than a sinner.'

'What did you say to him?'

'What I planned to do, Nick. I told him that he was distracting our fellows and causing a deal of misery. His answer was that they came to his table of their own accord, and that he had no power to stop them.'

'He said as much to me.'

'Did you know that James Ingram won a lot of money last night?' Nicholas shook his head. 'It convinced me that the man was no rogue. Philomen Lavery can lose as easily as he can win, it appears.'

'He's no real threat to us,' said Nicholas. 'He'll be quitting the city later this week so he'll not be able to inflict much more harm.'

'That's why I drew back from condemning him too harshly.'

'We'll soon forget all about him.'

Firethorn was wistful. 'Yes, I suppose that we will.' His mind wandered for a moment, then he became aware of Nicholas again. 'But why were you so anxious to catch me today?'

'To ask a favour of you.'

'You know that I would never refuse you.'

'This is a big favour,' said Nicholas. 'I may need to absent myself for a while.'

'But how can you do that when we rely on you so much?'

'Hear me out. We do not play here tomorrow, and on Tuesday we present *Love and Fortune*. George Dart can hold the book for that with his eyes closed.'

'George does *everything* with his eyes closed,' growled Firethorn. 'That's why he keeps bumping into things and breaking them. But why do you need to leave us, Nick? You must have a reason.'

'A pressing one. In brief, I must help to solve a murder.'

He gave Firethorn a concise account of what had happened and explained how he and Elias had become involved. The actor showed some compassion but he was not persuaded that his book holder should be spared to take part in an investigation.

'This is not your quarrel, Nick,' he argued. 'Keep out of it. Westfield's Men must come first. Let officers of the law look into these matters.'

'They would not bother to do so. Who cares about the death of a vagrant? Whether from disease, starvation or violent assault, beggars like Hywel Rees end up in the morgue all the time. Murder a wealthy man,' said Nicholas, 'and a hue and cry is set up. Kill a poor one and he vanishes into oblivion.'

184

'My fear is that you and Owen will vanish into oblivion.'

'You lose me alone. Owen will be here to play in *Love and Fortune*.'

'But Edmund will not,' said Firethorn. 'That means we shall have to rehearse someone else in his part. I want you there to do that, Nicholas.'

'A moment ago, you said you'd grant me any favour.'

'To my dear friend, I'd grant as many favours as he sought. But I've no obligation to a street girl who was arrested for begging. This favour is for Dorothea Tate, let's be clear about that.'

'Are you not moved by her plight?'

'Why, yes,' said Firethorn, defensively. 'I'm moved by the plight of any vagrant. I often toss them a coin as I pass them by. That's Christian charity. But I'd not turn my back on the company in order to help one of them arraign a man for stealing her virginity. The wonder is that she kept it so long.'

Nicholas was annoyed. 'Can you treat murder and rape so lightly?'

'No, Nick. Both are dreadful crimes. Those that commit them should be punished. But I still do not see that you should take it upon yourself to find the malefactors. To put it more plainly,' he said, 'why do you bother?'

'Because I gave my word.'

'And is that more important than your duty to Westfield's Men?'

'Yes,' said Nicholas, firmly. 'It is.'

* * *

185

Dorothea Tate had been so shocked to hear of the murder of Hywel Rees that she had been unable to speak for a long time. Sobbing quietly, she rocked to and fro on her seat as she contemplated a future without her dearest friend. Anne Hendrik sat beside her with a consoling arm around the girl's shoulders. Sharing her sorrow, she tried to offer words of comfort but Dorothea did not even hear them. She was consumed by her grief. At length, the girl sat up and made an effort to pull herself together. She used a hand to brush away the tears that had coursed down her face.

'I want to see him,' she announced. 'I want to see Hywel.'

'No, Dorothea.'

'It may not be him. Nicholas said that he could not be certain.'

'He and Owen were as certain as they could be.'

'But they might have made a mistake.'

'For your sake,' said Anne, 'I hope that they did. In that case, Hywel is still alive and he'll come looking for you. But you must prepare yourself for the worst.'

'That's what I've been doing.' She straightened her back. 'I'm ready for anything now, Anne. I want to visit the morgue. I want to see his face.'

'You heard what Nicholas said. He'd been in the water for days. That distorts the body horribly and changes the face.'

'I'd know him anywhere.'

'Spare yourself the horror.'

'It's my right,' insisted Dorothea. 'Hywel was my friend.'

'Then ask yourself this. Would he have wanted you to see him in that condition?'

The question made her pause. Doubts began to form in her mind. The girl brought a hand to her mouth as she searched for an answer. It was minutes before she turned back to Anne. There was a pleading note in her voice.

'I *have* to know the truth.'

'I fear that you already do,' said Anne, gently.

'What if it is not Hywel?'

'How many young men have that scar on the nose that Nicholas described? He recognised it at once. We know that Hywel was discharged from Bridewell. There's a record of that. Where did he go?'

'If only I knew!' exclaimed Dorothea.

'From what you've told me about him, Hywel was loyal and loving.'

'He was like a brother that I never had.'

'Then he would never dream of leaving you,' said Anne. 'However long it took, he would have waited until you were let out as well. Is that not so?'

'Yes. He swore he'd look after me.'

'Only one thing would stop him from doing that, Dorothea.'

The girl stared unseeingly ahead of her as she tried to fend off the truth of what she had just heard. She clung to the hope that Hywel might still be alive but her grasp was slowly weakening. In the end, after a long interval, her body sagged as she accepted the fact that her friend must be dead. She turned to Anne.

'I think that I'm ready to sleep now,' she murmured.

Edmund Hoode was also ready to sleep but the arrival of Nicholas Bracewell helped him to shake off his drowsiness at once. He sat up in the bed with a smile of relief.

'I feared that you'd forgotten me today.'

'I could never do that,' said Nicholas, lowering himself on to a chair beside the bed. 'I remembered you in my prayers at church and I came as soon as I could.'

'You must have had a busy day, then.'

'It has kept me occupied, Edmund.'

Nicholas gave no details. Hoode was a sick man who should not be burdened with additional anxieties. If he told his friend about the investigation on which he had embarked, Nicholas knew that the softhearted playwright would worry incessantly about what became of Dorothea Tate. He was not strong enough to cope with such tidings.

'Lawrence tells me that you were up and about this morning,' said Nicholas.

'Yes, Nick. I felt better than I had for a week or more.'

'And now?'

'I was fading badly when you came,' said Hoode. 'Doctor Zander warned me that the disease would ebb and flow like the sea.' He laughed grimly. 'Perhaps that is why I feel seasick most of the time.'

'I think the time may have come to seek another opinion on your health.'

'But that's already been done. Doctor Rime examined me and was able to identify the malady. Two doctors are in agreement here, Nick. How many more do we need?'

'Did either of them tell you how you first caught the disease?'

'That remains a mystery, though Doctor Rime felt that it must have been caused by something that I ate. The poison got into my blood.' His gaze switched to the papers on his table. 'Did Lawrence talk to you about *A Way to Content All Women*?'

'Yes,' said Nicholas. 'He mentioned that you might consider a co-author.'

'Not willingly, I admit. I have my pride and would not easily share the credit for a play of mine with someone else. But these are unusual times,' he went on. 'Illness keeps me from lifting my pen and I know how much a new comedy is needed. That being the case, I listened to Michael's offer.'

'The notion came from him, then?'

'Oh, yes. I'd not have thought of him at first. Other playwrights are much more well versed in the rules of comedy than Michael. But he was so persuasive, Nick. He said it would be an honour to work with me.' Hoode chuckled quietly. 'How the fellow has changed! When he first came to us, Michael Grammaticus was so shy that he could not even look us in the eye.'

'Success has emboldened him, Edmund.'

'I've half a mind to accept his offer.'

'Hear my device first,' suggested Nicholas. 'Lawrence

has given it his blessing so it needs only your approval. Before we engage Michael to finish the play, let him see what you have already written before adding a couple of new scenes to show us what he can do. That way, we do not commit ourselves too far too soon.'

'I'll happily agree to that,' said Hoode, 'on one condition.'

'What's that?'

'My plays are my progeny, Nick. I do not like to let them out of my sight. If Michael would read the new comedy, he must do so here where I can watch him. Do not tell him to take it away with him.'

'Nor will I,' said Nicholas, crossing to the table and picking up the sheets of parchment. 'You are right to guard your new child like a watchful parent.' He looked down at the Prologue, written in Hoode's neat hand. 'You give advice that every man longs to hear – *A Way to Content All Women*.'

'Lawrence boasted that he had already mastered the art.'

'I beg leave to doubt that. I've seen him enrage Margery a dozen times.'

'She's a choleric woman, Nick, and it is not easy to calm her when she's roused.'

'Then the secret is not to rouse her in the first place.'

Hoode laughed. 'You've hit the mark, Nick,' he said. 'That's the very moral of my new comedy. Why do I need Michael Grammaticus? *You* should be my co-author.'

* * *

The first two people to enter the room that evening were Frank Quilter and James Ingram, the first hoping to repair his losses while the second intended to exploit his good fortune. Philomen Lavery gave them a warm welcome and poured each a glass of wine. The cards were waiting on the table but there was no sign of the Bible now. While the visitors took their seats, Adam Crowmere ambled into the room.

'Do you come to join us?' asked Lavery.

'I'll watch a little before I play,' said the landlord. 'After bearing such losses last night, I'll be more cautious today. I want to study the cards first.'

'A sensible decision.'

'Do we play with the same pack as yesterday?' said Ingram.

'The very same.'

'Then I do not need to hesitate. I know that my luck will hold.'

'I pray that mine changes,' said Quilter, feeling his purse. 'You must not be allowed to rob us all again tonight, James. It's my turn to play the pickpocket.'

'Everyone at the table has the same chance to win,' said Lavery, sitting opposite the two actors. 'That's the beauty of the game. It makes us all equal.'

'Deal the cards,' urged Ingram. 'I want to savour another victory.'

'And I,' said Quilter, ruefully, 'to get my revenge.'

The cards were dealt and the game began. Before it was over, however, there was a tap on the door and it opened to reveal another player. As the man walked slowly into the room, Lavery looked up in astonishment.

'Come in, come in, sir!' he said with delight. 'This *is* a pleasant surprise!'

Henry Cleaton's office was small, musty and filled with books, documents and piles of papers. His desk was covered with so much clutter that it was impossible to see a square inch of the wooden top. Before his visitor could sit down, Cleaton had to move some writs off the chair for him. He grinned at Nicholas Bracewell.

'Take a weight off your feet,' he said. 'It's a long walk from Bankside.'

'I came to see if you've any news for me.'

'Then you come upon your hour. I've been a true bloodhound, Nicholas.'

'What have you learnt?'

'Where both of the men live,' he explained. 'When I put my mind to it, I soon saw how easily it could be done. Joseph Beechcroft is a weaver and Ralph Olgrave a tailor. I sent my clerk to enquire at the Weaver's Hall and he was given the address at once. The Merchant Tailors' Hall likewise supplied Olgrave's house and street.'

'Did they surrender the information so willingly?' asked Nicholas.

'We had to put bait on the hook. My clerk pretended that each man had been mentioned in a will and was due an inheritance. That quickly loosened tongues.'

'May I have the addresses?'

'As soon as I can find them,' said Cleaton, searching under the mounds of paper on his desk. 'I wrote them down and put them somewhere safe.'

Nicholas was amused. 'There's nowhere safer, Master Cleaton. You are the only man in the world who could find what you wanted in here.' Cleaton retrieved a few scrolls that fell from the desk and put them back again. 'I'll start with Joseph Beechcroft.'

'He lives in Basinghall Street, not far from the Weaver's Hall. Did you know that they are the oldest livery company in London? They received their first charter in 1155 and have a distinguished history.'

'It's a pity that Master Beechcroft did not uphold their high standards.'

'Ah,' said Cleaton, pulling out a scrap of parchment. 'Here it is, Nicholas.' He handed it over. 'Be wary of the fellow. If he can talk his way into such an advantageous position in Bridewell, he'll have a smooth tongue and a quick brain.'

'All that I mean to do at this point is to sound him out.'

'You'll do that better without Owen Elias beside you. He tends to be bellicose.'

'Celtic blood runs hot in his veins,' said Nicholas with an affectionate smile. 'Owen always prefers action over talk. The time will come when I need his strong arm and short temper.'

'Let me know how you get on.'

'I will, Master Cleaton. And thank you for all that you've done.'

'You'll need a lawyer again before you've finished, I daresay.'

'I'll know where to come.'

'Meantime, I'll make some more enquiries about Bridewell and see what I can find. I sniff a pungent scent here,' said Cleaton, beaming. 'My tail begins to wag.'

'I'm glad to hear that you are sanguine.'

'My optimism is tempered with hard fact. Hounds do not always catch the fox.'

'Oh, we'll catch this one,' said Nicholas with quiet determination. 'And his accomplice.'

Joseph Beechcroft was preening himself in a mirror when the servant brought him news of his visitor. Hearing that Nicholas Bracewell had come in the hope of discussing some aspect of Bridewell, the weaver agreed to see him. They met in the parlour, introduced themselves then weighed each other up. Nicholas was not invited to sit.

'What business brings you here?' asked Beechcroft. 'I was just about to set off for Bridewell. If you've an interest in the place, you should have sought me there.'

'I tried to do so,' lied Nicholas, 'but could not get past the gatekeeper.'

'We discourage random visitors.'

'I do not come by accident, Master Beechcroft. I have a purpose.'

'Tell me what it is.'

For a man who had started as a humble weaver, Beechcroft had a lordly air. He wore a gaudy doublet of blue and red with gold thread looped across the breast. In his buff jerkin and plain hose, Nicholas presented a sharp contrast.

'Well, sir,' nudged Beechcroft, irritably. 'I do not have all day.'

'How many people do you have inside Bridewell?' said Nicholas.

'That's private information.'

'I wondered if you had so many that you did not know who they all were.'

'I know the name of each and every one,' asserted Beechcroft. 'When someone works for me, I learn everything I can about them so that I can get the best out of them.'

'You assign the labour inside Bridewell, then?'

'What is it to you?'

'I wondered if you or Master Olgrave was in charge.'

'If you must know, we share the responsibility. Ralph and I are partners.'

'I'm told that you run the place with some efficiency,' said Nicholas with feigned admiration. 'It was not always the case under your predecessors. They often failed. You must be good administrators.'

'We are,' boasted the other. 'We know how to turn a profit. Is that why you've come to me, Master Bracewell? You wish to do some business with us?'

'That depends on how good your word is.'

'It's my bond, sir.'

'Tell me about one Hywel Rees,' said Nicholas, watching him carefully.

Beechcroft started. 'Who?'

'One of the inmates at Bridewell.'

'The name is unfamiliar to me.'

'A minute ago, you claimed to know everyone inside the institution.'

'Yes,' said Beechcroft, recovering his composure. 'And it's true. We did have a young man by the name of Hywel Rees with us but we discharged him days ago.'

'May I know the reason?'

'No, sir. You may not.'

'But I need to track him down,' said Nicholas, recalling the ruse that was used by Henry Cleaton's clerk. 'I've news that will mend his fortunes. Hywel Rees – if he be the man I seek – has been left some money by an uncle back in Wales.'

'Some money?'

'A substantial sum. I'm not at liberty to reveal the amount but it would buy the young man out of Bridewell or out of any debtor's prison. I heard that he had fallen on hard times and was convicted of vagrancy. There's a record of that, and of the fact that he was sent to you for correction.'

'No man was more in need of it!' said Beechcroft under his breath.

'What happened to him when he left your care?'

'He disappeared into the crowd.'

'I find that hard to believe, Master Beechcroft.'

'Why is that?'

'Because I understand that he was imprisoned with a friend,' said Nicholas. 'The two were arrested together and both were sent to you. Her name was Dorothea Tate. Do you remember her as well?'

'Yes,' replied Beechcroft. 'She, too, was discharged recently.'

'That seems odd, sir. When vagrants are committed to the workhouse, they expect to stay for some time. That's what the court enjoins. Do you have the power to override a judicial decision and dispatch any inmate you choose?'

Beechcroft scowled. 'Bridewell was not the right place for either of them.'

'So you sent them on their way?'

'Yes.'

'Do you have any idea where Dorothea Tate may have gone?'

'Back to the streets, I expect.'

'That means you discharged a beggar so that she could return to begging. What is the point of that, Master Beechcroft?'

'I'll not be criticised in my own house,' exploded the other, rounding on him. 'Why have you come here and what do you really want?'

'To learn the whereabouts of Hywel Rees. If you do not know where he is, it is possible that this girl does. Find her and we find the beneficiary of the will.'

'You are wasting your time, sir.'

'Am I?'

'I do not know exactly where he went,' said Beechcroft, 'but I can tell you this about Hywel Rees. He's not in London. Search as much as you like, you'll not catch sight of him again. He went back to Wales and we were glad to see the back of him.'

'I can see that you remember him very well.'

'He was a rebel. A stubborn, awkward, noisy fellow. A thorn in our sides. My partner and I can usually break the spirit of such rogues but he was too wilful for his own good. Hywel Rees had to go.'

'Back to Wales?'

'That's where he said that he was heading.'

'Without his closest friend, Dorothea Tate?'

'For all I know, the girl went with him. Good riddance to both of them!'

'Was she another rebel?'

'To some degree. Strict obedience is the rule inside Bridewell.'

'That depends on what people are asked to obey,' said Nicholas, levelly. 'Why did she flout your authority, Master Beechcroft? Can you answer that?'

'No!' retorted the other, crossing to open the door. 'I've answered too many of your questions, as it is. Hywel Rees is no longer in London, I can assure you of that, so you look in vain.' He pointed to the door. 'Good day to you!'

'Thank you for your help,' said Nicholas with the faintest hint of sarcasm. 'You've explained a lot to me. And as you say, your word is your bond. I can see now why Bridewell is in such safe hands.' He crossed to the door. 'Oh,' he added, pausing beside the man. 'You tell me that Hywel Rees went back to Wales.'

'I'm certain of it.'

'How would he get there? Do you think he might try to swim?'

Joseph Beechcroft turned pale and his mouth fell open. Nicholas had what he wanted. Before the other man could even speak, the visitor swept out of the house and left him in turmoil.

Chapter Nine

Lawrence Firethorn was in a vile mood that morning. Cantering into the yard of the Queen's Head, he brought his horse to a halt and glowered at everyone within range. When he dismounted, he tossed the rein to an ostler and barked an order. It was not the choicest moment for Michael Grammaticus to approach him.

'Good morrow, Master Firethorn,' he said.

'What do you want, sir?'

'Is there any news of the play?'

Firethorn was brusque. 'Nick has taken it to the scrivener and he is still copying it out. Forgive me, Michael, but I've far more important things to worry about than *The Siege of Troy*.'

'But I was talking about the other play.'

'What other play?'

'*A Way to Content All Women*. Has Edmund not spoken to you about it?'

'Oh, that,' said Firethorn, irritably. 'You believe that you can write a comedy.'

'Only with your consent.'

'Talk to Nick Bracewell. He knows my mind on this.'

'Edmund is agreeable,' said Grammaticus. 'We spoke about it yesterday.'

'Then why bother me? The only comment I can make on the play is that its title should be changed. Any man who believes that there's a way to content all women,' he said with rancour, 'has never met my wife. Are you married, Michael?'

'Only to my work.'

'Then I envy you.'

'Why?'

'Because I have learnt a grisly truth,' he confided. 'Women are *never* content. Give them what they want and they'll put a new demand upon you. Grant them that and they'll still not find contentment. Ignore their pretty faces and supple bodies. Eschew their blandishments. Women are no more than a breed of shrews and harpies.'

'If you say so.'

'I know it to be true.'

And on that sour note, Firethorn turned on his heel and strode out of the yard, leaving Grammaticus in his wake. No rehearsal had been called for that morning but a meeting of the sharers had been summoned. Only two of them were there when Firethorn stormed into the room that had been hired for the occasion. It gave him another excuse to lose his temper.

'Saints and serpents!' he howled. 'Where *is* everybody?'

'The others will soon be here, Lawrence,' said Elias.

'This is more than I can bear. I've lost our author, our book holder, our takings from *The Maid of the Mill*, and now I've lost most of the sharers. This is a conspiracy against me.'

'Be patient a while.'

'Patient!' cried Firethorn. 'Do not talk to me of patience, Owen. I've been far too patient with this company and look what happens. Everyone lets me down.'

'What's put you in this angry mood?'

'I spy a woman's hand here,' said Gill, mischievously. 'Or rather, the absence of it. Margery has not milked his epididymis this morning so Lawrence is full of bile.'

Firethorn glared at him. 'Be quiet, you prancing pestilence!'

'A rift in the marital lute?' teased Gill.

'Taunt me any more and I'll make a rift in *your* lute.'

'Calm down, Lawrence,' said Elias. 'We meet here as fellows.'

'Then show me some fellowship. Nobody else in this company will do it.'

'This is foolish talk. You know that we all love and respect you.'

Gill tossed his head. 'Do not include me in that, Owen.'

'You see?' said Firethorn, pointing at him. 'I'm surrounded by enemies.'

'How can one man surround you?' said Elias. 'This is the raving of a madman. Now, sit beside us and wait until the others come. A cup of Canary will improve your disposition.' He patted the chair beside him. 'Come now, Lawrence. Join us.'

Firethorn consented to sit down and sip from the cup of Canary wine that stood before him. He was sullen and distracted. Not wishing to provoke another outburst, the others said nothing. After a short while, James Ingram came into the room and greeted everyone with a pleasant smile.

'Forgive this lateness,' he said, lowering himself onto the settle beside Gill. 'My horse cast a shoe and I had to take it to be shod.'

Firethorn glared at him. 'Does the shoeing of a horse take precedence over the affairs of Westfield's Men?'

'No, Lawrence.'

'Then why were you not here on time?'

'We might ask the same of you, Lawrence,' said Gill with an impish grin. 'Owen and I had a long wait before you deigned to appear.'

'The meeting should start the moment that I walk through the door.'

'Then you'll have to walk through it again when the others arrive for we cannot begin without them.' Gill turned to Ingram. 'Take care, James,' he warned. 'Lawrence is like a wounded bull this morning. He'll charge you as soon as look at you.'

'Hold your noise, Barnaby!' snapped Firethorn.

'Hark! The beast is snorting again. He'll stamp his foot next.'

'Bait me any more and I'll stamp it on your overgrown testicles.'

'Peace!' chided Elias. 'If you are in this humour, Lawrence, there is no point in having any discussion this morning. Why do we not disband and return when you are in a more amenable mood?'

'That might take years,' said Gill.

'Stop goading him, Barnaby.'

'I merely speak the truth.'

'I'm surprised that vicious tongue of yours still knows how to do that,' remarked Firethorn, sharply. 'It's told so many wicked lies that it's in danger of dropping out. The day that Barnaby Gill turns honest man, the streets will sprout corn and the Thames will run with ale. You are nothing but a viper.'

'Then best beware my sting.'

'Enough of this!' protested Elias.

'Yes,' said Ingram, forcefully. 'There's no sport for us in watching you two at each other's throats. I thought we were met to talk about the future of the company, not to see a cock fight. Take off your spurs, I pray.'

'Well said, James.'

Firethorn and Gill stared across the table at each other but said nothing. The other sharers began to drift in until the full complement was assembled. The actor-manager rapped his knuckles on the table to gain everyone's attention. Before he could start the meeting, however, the door was flung open and a white-faced Hugh Wegges was standing before them. He pointed at Firethorn.

'There you are,' he said, 'I need to speak with you.'

Firethorn was curt. 'This is not the time, man. Be off with you!'

'But you'll want to hear what I say.'

'If it's to ask for your wages in advance again, then you waste your time. I spurn your request. How dare you interrupt us! Now, take that ugly visage out of my sight.'

'We've been robbed!' cried Wegges.

'What are you jabbering about?'

'I came to set out the costumes for *Love and Fortune*, that we play tomorrow, and half of them are not there. The finest costumes from our stock have gone. If you do not believe me, come and see for yourself.'

'I'll do just that,' said Firethorn, hauling himself up. 'If this be a jest, Hugh, I'll paint you yellow and hang you from the highest tree in England.'

'It's no jest, alas. I wish that it were.'

Wegges led the way with Firethorn at his heels. Elias and Gill were also in attendance. The tireman kept their costumes under lock and key in a room adjacent to the chamber that was used as their tiring-house. When they got there, Wegges threw open the door to reveal the evidence of the crime.

'See, sirs,' he said, 'what terrible losses we have suffered.'

The newcomers were dumbfounded. Several of their costumes had disappeared and those that were left behind were scattered all over the floor. It was obvious from a glance that the only richest garments had been stolen. Gill let out a cry.

'They've taken my doublet from *The Merchant of Calais*,' he gasped.

'And my cloak from *Black Antonio*,' complained Elias.

'What of my gown from *The Insatiate Duke*?' said Firethorn. 'It was a present from our patron and cost all of twenty pounds. A pox on these villains!' he yelled. 'They've taken our clothes and left us naked. Heads will roll for this.' He looked around in despair. 'Oh, where is Nick Bracewell when we need him most?'

Nicholas did not hesitate. Knowing that it was important to reach Ralph Olgrave before the man's partner did, he bounded through the streets until he came to Old Jewry. He did not even have to knock. A person he took to be Olgrave was talking to one of his servants at the threshold before departing. Nicholas had a moment to size the man up. Olgrave was older and shorter than his partner, but wider in the shoulders. Where Beechcroft had been gaunt, Olgrave was fleshy; where the one chose flamboyant apparel, the other had more sober taste. After giving instructions to his servant, Olgrave set off. Nicholas moved in to intercept him.

'Master Olgrave?' he enquired.

'Yes,' replied the other with smile. 'Who might you be, sir?'

'My name is Nicholas Bracewell and I crave a word with you.'

'Do you wish to employ me in some way?'

'Only to provide me with some information, Master Olgrave.'

'Concerning what?'

'Bridewell.'

'Ah,' said Olgrave with a chuckle. 'Master Bracewell asks about Bridewell, does he? Visit me there, if you wish, sir,' he went on, blithely. 'I do not like to be interrogated on my doorstep.'

'Does that mean you have something to hide?' probed Nicholas.

'Which of us does not, my friend? There's not a man alive who does not have something in his past he wishes to stay buried. Or if there is, he's lived a very dull life.' He appraised Nicholas shrewdly. 'I take you for someone who's seen excitement in his time. That means you'll have your share of dark secrets to conceal.'

'Nothing that I'd feel ashamed about, Master Olgrave.'

'Nor me. I've never had a twinge of guilt in my life.'

'Let me come back to Bridewell.'

'No, my friend,' said Olgrave, smoothly. 'Let *me* come back to Bridewell. Seek me there if you have any business with me. You'll find me there most days.'

'And some nights, too.'

'I have an apartment there, true. It's one of my privileges.'

'What do you do to earn those privileges, Master Olgrave?'

'I run the workhouse honestly and capably with my partner.'

'Yes,' said Nicholas, 'I've spoken with Master Beechcroft.'

'Oh? To what end, may I ask?'

'I've been commissioned by a lawyer to track down a man who has come into an unexpected inheritance. He's much in need of it, too, for the last I heard of him, he was sent to Bridewell as a punishment.'

'We provide work as well as correction. Who is this man you seek?'

'His name Hywel Rees.'

'No,' said Olgrave without a flicker. 'I do not recall the fellow.'

'Master Beechcroft knew him instantly.'

'Then why do you come to me? If Joseph recognises the name, speak to him. Had I met him, I think I'd remember someone called Hywel Rees, but I do not.'

'What of Dorothea Tate?'

'What of her?' replied Olgrave, easily. 'The name is new to me.'

'She was a friend of Hywel Rees, and also sent to Bridewell.'

'You seem to know more about our inmates than I do, Master Bracewell. Do you have any more names to scatter before me or may I continue on my way?'

Nicholas paused. Ralph Olgrave had more self-possession than his partner. Unlike Joseph Beechcroft, his expression did not betray his thoughts. The same complacent smile had played around Olgrave's lips from the start. Nicholas could not remove it.

'How often are your inmates discharged?' he said.

'As often or as seldom as we wish.'

'I learn that Hywel Rees was thrust out after only a short time in Bridewell.'

'You've learnt more than me,' said Olgrave. 'My partner signs the discharge papers. I've no knowledge of this man or of his release.'

'Dorothea Tate was let out more recently.'

'Then she'll have vanished back into the eternal army of beggars who besiege the capital. Bridewell does a valuable service, my friend.'

'Does it?'

'We try to sweep the streets clean of vagrants so that worthy citizens like you can walk them with safety.'

'How much safety do the vagrants have once inside Bridewell?'

'There's only one way for you to find out.'

'Is there?'

'Yes,' said Olgrave with a teasing grin. 'Come there as our guest. All you have to do is to live on the streets and beg for your food, and we'll be pleased to invite you to our table. We may need to whip you first but I see you have a broad back that will survive the punishment. Nicholas Bracewell, is it?' he went on, looking him up and down. 'Now, that's one name I will remember. Adieu, good sir.'

Olgrave raised his hat in mock farewell, then sauntered off down the street. Nicholas watched him go. He had not been able to penetrate the man's smugness but he was nevertheless glad of the encounter. It showed him what he was up against. Having met Joseph Beechcroft, he was more than ready to accept Dorothea's assessment that the man was a devil, but he remembered what she had said about his partner. In her view, Ralph Olgrave was even worse. As he saw the jaunty figure moving away from him, Nicholas had no difficulty in believing it.

'Saints preserve us!' exclaimed Adam Crowmere. 'How on earth did *this* happen?'

'I put that same question to you,' said Firethorn, angrily. 'Do you not keep your doors locked at night?'

''Tis an article of faith with me. I check them myself before I retire to bed.'

'And was the door to our wardrobe secure?'

'Completely. I remember trying the latch.'

'What time was that?'

'Around midnight, as I recall.'

'Then our thief came calling in the darkness.'

Summoned by Firethorn, the landlord gaped at the half-empty room where the costumes had been stored. Elias and Ingram had withdrawn but Hugh Wegges, as the tireman, lingered at the door. Crowmere ran a worried hand across his brow.

'This is a tragedy, Lawrence,' he said. 'What must you think of me?'

'That depends on whether or not you were at fault.'

'I wish that I were, then we'd have an answer to this riddle. Only two keys will open that door. I have one of them and the other is kept by your tireman here.'

'It never leaves my belt,' said Wegges.

'Then my key must have done the damage,' admitted

Crowmere, 'unless this is the work of some cunning picklock. But how would he know what was in the room? He would hardly worm his way in there at random.'

Firethorn was rumbling with suppressed fury. 'This crime was planned,' he said. 'The thief knew where to come and what to steal. Our costumes are our livelihood, Adam. Take those away and we are plain men, shorn of any authority.'

'Some are left, Lawrence. There's comfort in that.'

'Only if I wish to lower myself to play the part of a beggar, a headsman or a common soldier. Look here,' he said, picking up a leather apron. 'This is worn by a blacksmith in *Cupid's Folly*. Will I be reduced to wearing that? How can I play a king or an emperor or a cardinal in a leather apron? I'd be a laughing stock. My father was a blacksmith, Adam,' he explained, tossing the apron aside, 'and I worked hard to escape the forge. I swear, I'll not go back to it.'

'Can you put an exact price on the loss?' asked Crowmere.

'Some items were gifted to us,' said Wegges. 'We did not have to buy them.'

'What of those you did have to purchase?'

'Fifty pounds would come nowhere near covering the cost.'

The landlord gulped. 'I can see why it cuts so deep. Well, let me offer some balm at least for your wound. Fifty pounds is too much for me to spare but I'll insist you take five at least by way of consolation.'

'The only consolation I seek is to find the villain who did this,' said Firethorn. 'It must be someone who frequents the Queen's Head and knows where our wardrobe is.'

'He also knows where I keep my keys, Lawrence, for he may have borrowed one when my back was turned. Yes,' he said, pensively, 'that may be it. Some light-fingered varlet must have taken the key and had a replica made. That way, he could get into the room at will.' His eyebrows formed a chevron. 'Let me speak to my servants. One of them may be able to enlighten us.'

'One of them may be the culprit,' said Firethorn.

'If that's the case, I'll tear him limb from limb.'

'Leave his entrails to me, Adam. I'll roast them over a fire.'

'What am I to do now?' asked Wegges, tamely. 'Am I to lock the door again?'

'When there is nothing left worth stealing? No, Hugh. Search the place for clues. Talk to all who haunt the taproom to see if they can help. We'll get those costumes back somehow. And when we do,' said Firethorn, 'you'll sleep outside this door all night.'

Henry Cleaton sat back in his chair and chewed on the stem of a pipe that had no tobacco in it. After hearing all that his visitor had to say, he removed the pipe to speak.

'You found no more than I expected, Nicholas,' he said.

'Two arrant knaves, who revel in their wickedness.'

'I doubt if they will revel in it today. You ruffled their feathers.'

'I may have done so with Master Beechcroft,' said Nicholas, 'but his partner must have ice in his veins. He remained cool to the end. Had I gone there with Dorothea on my arm, Ralph Olgrave would not have turned a hair.'

'That's because he feels secure in his villainy, and he's right to do so.'

'But we have a witness.'

'He'll find a dozen willing witnesses, whose voices will drown out anything that Dorothea Tate has to say. Look not to her, Nicholas. Certain proof is needed.'

'We know that a feast was held in Bridewell, and that visitors were entertained by prostitutes imprisoned there. Is that not in defiance of the contract they have to run the institution?'

'Yes,' agreed Cleaton.

'Could they not be arraigned for keeping a disorderly house?'

'Possibly.'

'You do not sound convinced, Master Cleaton.'

'I'm a lawyer and the only thing that convinces me is the weight of evidence. Yet what is your evidence here?' he asked. 'The word of a frightened girl with a grudge against Bridewell. Yes,' he continued before Nicholas could object, 'I accept that she has good reason to bear a grudge but put yourself in the position of the other women in the case. Dorothea refused to join in the merriment but my guess is that those harlots were only too ready to eat, drink and oblige the gentlemen. They are locked in a workhouse, remember. What would they prefer to do, Nicholas? Make

213

ticking for feather beds or do the work that they know best by lying on those feather beds?'

Nicholas was forced to agree. When he called at the lawyer's office to report on his conversations with the two men, he hoped that Cleaton would feel that definite progress had been made. All that Nicholas had actually done, however, was to satisfy himself that Dorothea's descriptions of Beechcroft and Olgrave were accurate ones. It was one thing to jolt the former by asking if Hywel Rees might have swum back to Wales, but finding hard evidence that he was involved in the murder was quite another. Nicholas was frustrated. Slapping his thighs, he rose from his chair

'They are corrupt men,' he argued. 'Others who used Bridewell for their own purposes were either dismissed or imprisoned. Can it not be so for them?'

'Only if they are found out,' said Cleaton. 'In the past, wayward treasurers were caught when the account books were inspected. Beechcroft and Olgrave are too clever to be snared that way. Their accounts will be above reproach.'

'Is there no way to get into Bridewell to verify the facts?'

'Not without a warrant, Nicholas, and who would give us that?'

'Dorothea has given me my warrant.'

'I admire the sentiment, but deplore its lack of legality. Bridewell is a fortress. Inside that, Beechcroft and Olgrave are beyond our reach.'

'Then we must lure them out.'

'I think they'll be more wary of Nicholas Bracewell in the future,' said Cleaton. 'Especially since you used the same trick as my clerk to extract information. The two men will have realised by now that you played false with them.'

'To good purpose.'

'Granted. But it will mean they'll not be fooled again.'

'Then I'll have to work another way.'

'If only I knew how, Nicholas. The problem with being a lawyer is that I am shackled by the law. I can only envisage legal ways of achieving my ends.'

'Was it legal to ask your clerk to obtain addresses the way that he did?'

'More or less,' said Cleaton, happily. 'We did not break the law so much as bend it slightly. In a sense, my clerk spoke the truth. Joseph Beechcroft and Ralph Olgrave were mentioned in a will. It was the unwritten testament of Hywel Rees, who bequeathed the pair of them his hatred.'

'Then I'm the executor who must enforce the terms of that will.'

'How do you propose to do that?'

'By taking advice from Master Olgrave.'

'What kind of advice?'

'I'll explain that in a moment,' said Nicholas. 'First, I must ask a favour of you.'

'Is it within the bounds of the law?'

'It could not be more so, Master Cleaton. It will appeal to a legal mind.'

Michael Grammaticus read the play with growing excitement. He was seated at the table in Hoode's lodging so that he could turn over the sheets of parchment more easily. The author of *A Way to Content All Women* sat opposite him, observing his reactions and disappointed that no laughter came from his visitor. Grammaticus came to the last page and read it through with the same grim concentration.

'Oh!' he sighed, looking up. 'It has come to a premature end.'

'Did you like the play, Michael?'

'I loved every word of it. You have written a small masterpiece.'

'There was not even a hint of a smile in your face.'

'Inwardly, I promise you, I was all mirth. The wit and humour flow so smoothly from your pen, Edmund. There is no sense of effort.'

'There was when I tried to read the play myself,' said Hoode. 'I got up early and forced myself to do it, but I dozed off before the end of the first act.'

'No spectator would ever do so. Every speech has a sparkle to it.' Grammaticus shook his head. 'I'm not sure that I can emulate that.'

'I've told you Nick's suggestion. Write two more scenes to complete Act Four, then we can judge how well you disguise yourself as Edmund Hoode.'

'The next scene, as I take it, shows Vernon's proposal to Maria?'

'I think that's what I intended.'

'Then the act must surely end with the discovery of Will Lucifer in Rosalind's bedchamber on the eve of her marriage to Timothy Gull.' He tapped the parchment. 'That's the logical development of the comedy because it brings yet another round of misunderstandings. Is it not so, Edmund?'

Hoode scratched his head. 'As far as I can recall.'

'Think more upon it, if you will,' said Grammaticus. 'I'll need all the help that you can give me. I'll be an apt pupil, be assured of that.' There was a knock on the front door. 'You have another visitor, I think. I'll leave you alone with him while I go to the market to buy you some more fruit. Doctor Zander insists that you eat it.'

'You are too kind to me, Michael.'

'I could never repay what you've done for me.'

He got up from the table and looked down covetously at the play again. Knuckles tapped softly on the door then Nicholas Bracewell came into the room. He exchanged warm greetings with the two playwrights. Grammaticus then excused himself and went on his way. Nicholas ran a careful eye over Hoode.

'You look better than you have for weeks,' he said.

'I feel that the worst is over, Nick,'

'That's good to hear. We may not need Michael's help with your new comedy, after all. You'll soon be able to finish it yourself.'

'Oh, I doubt that,' said Hoode. 'My mind is like a morass. When Michael talked just now of the characters in *A Way to Content All Women*, I could barely recall who they were. It was almost as if the play were not mine.'

'It is, Edmund, and will always remain so.'

'Michael has agreed to write the two scenes, as you

advised. But he insists on doing so at his lodging, even though I'll not let the play out of my sight. He says that he can only work at his own desk.'

'You need to be at his elbow, to guide his pen in the right direction.'

'That's what I'd hoped to do,' said Hoode. 'I even offered to take the play to his lodging, if someone could be found to carry me there, but he'd not hear of it.'

'Why was that?'

'Michael is a very private person. His imagination only flowers when he's alone.'

'Where does he lodge?'

'Somewhere in Cornhill, I believe.'

'Not far away from here, then,' said Nicholas. 'We could easily transport you there with the play in your hand.' A memory nudged him. 'When I offered to go with Michael to fetch his copy of *The Siege of Troy*, he refused to let me go with him. Now, he keeps you away from his lodging. Is he ashamed of where he lives?'

'That can hardly be so. There must be another reason.'

'A mistress with whom he lives?'

Hoode laughed. 'I think that we can absolve him of that sin, Nick.'

'He's shown great care for you, Edmund, and that earns him my admiration. He never fails to call. Who else has been here this morning?' asked Nicholas. 'I daresay that Owen was the first. What of Lawrence?'

'He came and went in a towering rage, Nick. Your name was taken in vain.'

'Was it?'

'Lawrence said that you should have been there when the discovery was made.'

'What discovery?'

'Our wardrobe has been raided and our finest costumes stolen.'

Nicholas was shocked. 'But they are locked securely in a room.'

'Nevertheless, they've gone. It seems that Hugh Wegges found the place in disarray this morning. He was upset, the landlord was distraught and Lawrence is in a fury. Keep clear of him,' said Hoode. 'He blames you for being absent.'

A long day had done nothing to still her fears or to extinguish her hopes. Dorothea Tate asked time and again if she could visit the morgue. It was the only way to make sure that the dead body fished out of the Thames did belong to Hywel Rees. Though she sensed that her friend had been murdered, she could not let go of the vain hope that he was still alive. Anne Hendrik tried to reason with the girl.

'What can be gained, Dorothea?' she said. 'Go to the morgue and you only inflict needless pain upon yourself.'

'I'm in agony, as it is.'

'Try to get some rest.'

'How can I do that, Anne? I lay awake all night, thinking about Hywel.'

'Do you have fond memories of him?'

'The fondest. He was a true friend.'

'Then do not sully those fond memories by looking on

him now. Nick and Owen Elias have strong stomachs but even they were revolted by what they saw. Hywel is not the young man you knew.'

Dorothea sagged back in her chair. Without help, she knew that she would never be admitted to view a dead body. Nicholas would have to take her and he was as keen as Anne to keep her away from the horrid sight. There was nothing that the girl could do. It was a paradox. In the most comfortable house she had ever stayed in, she felt somehow constrained. While she was enjoying the kindness of friends, she was beginning to view them as enemies who stopped her from doing the one thing of importance to her.

Anne had made such efforts to distract her, taking her into the workshop next door so that she could watch hats being made, visiting the market with her, dining with her, listening to her, watching over her. The only time that Dorothea could be alone was if she went to her room and there she was assailed by worries about Hywel. A sense of guilt developed. Why should she have such comforts when the young Welshman might be lying on a slab? For the first time in her life, Dorothea wore clean clothing and ate as much food as she wished. Yet the very fact that she was protected and cared for made her uneasy. She did not belong.

The return of Nicholas made her rise expectantly from the chair. Anne, too, got up to greet him, glad that he had come back so early in the evening and seeing from his face that he had news to impart.

'Where have you been?' she wondered.

'To several places,' he replied. 'I began at the lawyer's office and ended up at the Queen's Head, where Lawrence had to be pacified. He was incensed because the company has been dealt another bitter blow.'

'Your old landlord is returning?'

'No, Anne. We've been spared that horror, though it will surely come if our run of bad luck continues. Someone raided our wardrobe and made off with the better part of it. They'll raise a tidy sum by selling those costumes.'

'Who would do such a thing?'

'Rivals. Someone who had a grudge against us. Or simply a thief in search of making a profit. Lawrence is maddened. It took me an hour to calm him down.'

'What of the lawyer?' asked Dorothea, impatiently. 'You said before you left that he might be able to help us.'

'He did, Dorothea. Sit down again and I'll tell you how.' She and Anne resumed their seats. 'Master Cleaton worked quickly,' said Nicholas, remaining on his feet. 'He found out where Joseph Beechcroft and Ralph Olgrave lived.'

'They have chambers at Bridewell.'

'Yes, but they also have homes and families.'

Dorothea goggled. 'Master Olgrave has a *family*? A wife and children?'

'Judging by the size of his house, I think it very likely.'

'Then how could he do what he did to me?' she said in bewilderment. 'That was not the action of a married man. What of his vows to his wife?'

'I think that he forgets them when he chooses,' said Nicholas, 'and does so without compunction. He boasted to me that he never felt a twinge of guilt.'

'You *met* him?'

'I met the both of them, Dorothea. They are a well-matched pair.'

'What did they say?'

'The one assured me that Hywel had gone back to Wales, the other pretended that he had never heard the name. He also denied all knowledge of you.'

'That's shameful!' cried Dorothea. 'After what he did to me, that's cruel.'

'Cruel and disgraceful,' said Anne, touching her hand in sympathy. 'What did you do, Nick – confront the villains with their crimes?'

'No,' he replied, 'I merely wished to take their measure. Master Beechcroft was inclined to bluster but his partner kept his feelings under control. I took him to the more dangerous of the two.'

'Oh, he is, he is!' said Dorothea with passion.

'Then you must help me to bring him down.' He turned to Anne. 'If you will, please, fetch paper and pen. I want Dorothea to become an artist and draw as much of Bridewell as she can recall.'

'I've no skill with a pen, Nicholas.'

'But I do,' said Anne. 'I sit here and draw pretty hats all day.' She headed for the door. 'I'll hold the pen and you can tell me where it should go on the paper.'

'But why do you need a drawing of Bridewell, Nicholas?'

'Because I need to understand where you were when the outrages happened.'

'I was in the hall at first, then in Master Olgrave's chamber.'

'Show me where both of them are on a sketch,' said Nicholas. 'They are vile men, Dorothea, but they are also slippery. I'd gain nothing by accusing them to their faces. If I did so in public, they'd bring an action of slander against me.'

'But I was *there*. I know what sort of men they are.'

'And so do I, now that I have met the rogues.'

She was aggrieved. 'Can we not have them arrested and taken to court?'

'Not until we have more proof, Dorothea,' he said, 'and the one certain way of doing that is to get a lot closer to Joseph Beechcroft and Ralph Olgrave.'

Beechcroft paced up and down the room like a caged tiger. Ever since he had arrived at Bridewell, he had been in a state of agitation. Olgrave, on the other hand, was relaxed and cheerful. Reclining in a chair, he sipped a cup of wine.

'He *knows*, Ralph,' said his partner with alarm. 'The fellow knows.'

'How can he know? There were only two of us there.' He grinned. 'Well, three of us to be precise but that turbulent Welshman could not stay. The river called him.'

'Why did he ask me if Hywel Rees had swum back to Wales?'

'To see if he could chase the colour from your cheeks, and he succeeded. You are too easily shaken, Joseph. Learn from me to keep a straight face.'

'When I am accused of a murder?'

'That's not what happened,' said Olgrave. 'Nicholas Bracewell was guessing. He has a little knowledge, I grant you, and tried to augment it by frightening you. Thanks to your folly, he now has more to bite upon.'

'My heart pounded when he mentioned swimming.'

'Only because you rely on your emotions instead of your brain. Think, Joseph. Use your head and you'll see that we are not in imminent danger.'

'I believe we are,' said Beechcroft, stopping beside him. 'Nicholas Bracewell is on our trail, Ralph. He used that ruse to get into my house then suddenly produced two names out of the air that I hoped never to hear again.'

'And how do you suppose he did that?'

'He must have been acquainted with the pair of them.'

'Yes,' said Olgrave, 'but they were both out of his reach inside Bridewell. How could he know that Hywel Rees had been killed and tossed into the Thames?' Tapping his head with a finger, he stood up. 'Think, man. Do as I bid you. Use your brain.'

Beechcroft shrugged. 'It must have been a wild guess.'

'I fancy not. There is another explanation.'

'I do not see it, Ralph.'

'But it stands right before you, man. The only way that Nicholas Bracewell could be aware of the Welshman's death, was if the body had been washed up out of the river. In short, he was clever enough to go to the morgue in order to check.'

'And *was* the body found?'

'I suspect that it might have been. When I've calmed you down, I mean to visit the morgue myself in order to be certain. Yes,' he added, draining his wine, 'and I shall ask the coroner who else has shown an interest in Hywel Rees. I believe that I know the name he'll give me.'

'Nicholas Bracewell,' said Beechcroft, curling his lip. 'Who *is* the fellow?'

'We'll find out somehow, Joseph, and he will lead us to her.'

'Who?'

'Dorothea Tate. He must be working in league with that little scorpion.'

'We were wrong to discharge her.'

'We could hardly keep her here to rant and rave. Besides,' said Olgrave with a cackle, 'I'd had my sport with her. When we turned her out, I thought she'd end up in the stews of Bankside. Dorothea would make a lively trull now that I've introduced her to the trade. She fought like a terrier,' he recalled. 'I still have the scratches down my back. Until they heal, I'll not dare to lie with my wife.' He cackled again. 'I only lie *to* her.'

Beechcroft was on the move again. 'And you believe that she and that man are confederates? That disturbs me, Ralph. They could bring us down.'

'Not if we keep our nerve.'

'I lost mine for a second when he called at my house.'

'He'll not come again, I warrant you. And he can hardly reach us here,' Olgrave reminded him. 'Bridewell is our kingdom. No power in the land can threaten us.'

'Dorothea Tate might do so, if she has enough help.'

'Then we'll have to make sure she does not get it. Nicholas Bracewell paid a visit to our houses. When we find out where he lives, we'll do the same to him. My guess is that the girl will be staying there as well. Relax, Joseph,' he said, confidently. 'We'll do what we should have done before.'

'What's that?'

'Hit two marks with the same shot.' His eyes shone. 'We'll kill the pair of them.'

Chapter Ten

Margery Firethorn was smouldering with anger as she sat in the half-dark of her parlour. There was a single lighted candle beside her. It was the second night in succession when she found herself waiting up for an errant husband and that served to sharpen the edge of her temper. Everyone else in the house in Shoreditch had retired to bed but she was determined to sit up for her spouse, no matter how long it might take. Such was the strength of her resolve that there was no danger of her falling asleep. A hundred candles burnt brightly inside her.

At long last, she heard the sound of a horse's hooves, clacking on the hard surface of Old Street. She blew out the flame and plunged the room into darkness, listening to Firethorn dismount, stable the animal and, after some delay, let himself into the house. Leaving his hat on the wooden peg behind the door, he stole into the parlour on tiptoe, intending to creep up the stairs with the least possible noise. Firethorn had just reached the first step when a voice shattered the silence.

'Lawrence!' snarled his wife.

'My God!' he exclaimed, a hand to his chest. 'Is that you, Margery?'

'Who else would bother to stay up for a worthless husband like you?'

'Ah,' he said, as she was conjured out of the gloom to stand a few inches away from him. 'There you are, my angel.'

'Angel me no angels,' she warned. 'Where have you been?'

'Business affairs kept me away from your warm bosom.'

'That was your excuse yesterday and I did not believe it then. You swore to me that you'd return early this evening so that you could welcome Jonathan.'

'Jonathan?'

'Have you forgotten that my brother-in-law was arriving today?'

'It went quite out of my mind,' he confessed. 'I've had such a day at the Queen's Head that all else fled from my busy brain.'

'So I am left alone to feed the children, the apprentices and our visitor, while you are revelling with the other actors. It's not fair, Lawrence. It's not kind.'

'A thousand pardons, my love,' he said, reaching out to embrace her, only to have both hands smacked away. 'Instead of scolding me, you should pity me.'

'Pity you!' she echoed. 'I'd sooner beat you black and blue.'

'If that relieves your anger, you may do it. I've suffered so much today already that I'll not even feel the blows. I've been knocked about until I am quite numb.'

Margery grabbed his beard. 'What's her name, Lawrence?'

'Who?'

'The woman who has kept you out late for two nights. Who is this jade? Come, sir,' she demanded, tightening her grip, 'who is this wanton hussy?'

'She goes by the name of Dame Fortune,' he groaned, 'and she's battered me harder than you could ever do. It was not enough for her to deprive me of Edmund, Nick and the takings from *The Maid of the Mill*. She also robbed us of our costumes and took away my sanity.'

Margery released him. 'What are you talking about?'

'The slow death of Westfield's Men.'

'Your costumes were stolen?'

'All that were of any value,' he said. 'Hugh Wegges discovered the theft this morning. The landlord offered us five pounds to cover our loss but we'd need ten times that amount at least. And the worst of it is, Nick Bracewell was not there to help.'

'Why not?'

'It would take too long to explain, Margery.'

'He's never let you down before.'

'No, that's why I summoned him. I knew that he'd call on Edmund at some time so I left a message there about the loss of our wardrobe. How can we play *Love and Fortune* tomorrow if we have nothing to wear?'

'Nick is the only person who could answer that question.'

'He's promised to try,' said Firethorn, wearily. 'And, since we are so embattled, he's agreed to hold the book for us tomorrow afternoon instead of deserting us.' He gave a low moan. 'I never hope to see a day as bad as this again, Margery.' A mirthless laugh followed. 'And there's my wife, thinking that I'm lying in the arms of some buxom wench. Dame Fortune keeps a cold bed, I can tell you. I've had no pleasure between her thighs today.'

'Oh, you poor man!' she said, embracing him. 'I misjudged you, Lawrence.'

'I've been bound to Ixion's wheel.'

'Why did you not send word of all this trouble? I'd then have been able to explain to Jonathan that you were delayed. He was so anxious to speak to you.'

'I had anxieties of my own to occupy me.'

'You can see my brother-in-law tomorrow, and travel with him into the city.'

'Must I?' protested Firethorn.

'Jonathan wishes to go to the Queen's Head so that he can watch the rehearsal.'

'When we are in such confusion? Keep him away, Margery. He'll see us at our worst and take a low opinion of our work back to your sister in Cambridge. Instead of watching *Love and Fortune*, your brother-in-law will see only *Hatred and Misfortune*.'

'You'll rally somehow.'

'Even Lazarus could not rise again from this. Help me, my dove. Jonathan Jarrold is a tedious fellow at the best of times. Spare me his company.'

'Leave we that decision until the morning. Our bed calls us.'

He smiled hopefully. 'Are we reconciled, then?'

'No,' she whispered in his ear. 'But we soon will be.'

Nicholas Bracewell rode into the yard of the Queen's Head on the horse that he had borrowed from Anne Hendrik. Across the pommel were several garments that he had managed to collect from Anne and from some of her neighbours. She had also supplied the selection of hats that he had carried in a bag. George Dart came scurrying across to him to take everything he had brought. He took it off to the tireman. Nicholas dismounted and gave the reins to the ostler who stood by. He was pleased to see that their makeshift stage had already been erected but even more delighted to note that Owen Elias was there so early in the morning. The Welshman came across to him.

'Good morrow, Nick,' he said. 'More costumes, eh? That's good. I've loaned a rag or two from my own meagre wardrobe. They'll serve for a rustic comedy like *Love and Fortune*. But what news of Dorothea?'

'She frets, Owen.'

'Who would not, in her position? I long to help the girl but I'm forced to chafe at the bit here. Lawrence sorely needs us.'

'That's why I'm here,' said Nicholas, 'but I've not forgotten Bridewell.'

'Nor have I.'

'When we have a moment, I'll divulge my plan.'

'I hope that it involves slitting the throats of those two villains.'

'Joseph Beechcroft and Ralph Olgrave are certainly my targets. But, now that I've met the pair, I know that it will not be so easy to hit them.' He saw Firethorn ride into the yard with a stranger. 'We'll talk anon, Owen.'

'I hope that Lawrence is in a better mood today. He was roaring like a lion yesterday and James told us the reason for his distemper.'

'Oh?'

'Lawrence ventured into Master Lavery's room and lost heavily at cards.'

Nicholas was taken aback. 'But he spoke so strongly against it.'

'Temptation got the better of him, Nick. I thought I saw him sneaking off upstairs last night. If he lost again, our ears are in for another roasting.' He saw Firethorn bearing down on them. 'Here he is,' he noted, 'and his eye is still inflamed. That means he had another defeat at the card table.' He moved away. 'I'll leave him to you, Nick.'

Having given his horse to an ostler, Firethorn abandoned his companion and marched across to the book holder. The actor was torn between fury and resignation.

'We are doomed,' he said, waving a hand. 'Every way I turn, I spy disaster.'

'Then you have not looked at our wardrobe,' said Nicholas with smile. 'Owen and I have brought some new costumes and others have promised to do the like. We'll have enough to dress the play this afternoon.'

'But what about tomorrow's, Nick? *The Knights of Malta* calls for better apparel than we can ever muster, and *The Loyal Subject*, that we play on Friday, needs a queen in all her glory. Are we to put Dick Honeydew on stage in sackcloth when he takes the part? How regal will the lad look in that?'

'By then, we may have our own wardrobe back.'

'How can that be? It will already have been sold.'

'To whom?'

'To anyone who'll buy it. Our rivals would seize on such a purchase.'

'Then they'd be foolish to do so,' said Nicholas. 'We'd recognise our wardrobe anywhere. As soon as one of us went to The Curtain, The Theatre or The Rose, we'd know who had our costumes and demand them back. No,' he went on, 'they'll have to be sold singly to individuals. That will take time. No shop would buy such a range of attire. And there's another thing to remember.'

'What's that?'

'Hugh Wegges showed me the full inventory of what was taken. Some of those cloaks and gowns were heavy to wear. No one man could carry them all away himself.'

'He had accomplices?'

'Either that or one man made a number of visits to our wardrobe.'

'What thief would risk doing that?'

'One who knew where to hide his booty nearby,' said Nicholas. 'It may even be someone who is staying at the inn. Our landlord has opened up more rooms to guests. I mean to ask what their names are.'

'I'll do that office, Nick,' volunteered Firethorn. 'It never occurred to me that our costumes might be hidden right in front of us. That's the last place we'd think to look. Let me speak to Adam. I'll have him search every room.'

'Cautiously, though. We must not spread commotion.'

Firethorn bristled. 'I'll spread much more than commotion if I find that the thief is still here.' He became aware of a figure standing nearby and gave him a token smile. 'One moment,' he said. 'I'll just speak to my book holder.' He lowered his voice. 'Here's another scourge for my back, Nick. This fellow is Jonathan Jarrold, a bookseller from Cambridge, the dullest creature on two legs. But he's Margery's brother-in-law so I must indulge him.'

'What does he want?'

'To watch us at rehearsal. He has appointments with other booksellers this afternoon so he cannot see the performance itself. Margery insisted that I let him view our morning's turmoil.'

Nicholas was confident. 'We'll give a better account of ourselves than you fear.'

'Get him from under my feet, that's all I ask. The fellow unnerves me.' He swung round to beam at the visitor. 'Come and meet Nick Bracewell,' he said. 'He'll look after you, Jonathan. I must away.'

Firethorn headed for the tiring-house and left the two men to exchange greetings. Nicholas had heard mention of Jonathan Jarrold before and he knew that Firethorn had little time for the man, even though he had great admiration for the actor. Jarrold was short, thin and studious, his nervous eyes glinting behind spectacles, his body hunched apologetically in its plain garb. He rubbed his palms together.

'I fear that I come at an inopportune moment,' he said.

'Rehearsals are always prone to misadventure,' explained Nicholas, 'so you'll have to bear with us. Lawrence will have told you of the troubles we face.'

'He talked of nothing else over breakfast.'

'Then you'll understand our shortcomings.' Nicholas glanced upwards. 'The best place to sit is in the lower gallery. It commands a fine view and you'll have it all to yourself.' He turned back to Jarrold. 'Have you seen Westfield's Men before?'

'Oh, yes,' said Jarrold, nodding enthusiastically. 'On my rare visits to London, I always come to the Queen's Head, and you played at Cambridge last year.'

'The plague forced us to go on tour.'

'I'll not forget your visit. We saw *The Merchant of Calais*, as fine a play as I've ever had the privilege to witness. Comedy, tragedy and romance were so sweetly co-mingled. Lawence was kind enough to introduce us to the author.'

'Edmund Hoode.'

'I'd hoped to renew the acquaintance today, but I hear that he's indisposed.'

'Illness keeps him from us,' said Nicholas, 'but we've a

new playwright to fill his absence. As it happens, he hails from Cambridge as well.'

'Oh, what is his name?'

'Michael Grammaticus.'

'But I *know* him,' said Jarrold, clapping his hands together. 'A true scholar, if ever there was one. When he was in Cambridge, he was always in my shop, searching for Greek and Latin texts. The both of them were.'

'The both of them?'

'Michael and his friend, Stephen Wragby. They were never apart. They lived together, studied together and taught together. Michael was the finer scholar but Stephen had the better imagination. I miss him so much,' he went on, stifling a sigh. 'He was far too young to die.'

'Stephen Wragby is dead?'

'Of the plague. It is not confined to London, alas. It reached out its long hand and snatched him away from us. Michael was utterly destroyed,' recalled Jarrold. 'Careless of his own health, he nursed Stephen until the bitter end. One friend died, the other was somehow spared. And I lost two of the best customers I ever had.'

'Is that why Michael decided to leave Cambridge?'

'He could not bear to stay without Stephen.' He adjusted his spectacles. 'Yet you say that Michael is a playwright now?'

'Yes,' replied Nicholas. 'One of his plays has already been staged and a second will be back from the scrivener any day. It's a pity you missed *Caesar's Fall*. It was the work of a brilliant intelligence.'

'That is an accurate description of Michael Grammaticus.'

'His new play is called *The Siege of Troy*.'

Jarrold laughed. 'That proves my point. They were like twins. Michael and Stephen did everything together. Their minds coalesced into one.'

'In what sense, Master Jarrold?'

'Look at the title of this new play.'

'*The Siege of Troy*?'

'I saw a play by Stephen Wragby performed at Cambridge only a few years ago. It was on exactly the same subject,' said Jarrold. 'Except that it was written in Greek.'

Ralph Olgrave would never have identified the man on the slab at the morgue if it had not been for the damage to his skull. He moved some yards away from the stink of decay to speak to the coroner.

'And they gave his name as Hywel Rees?' he asked.

'Yes, Master Olgrave.'

'Did they give you their names as well?'

'I insisted on it,' said the coroner, fussily. 'I do not admit strangers to the morgue to view the cadavers. That's a ghoulish occupation and I'll not allow it.'

'So who were they? Was one of them called Nicholas Bracewell?'

'Yes, I believe that he was.'

'And the other?'

'A sturdy Welshman by the name of Owen Elias.'

'A Welshman?'

Olgrave was unhappy to hear that. It suggested that the dead man had a relative or friend who was searching

237

for him, someone who would feel obliged to join the hunt for the killer of Hywel Rees. That was worrying. Nicholas Bracewell had an assistant.

'How would I find these gentlemen?' said Olgrave.

'They left no address with me, sir.'

'Have you any idea where they might have come from?'

'I cannot answer for the one,' said the old man, 'but I could hazard a guess about the other. The Welshman is an actor. There was something about the way he dressed and spoke and held himself. Owen Elias belongs on a stage. If you wish to find him, search the playhouses for that is where he'll be.'

'I fancy that Nicholas Bracewell might be there as well,' said Olgrave to himself, as he remembered their earlier encounter. 'For he is no mean actor.'

Adversity usually brought out the best in Westfield's Men but that was not the case with *Love and Fortune*. Dressed in assorted costumes that were visibly the wrong size, shape and colour, the actors were inexplicably tentative in a play that they had performed many times. Entrances were missed, lines forgotten or gabbled too quickly, and properties knocked clumsily over. None of the actors rose above competence. Lawrence Firethorn was uninspired, Barnaby Gill lacklustre and Owen Elias strangely out of sorts. Even the reliable Richard Honeydew, taking the role of the heroine in a wig and a borrowed costume, was unable to lift the play. The audience grew restive.

Some of the unintended humour worked to their advantage. Spectators who were unfamiliar with the play, shook with glee when James Ingram inadvertently dropped a chalice to the floor or when Frank Quilter came onstage too soon and collided with the departing George Dart, sublimely unsuited to all three of the small parts allotted to him. Those who had seen the comedy before, however, found it disappointing fare and several began to drift away long before the performance ended. A tepid round of applause told the company what it already knew. They had failed.

Firethorn was relieved to escape into the safety of the tiring-house. Flinging himself down on a bench, he put his head in his hands. Nicholas came over to him.

'It might have been worse,' he observed.

'Yes,' moaned Firethorn, 'Lord Westfield might have been here to witness our shame.'

'You redeemed yourselves in the last act.'

'That was fear and not redemption, Nick. We had to get *something* right or they'd have started throwing things at us. As it was, the insults were beginning to fly.'

'We'll make amends tomorrow.'

'How? By playing *The Knights of Malta* in these borrowed costumes?' He plucked at his doublet. 'Whoever heard of a proud knight in remnants such as these?'

Elias heard him. 'Do you mind, Lawrence?' he said, indignantly. 'You happen to be wearing my finest apparel.'

'It was certainly not tailored to fit me, Owen. It ruined my performance.'

'It's a poor actor who blames his costume.'

'And a poor judge of taste who chooses *this* as his best doublet?'

'I'll not be insulted,' warned Elias, pugnaciously.

'Stand off, Owen,' said Nicholas, easing him away. 'He does not mean to upset you. The fault lies not in our wardrobe but in the effect that our losses have had upon us. To lose Edmund was bad enough. To have our takings stolen and our wardrobe plundered has put a strain on all of us. We'll vindicate our reputation tomorrow.'

'Our reputation as *what*?' asked Firethorn. 'Fools and imbeciles? Did you see what happened out there today? We were all blundering about the stage like so many demented George Darts.'

'I did my best, Master Firethorn,' said Dart, meekly.

Nicholas gave him a kind smile. 'You always do, George. Thank you.'

'That was the idiot you designated to hold the book today,' remarked Firethorn. 'Imagine how much worse it would have been if that had happened. Fire and brimstone! They'd have skinned us alive for our mistakes.'

'Tomorrow, we'll improve,' said Nicholas. 'Crying over our mistakes achieves nothing. We must strive to put them right.'

'How can we do that, if our book holder wants to leave us?'

'I'll be here. I give you my word.'

'That's some relief at least.'

'You'll gain some more, if you go home early this

evening,' advised Nicholas, quietly. 'Master Jarrold told me how late you returned last night. I think we both know the reason why.' Firethorn looked guiltily up at him. 'How can you condemn others for going astray when you take the same path yourself?'

'But I came so close to *winning*,' said Firethorn in a whisper.

'Would that have made it right to set such an example to the others?'

'No, Nick. I'm justly reproached. The lure of gain blinded me to all else. Margery must never find out, or she'll ban me from her bed in perpetuity.'

'She'll hear nothing from me.'

'Nor me.' He pursed his lips in recrimination. 'Oh, I rue the day that Philomen Lavery came to stay at the Queen's Head. He corrupted all our judgements.'

'Put him and his pack of cards behind you. He'll soon be gone.'

'So will Margery's brother-in-law, thank heaven. Dear God! Why did Jonathan have to visit us now when we are at our wits' end? He's one more burden on my back. Let him go back to Cambridge and stay there.'

'I was pleased to meet him at last.'

'Jonathan Jarrold? The man is tedium made manifest.'

'Not so,' said Nicholas, recalling what he had been told about Cambridge. 'I found his conversation very illuminating.'

He broke away to supervise the dismantling of the stage and the storing of costumes and properties. Since so many garments had been borrowed, he asked Wegges to take particular care of them. Nicholas was following an established routine but he was impatient, tied to his duties at the Queen's Head when he wanted to be investigating a murder. While he laboured for Westfield's Men, his mind was on Bridewell.

Joseph Beechcroft was still perturbed. He and his partner were in the room at Bridewell that they used as an office. Beechcroft drummed his fingers nervously on the table.

'How do we even know that the fellow was an actor?' he said. 'That was only the coroner's guess. Owen Elias could just as easily have been a weaver or a tailor.'

'No,' said Olgrave. 'Have faith in the coroner. His whole life is spent in making judgements of character. He'll weigh a man up, whether he be alive or dead. If he picked this one out as an actor, then I trust his word.'

'But we sent someone to enquire at The Rose and they came back empty-handed. It was so at the two playhouses in Shoreditch. Owen Elias was not there.'

'That still leaves the company that plays at the Queen's Head.'

'No, Ralph,' said Beechcroft. 'I think we are following a false trail.'

'Only because you did not speak to the gatekeeper, as I just did.'

'The gatekeeper?'

'Yes,' replied Olgrave. 'I reasoned that, if anyone wanted to know more about us, and the way that we run Bridewell, they'd come knocking at the door. And that's exactly what a certain Welshman did.'

'Owen Elias?'

'He did not give his name, it seems, but claimed to be the cousin of Hywel Rees. When told that the fellow had been discharged, he produced the name of Dorothea Tate.'

Beechcroft was alarmed. 'They are closing in on us!'

'The gatekeeper gave nothing away.'

'He did not need to, Ralph. They know that that troublesome Welshman was killed and hurled into the river, and they have the girl to help them.'

'Her voice will not convince any court in the land.'

'It might, if they provide the evidence to back it up.'

'How can they do that?' asked Olgrave with a mocking laugh. 'Take us to the torture chamber and wring confessions out of us, as if we were scheming Papists? For without that, they have nothing.'

'They have enough to unsettle my stomach, I know that.'

'The cure is at hand. We simply remove Nicholas Bracewell and the girl.'

'What of this other man, Owen Elias?'

'He's Welsh,' said Olgrave with a sneer. 'I'll send him to join his countryman.'

Nicholas Bracewell was kept waiting at the lawyer's office until Cleaton had finished talking to a client. The book holder spent the time examining the sketch of Bridewell that Anne Hendrik had drawn under the guidance of someone who had actually been inside the institution. How accurate

Dorothea Tate's memory had been, Nicholas did not know, but the sketch gave him an idea of the basic design of the building with its three courtyards and its wharf beside the Thames. The girl had marked the position of the room where she had slept, and of the hall where the feast had taken place. A small cross told Nicholas where Ralph Olgrave's private chamber was located.

Henry Cleaton appeared from his office and shepherded an elderly woman to the front door. After greeting Nicholas, he invited him into the cluttered room and both of them sat down.

'I still have qualms about this,' admitted the lawyer.

'All that you are doing is to give advice, as you would to any client.'

'I'd never urge them to break the law, Nicholas.'

'I believe that I'm working strictly within it.'

'A magistrate might take a contrary view.'

'Then I'll make sure I do not come up before one,' said Nicholas with a grin. 'What do you have for me, Master Cleaton?'

'Only this.' The lawyer handed him a writ. 'It's the paper that will commit you to Bridewell, but mark this well: I can simply get you inside the place. You'll have to get out again yourself.'

'I accept that.' Nicholas studied the wording of the writ. 'Is this a forgery?'

'I'd never stoop to such a thing. What you hold there is quite authentic. I had it of a friend of mine who sits on the Bench. You'll see that there is a gap where a name is to be inserted,' said Cleaton. 'Had I filled that in, I *would* have been guilty of forgery and I drew back from that.'

'In any case, you would not know what name to use for I'll have to invent a new one. If I'm committed to the workhouse as Nicholas Bracewell, I'm likely to suffer the same fate as Hywel Rees. They must not know who I am.'

'You go there as a counterfeit.'

'Only to reveal a much greater counterfeit,' said Nicholas. 'Joseph Beechcroft and Ralph Olgrave pretend to be honest men, engaged in a worthy enterprise, but they are guilty of the most dreadful crimes. I mean to rip away their disguises.'

'I fear for your safety, Nicholas. They are evil men.'

'Then that evil must be exposed to the world, and I can only do that by getting cheek by jowl with them. Master Olgrave gave me the notion. If I would know how Bridewell is run, he told me, I've only to get myself imprisoned there.'

'That puts you at their mercy.'

'Only if they discover who I am,' said Nicholas. 'By the time that they do that, it will be too late. Now, Master Cleaton, teach me the way of it. What is the correct procedure when a vagrant is convicted in a court?'

With some reluctance, the lawyer told him what he wanted to hear, describing the process from the moment a vagrant was arrested until he or she was committed to Bridewell. Though he warned Nicholas of the dangers, the latter was not deterred in the slightest. He was adamant that, whatever the risks involved, someone had to answer for the murder of Hywel Rees and the rape of Dorothea

Tate. When the instruction was over, Cleaton took him to the front door.

'Are you a lucky man by nature?' he said.

'Why do you ask?'

'Because luck is what you'll need once you are inside Bridewell.'

Nicholas pondered. As he looked back, he could see nothing but a continuous stream of bad luck, culminating in the poor performance at the Queen's Head that afternoon. Like those who had been enticed to the card table, he was involved in a game of chance. The difference was that he stood to lose far more than his money.

'I am due some good luck, Master Cleaton,' he said.

'Then I hope that you get it, my friend.'

Nicholas took his leave and mounted the horse that he had left tethered outside. He had intended to pay a visit to Edmund Hoode and the most direct way was to ride along Cheapside. But the conversation with Jonathan Jarrold suddenly came into his mind and sparked his curiosity. Since he had the horse at his disposal, he could go by a much longer route without too great a loss of time. Accordingly, he kicked the animal into a trot and headed in the direction of Cornhill, wondering if he might be able to single out the lodging to which Michael Grammaticus somehow never invited visitors.

Cornhill was the highest hill in the city, the site of an ancient grain market that gave it its name, and a place where the pillory and stocks were rarely uninhabited. The early evening had not thinned out the bustle. As Nicholas trotted along the thoroughfare, he had to pick his way past carriages, carts, mounted riders and the hordes on foot. Moving his head to and fro, he scrutinised the properties on both sides of the road and was impressed by their size and state of upkeep. If the playwright lodged in Cornhill, then he had no need to be embarrassed about his address.

Nicholas rode on until he reached a large house that soared above the buildings all around it with an almost aggressive ease. He decided that it must be the home of a rich merchant or a leading politician. Its owner would not have been popular with those who lived in the cottage immediately opposite because their light was obscured. Indeed, although it was still early evening, candles burnt in the windows of the cottage. As he glanced up at a window on the second floor, Nicholas realised that his journey had not been in vain. Quill pen in hand, a figure was crouched over a table. Though he could only see the man in a fleeting profile, Nicholas recognised him as Michael Grammaticus.

A short distance beyond the cottage, he reined in his horse and looked back over his shoulder, wondering whether or not he should call on the playwright. Certain that the man would be working on the new scenes for *A Way to Content All Women*, he decided that it would be unwise to interrupt him, and he suspected that Grammaticus would be discomfited by an unheralded visit. Nicholas swung his horse around. He was about to ride back down the hill when he saw another familiar figure. The man was cantering towards him on a bay mare. Before he reached Nicholas, he brought the animal to a halt and dismounted in front of the cottage where Grammaticus was working. Almost immediately, a servant emerged to take charge of the horse and lead it to the stables at the rear. The man, meanwhile, entered the cottage with a proprietary strut.

It was Doctor Emmanuel Zander.

When the stage had been dismantled and put away, all trace of the players may have vanished but not of the performance itself. The yard into which the spectators had been crammed was littered with discarded food and other rubbish. One of Leonard's many tasks was to sweep the yard with a broom so that it was relatively clean when the audience filled it on the following afternoon. It was lonely and repetitious work but he did it with his customary zeal, using his strength to sweep everything into a huge pile that he could load into his barrow. As he brushed away with rhythmical strokes, Leonard sent a small shower of dust into the air. He did not see the man who came into the yard.

'One moment, friend,' said the stranger. 'Do you work here?'

'I do, sir,' said Leonard, pausing to lean on his broom.

'Then you'd know of the company that performs here.'

'Westfield's Men, the best players in London. And I'm part of the troupe, sir, for I sweep up after them.' Leonard glanced around the yard. 'This mess was made this afternoon during *Love and Fortune*.'

'Do you know any of the actors?'

'Know them, sir? Why, I'm friends with each and every one.'

The stranger, a small weasel of a man in his thirties, stepped in closer.

'Would they include a fellow by the name of Owen Elias?' he asked.

'Yes, they would. Owen's among the finest of them.'

'A fiery Welshman, as I hear.'

Leonard chuckled. 'Then you hear aright. Owen will let no man put him down. If you meet him in the taproom, be sure to treat him with respect or he'll buffet you for certain.' He looked down at the man. 'What's your business with him?'

'The person I really seek,' said the stranger, 'is a friend of his, who may or may not have any dealings with Westfield's Men. Have you ever heard tell of one Nicholas Bracewell?' Leonard burst out laughing. 'What did I say to set you off?'

'Anyone who knows Westfield's Men will know Nick Bracewell, sir.'

'Why?'

'Because he holds them all together,' said Leonard, proudly. 'Nick is the best friend that I have in the company. He's their book holder.'

Owen Elias juggled with three apples and kept them spinning through the air. As soon as Hoode applauded him, however, he lost his concentration and his timing. All three apples tumbled to the floor. Hoode bent down to retrieve them.

'No, no, Edmund,' said Elias. 'I dropped them, so I must pick them up.'

'It was my fault that they fell to the floor.'

'I should not have been so easily distracted. It was Barnaby who taught me how to juggle. He can keep five apples in the air at one time and they are never in any danger of being dropped.' He gathered up the fruit and replaced it in a bowl. 'You may judge what that proves.'

'Barnaby has quicker hands than you.'

Elias gave a coarse laugh. 'Many young men have learnt that.'

After a long day without visitors, Hoode was relieved when the Welshman called to see him, but distressed to hear of the calamitous performance of *Love and Fortune* that afternoon. Hoode had felt well enough to get out of bed and dress, but he was tiring as the evening wore on. Elias did his best to entertain his friend with antics and anecdotes. They were both pleased when Nicholas Bracewell joined them.

'I was beginning to think my friends had forgotten me,' said Hoode.

'We could never do that,' promised Nicholas. 'Owen will have told you of our tribulations today. We barely got through the play.'

'I should have been there to help you.'

'Not while you are still unwell,' said Elias. 'But what's this I hear about Michael Grammaticus stealing your play away from you?'

'That's not the case at all, Owen.'

'No,' said Nicholas. 'He's merely writing a couple of scenes to see if he can pick up Edmund's voice. Michael believes that he can work just as well in a comedy.'

'How?' wondered Elias. 'Comedy is about laughter and I've never seen the fellow crack his face. I've seen happier countenances on a slab at the morgue.'

Nicholas shot him a look of reproof. By prior arrangement, they had agreed to say nothing about Bridewell in Hoode's presence, nor to worry him with details of what had been taking place there. Elias gave the book holder an apologetic shrug. After a few minutes, he bade farewell to his friends and went off. Left alone with him, Nicholas was able to take a closer look at Hoode.

'How do you feel now, Edmund?'

'I am well in the morning, when I take my medicine, then drowsy after I've dined. The medicine revives me again towards the end of the afternoon but I'm unable to stay awake late into the evening.'

'There is a definite pattern, then?'

'Oh, yes. Doctor Zander said that there would be.'

'Has he called on you today?'

'Not yet,' said Hoode, 'but he promised to come today or tomorrow. I worry about his frequent visits. It must be costing Michael so much money, yet he'll not hear of my paying the bills. The wonder is that *he* has not been here today either, though he did warn me that he'd only come when he'd finished a scene for my comedy.'

'Has Michael ever mentioned a friend called Stephen Wragby to you?'

'No, he so rarely talks about himself.'

'Did he tell you anything about his time at Cambridge?'

'Very little, Nick – except that he was glad to escape from it.'

'Why should a scholar want to flee a seat of scholarship?'

'He yearns for the excitement that only a playhouse can offer.'

'It's offered us excitement of the wrong sort today,' said Nicholas. 'We've had mishaps before but nothing to rival this afternoon's parade of accidents. We let our audience down badly, Edmund.'

'Owen had even harsher criticism than that.'

'Had Michael been there, he'd have doubted that we had a talent for comedy.'

'Only one thing would keep him away from the Queen's Head,' said Hoode. 'He must be penning that new scene for my new play.'

Nicholas thought about what he has seen earlier, Grammaticus bent over his work while someone stepped familiarly into the cottage as if he owned it. He also recalled that it was the playwright who had rushed to fetch a doctor when Hoode was stricken during the rehearsal of *Caesar's Fall*. Nicholas came to a sudden decision.

'I'll bring someone else to see you, Edmund,' he said.

'But Doctor Zander is my physician.'

'We need another opinion.'

'We've already had that from Doctor Rime.'

'A third pair of eyes will do no harm.'

'Doctor Zander will be very hurt if we turn to someone else, Nick.'

'Then we must make sure we do not tell him,' said Nicholas.

* * *

Three glasses of Canary wine made Lawrence Firethorn feel much better about himself and the company that he led. As he sat in the taproom with Barnaby Gill and some of the other sharers, he felt almost strong enough to return home to endure an evening of boredom with Jonathan Jarrold.

'The strange thing is,' mused Gill, 'that the rehearsal was so much better than the performance itself. We should have invited the spectators to that.'

'We had an audience of one, as it happens,' said Firethorn. 'Margery's brother-in-law is visiting us from Cambridge, filling the house with the musty smell of old books. He liked what he saw in rehearsal so will bear a kind report back to his wife.'

'We earned no kind reports this afternoon, Lawrence.'

'I blame you for that.'

Gill flared up at once. 'Me! I was the company's salvation.'

'Not when you fell on your bum in the middle of a jig.'

'That was the fault of the costume. It was far too big for me.'

'The costume was the right size, Barnaby. You were too small for it.'

'I demand the right to be dressed properly on stage,' said Gill, rising to his feet. 'How can I dance when I have breeches that trip me up like that? Find me something that fits me or I'll not play at all tomorrow.'

Firethorn grinned wickedly. 'We'll offer up a prayer of thanks.'

But the barb was lost on Gill, who had already flounced

out. Firethorn drained his cup and thought about leaving. Adam Crowmere sauntered across to him.

'We found nothing, Lawrence,' he said with regret. 'I've searched every room here and there's no sign of your wardrobe. It could be miles away by now.'

'Nick was wrong for once, then.'

'I fear so.' He nudged Firethorn. 'Shall we see you again tonight, Lawrence?'

'No, Adam. I'm done with it.'

'But you might win back all that you lost. That's what I did last night.'

'Yes,' said Firethorn, mournfully. 'I watched you doing it.'

'My luck will doubtless change tonight. Why not find out?'

'There's no pleasure in watching someone take my money from me. I might as well have tossed it in the Thames as risk it on the turn of a card.'

'But you *enjoyed* the game,' Crowmere reminded him. 'I could see it in your face. It set your pulse racing. Master Lavery will be leaving soon,' he added. 'Come now or you lose your opportunity to get your revenge on me. I, too, will be away.'

Firethorn was concerned. 'You, Adam? But you are the best landlord that the Queen's Head has ever had. We want you to stay forever.'

There was vocal agreement from the others at the table. Crowmere gave a bow.

'My thanks to you all,' he said, 'but I, alas, do not own

the inn. Alexander does, and the letter I received today made that clear.'

'Why?' asked Firethorn, anxiously. 'What does he say?'

'His brother died in his sleep, it seems. Alexander will stay in Dunstable until the funeral then return to London post-haste.' He gazed around the table with a benign smile. 'You'll soon have your old landlord back in the saddle again.'

Chapter Eleven

Another day had done nothing to calm Dorothea Tate's frayed nerves. She was still very apprehensive and constantly troubled by pangs of guilt. Though Anne Hendrik did her best to keep the girl occupied, she could not divert her for long. As the evening wore on, and the first candles were lighted in the house, Dorothea remained restless and unhappy. The two women were sitting in the parlour. Anne was sewing a dress.

'Where is Nicholas?' asked Dorothea, getting to her feet.

'He will be back again soon.'

'I pray that nothing untoward has happened to him.'

'Nick can take care of himself,' said Anne, looking up from her sewing. 'Have no fears on his account, Dorothea.'

'But the men who run Bridewell are so dangerous. They'll stop at nothing.'

'All the more reason to bring them to justice.'

'What can one man do against them and the keepers at the workhouse?'

'We shall see.'

'I'm frightened for his safety, Anne.'

'That's only natural.'

'I've lost one dear friend already,' said Dorothea. 'I'd hate to lose another.'

'I'm glad that you see Nick as a friend. When he first brought you back here, you had grave doubts about him. You were afraid that he was trying to lead you astray.' Anne smiled fondly. 'Nick would never do that.'

'I know. He's such a kind man. But I worry about him – and so do you.'

'Me?'

'Yes, Anne,' she said. 'I've been watching you all evening. You pretend to be calm and collected but every time you hear a horse in the street you look up at the door. I think you are as worried as I am.'

'I would like him back home, I admit that.'

'You see? You call it his home, not his lodging.'

'Nick is rather more than a lodger to me,' said Anne, discreetly. 'He's a close friend. That's why he knew I'd take you in and look after you.' She finished her sewing and held up the dress. 'Here we are. Wear this tomorrow. It's an old dress of mine that I was going to throw out, but I've mended it instead.'

Dorothea took the dress from her. 'Thank you, Anne.'

'Try it on.'

'I can see that it fits,' said the girl, holding it against herself. 'I've never worn anything as nice as this. You are so generous.'

'There was a time when I was slim enough to wear it,' said Anne, wistfully, 'but no more, alas. I'd much rather you have it.' She saw the remorse in Dorothea's face. 'Is something wrong?'

'Yes,' replied the girl. 'I wonder what I have done to deserve this.'

'You need help. It would be cruel to turn you away.'

'Yet that's what everyone else did. Hywel and I begged on the streets for days and most people walked past without even noticing us. Some of those who did spat on us or called us vile names. London is a cruel city.'

'Some people can be very selfish,' agreed Anne, sadly.

'If only Hywel could have lived to enjoy all this,' said Dorothea, looking around the room. 'To wear clean clothes and eat good food and have a roof over his head. It's not fair that I should have it while he lies dead in the morgue.'

'Do not see it that way, Dorothea.'

'But I must. I still feel so guilty about what happened to him.'

'Without reason.'

'He came to my rescue,' said Dorothea with feeling. 'When Master Beechcroft was scolding me, Hywel attacked him and beat him to the ground. That's why they killed him. It was because of me. And I fear that they'll do the same to Nicholas. Stop him from going to

Bridewell,' she implored, coming across to Anne. 'Please, stop him. I don't want his blood on my conscience as well.'

Doctor John Mordrake removed the cork from the tiny bottle and sniffed it. He was a big man whose face and body had suffered the ravages of time. His long, lank, silver-grey hair merged with a straggly beard. He wore a capacious black gown, black buckled shoes and a large gold chain that hung down to his chest. Astrologer, alchemist, wizard, seer and royal physician, he exuded a strange power. Nicholas Bracewell had befriended him years before and turned to him on more than one occasion. This time, he had brought Mordrake to examine Edmund Hoode.

Seated on the bed in his nightshirt, the patient watched with some trepidation. He feared that Doctor Zander might make an evening call at the house and catch him seeking another medical opinion. Seeing his concern, Nicholas gave him an encouraging smile. He wanted the playwright to be treated by a doctor who was not so closely connected to Michael Grammaticus. Some people thought Mordrake a mountebank, others decried him as a necromancer, but Nicholas had every faith in him. He turned to watch as the old man dipped his finger into the bottle, then tasted the medicine on the tip of his tongue. With a grunt of satisfaction, Mordrake put the bottle aside. He reached for one of the candles and held the flame close to Hoode's face, moving it around so that he could conduct a detailed scrutiny.

'Put out your tongue, sir,' he ordered.

'Yes, Doctor Mordrake,' said Hoode, obeying.

The old man peered at it. 'You feel no pain?' Hoode shook his head. Mordrake felt both sides of the patient's neck. 'No swelling of the glands?'

'Only at first, when the fever was upon me.'

'What have you been eating?'

'Lots of fruit,' said Hoode, indicating the bowl. 'Doctor Zander advised it.'

Mordrake selected an apple, took a large bite from it, then removed the piece from his mouth. He sniffed it and the rest of the apple before putting both on the table.

'I'll need to see your water, Master Hoode.'

'The chamber pot is under the bed. It's not been emptied.'

'Good,' said Mordrake, lowering himself with some difficulty to his knees and extracting the chamber pot. 'I'll take a specimen, if I may.'

From a pocket somewhere in his gown, he pulled out a stone bottle and uncorked it before filling it with urine. Once again, his nose made the diagnosis. Corking the bottle, he slipped it back into his pocket and eased the chamber pot beneath the bed. Nicholas stepped forward to help him up.

'Thank you, Nicholas,' said Mordrake, leaning heavily on his arm. 'I can cure the plague, the pox and the sweating sickness, but I've yet to find a remedy for old age.'

'Do you think that you can cure Edmund?' asked Nicholas.

'Without a doubt.'

Hoode was heartened. 'That's cheering news, Doctor

Mordrake,' he said. 'How long will it take? Doctor Zander said that it would take several weeks, perhaps even longer.'

'Leave yourself in the hands of that impostor,' warned Mordrake, raising a long finger, 'and you may never recover. You suffer from no disease, Master Hoode.'

'No? Then what is wrong with me?'

'You are being poisoned.'

Margery Firethorn had run out of apologies. Expecting her husband to return in order to spend time with their guest, she was mortified to be left alone again in Shoreditch with her brother-in-law. They had always had an uneasy relationship. She found Jonathan Jarrold far too mild and self-effacing for her taste whereas he was patently intimidated by her potency. To be left alone in a room with Margery made him feel shy and inadequate, and he was eternally grateful that he had married the quieter of the two sisters. Since she had little interest in books, and even less in this particular bookseller, Margery had little to say to him. Their conversation was punctuated by long silences.

'Lawrence will be back soon,' she said for the fifteenth time.

'I want to congratulate him on his performance at the rehearsal.'

'As long as you do not mention this afternoon. According to the apprentices, it was a sorry affair. That will have put Lawrence in a choleric mood.'

'He was not very cheerful this morning,' he recalled with

a diffident smile. 'How he yelled at his actors! I'd never heard such curses.'

'He always snaps at their heels,' said Margery.

'Putting on a play is more difficult than I imagined. This is the first time I've witnessed a rehearsal and it opened my eyes. Lawrence was in fine voice himself, so was Barnaby Gill, the clown. I remember seeing him at Cambridge.'

'Who else did you meet? Nick Bracewell, I daresay.'

'Oh, he was most helpful,' said Jarrold. 'That was another revelation. I thought that a book holder simply prompted the actors, but this one did so much more than that. He even told people where to move and stand onstage.'

She gave an affectionate smile. 'Nick is a jewel.'

'It was he who told me about Michael Grammaticus. I knew him at Cambridge.'

'Was he any livelier there? Lawrence says that the fellow is so morose.'

'I think that Michael still mourns the death of his friend.'

There was another strained silence. Margery's ears pricked up hopefully at the sound of a horse in the street outside, but it trotted past the house. She settled back in her chair with a grunt of annoyance. Jarrold was perched on the edge of his stool, conscious that his presence was irritating her yet unable to find words to win her over. Even at her most quiescent, he was wary of Margery. When she was fuming, as now, with barely contained rage, he found her nothing short of terrifying. The thought of sharing a bed with such a termagant made him shudder. Jarrold sensed that he would be devoured alive.

Feeling that it was his turn to initiate further conversation, he fell back on a sentence that she had already uttered time and again.

'Lawrence will be back soon,' he said.

Margery exploded. 'Where, in the bowels of Christ, *is* the rogue?' she howled.

Lawrence Firethorn watched from a corner as Philomen Lavery dealt the cards. Still reeling from the news of Marwood's return, Firethorn had drunk far too much wine to be able to resist the landlord's persuasive tongue. Adam Crowmere had taken him up to the room where three guests were playing cards with Lavery. The landlord advised Firethorn to watch while he took the empty chair at the table. It soon became clear that Crowmere's run of luck had expired. Time after time he lost a game yet somehow maintained his good humour.

'I'll withdraw,' he said with a chuckle, 'while I still have money enough to feed myself. Take my place, Lawrence,' he invited. 'You can do no worse than me.'

Firethorn shook his head. 'I'll not play again.'

'One game,' suggested Lavery, gathering up the cards. 'Just one game.'

'One always leads to another.'

'Not if your will is strong enough, Master Firethorn.'

'My will is like iron,' boasted the other.

'Then you can play a single game and walk away.'

'Yes,' said Firethorn. 'I could, if I wished.'

'Prove it,' coaxed Lavery. 'Take the empty chair.'

With obvious misgivings, Firethorn lowered himself into the seat. Lavery dealt the cards to all the players. Crowmere stood directly behind Firethorn as the actor studied his cards. Seeing what the actor had been dealt, the landlord chortled.

'Well done, Lawrence,' he said, patting him on the back. 'With those cards, I think you'll win at last. I told you that your luck would change.'

Michael Grammaticus was still poring over his table when the servant entered the room to tell him that he had a visitor. The playwright was puzzled and disturbed. Few people in London even knew where he lodged. When he heard that the caller was Nicholas Bracewell, he relaxed somewhat but he was far from pleased at the intrusion. He told the servant to bring the visitor up then he glanced down again at the scene on which he had been working for so long. When Nicholas was shown in, Grammaticus gave him a guarded welcome.

'I know why you've come,' he said, getting up from his chair. 'Edmund has sent you to chide me for not calling on him today, but I promised to finish this scene for his play first.'

'How much have you written?' asked Nicholas.

'Far too much. Enough to furnish three scenes, in fact, but none of it worthy enough to show to anyone else.' He gave a gesture of hopelessness. 'Perhaps I do not have a gift for comedy, after all.'

'What do you consider to be your strength as an author, Michael?'

'My sense of drama, Nick. I believe that I have an eye for conflict.'

'You have an eye for something,' conceded Nicholas, 'though I am not yet sure what it is. But forgive me for calling so late in the evening. It was important to see you.'

'Does it concern *The Siege of Troy*?'

'Yes, it does.'

'I knew that Lawrence would require more changes.'

'This has nothing to do with Lawrence, but rather with his wife, Margery. Did you know that her sister lives in Cambridge?'

'No. Why should I?'

'Because her brother-in-law is an acquaintance of yours, one Jonathan Jarrold.'

'The bookseller? Yes, I know Master Jarrold well. He keeps a good stock.'

'He's visiting London,' said Nicholas, 'and chanced to attend our rehearsal this morning. We talked at length. Master Jarrold was surprised to learn that you had turned playwright. That was always the ambition of your friend, Stephen Wragby.'

Grammaticus tensed. 'Why have you come here, Nick?'

'To find out who really wrote *Caesar's Fall*.'

'I did!' said the other, defiantly.

'What of *The Siege of Troy*?'

'Every word of it is mine.'

'The Epilogue was certainly penned by you,' agreed Nicholas. 'That's why you took so long to finish it, is it not? And why it is such a poor addition to a rich drama. It was the Epilogue that planted the first seed of doubt in my mind, Michael.'

'If it will not serve,' said Grammaticus, 'I'll write a new and better one.'

'Do you really have the skill to do that?'

'You know that I have!'

'What I know is that *The Siege of Troy* was first written in Greek by Stephen Wragby. Every word of it may be yours, but only in the sense that you translated it.'

'I worked on the play *with* Stephen,' insisted the other. 'I was a co-author.'

'Taking the credit for someone else's genius,' said Nicholas, pointing to the sheets of parchment on the table. 'As you are trying to do with *A Way to Content All Women*. Your friend was dead, and unable to stop you, but Edmund Hoode is still alive. So you had to render him helpless.'

Grammaticus was appalled. 'What are you talking about? I *love* Edmund.'

'No, Michael. You only love and covet the position that he holds.'

'He has ever been my inspiration.'

'Is that why you and Doctor Zander conspired to poison him?' said Nicholas, calmly. 'I wondered why you were so loath to let anyone visit your lodging. We'd have discovered that you and the doctor slept under the same roof. It also explains why you paid the bills and bought all of Edmund's food. You were never caring for him, Michael, only making sure that he did not recover.'

'He *was* recovering,' argued the playwright. 'Edmund

improved a little each day. You saw that, Nick. It was thanks to the medicine that Doctor Rime prescribed. Or do you accuse *him* of being in league with us as well?'

'No, I do not. To call in a second doctor was a cunning trick. It made me think that Edmund's malady was genuine. When I chanced upon the fact that you and Doctor Zander shared a cottage,' said Nicholas, 'my suspicion was aroused. I decided to ask for a third opinion on Edmund's condition.' Grammaticus was becoming agitated. 'I fancy that you'll have heard the name of Doctor Mordrake?'

The other man gulped. 'Doctor John Mordrake? The Queen's physician?'

'The very same. He's a friend of mine and, since I was able to do him a favour when we travelled to Bohemia, he felt that he was in my debt. That debt,' explained Nicholas, advancing on him, 'has been handsomely repaid. The medicine that Edmund has been taking is an antidote to poison.'

'That's what Doctor Rime told us.'

'Yes,' said Nicholas, 'but he did not realise that you had been supplying the poison in the first place. You first brought Edmund to his knees, then you kept him weak by feeding him more venom day by day.'

'No, no!' exclaimed the other. 'Why on earth should I do that?'

Nicholas pointed to the table. 'There lies your answer, Michael. You wanted to get your hands on Edmund's work and usurp his position. The antidote may have revived him a little but you hindered his recovery by administering more poison in the fruit and in the broth that you brought for him.'

'I worshipped the man, Nick. I'd not harm him for the world.' He crossed to the door. 'Let Emmanuel explain it to you. He'll convince you that we acted for the best.'

Grammaticus let himself out and clattered down the stairs. Nicholas crossed to the table, standing in its own pool of light. Sheets of parchment had already been covered in words but to little effect. When he read one attempt at the new scene, Nicholas found scant wit and feeble humour. Evidently, *A Way to Content All Women* had found the would-be author out.

The door swung open again and Grammaticus returned with Doctor Zander at his elbow. Because they were at the darker end of the room Nicholas could only see them in shadow. Zander was pulsing with righteous indignation.

'What's this I hear?' he demanded. 'You called in a doctor behind my back when I was engaged to treat the patient? That's unforgivable.'

'It was essential,' returned Nicholas. 'Doctor Mordrake unmasked you both.'

'Mordrake! Ha! That old fool is no doctor. He's a mad alchemist who believes he can turn base metal into gold.'

'Her Majesty sees fit to retain him, Doctor Zander. Can you claim that honour?'

'I dispute Mordrake's conclusion.'

'Then let us call in a fourth and fifth doctor to examine Edmund,' said Nicholas. 'They'll only find what Doctor Rime and Doctor Mordrake did. The patient was being poisoned to keep him away from Westfield's Men.'

Zander stamped a foot. 'Do you dare to insult my reputation?'

'You no longer have a reputation. Before I've finished, I'll see the pair of you behind bars for this. You put a friend of mine through a dreadful ordeal to satisfy your own designs. Heavens!' said Nicholas. 'You might have killed him.'

'We'd never have done that,' insisted Grammaticus. 'I swear it.'

'Be quiet, Michael,' said Zander.

'No, Emmanuel. What is the point? He knows too much.'

'Admit nothing, man. He has no proof.'

'I've ample proof,' said Nicholas. 'There's even more on that table. Michael has been humbled. He's no Edmund Hoode, and it appears that he's no Stephen Wragby either.' Grammaticus lowered his head. 'Who *did* write those plays, Michael?'

'Stephen did,' confessed the other.

'Wrote them and translated them?'

'Yes, Nick. But I helped him every inch of the way. I simply wanted to preserve his memory by having Stephen's work performed upon a London stage.'

'Then why not leave his name on the plays?'

'Because they were bequeathed to me. Don't you see? They were *mine*.'

'Listen,' said Zander, changing his tone. 'There is a way out of this unfortunate dilemma. What we did was wrong, I grant you, that but there was no malice in it. Why,' he added with a forced laugh, 'we kept Edmund Hoode alive to write another day. Do not destroy Michael's ambition like this. Let his new play be performed.'

'Yes,' pleaded Grammaticus. 'We'll pay you anything, Nick. It's my dearest wish that *The Siege of Troy* is seen at the Queen's Head. Let me have but that and you'll see no more of me.'

Zander felt his purse. 'Come, sir, how much will it cost to buy your silence?'

'We are friends, Nick. Do it as a favour to me.'

'The only favour I'll do is for Edmund Hoode,' said Nicholas, firmly. 'The two of you will be arrested, tried and convicted. What you did was evil and unpardonable.'

'You are a very foolish man,' said Zander, putting a hand to his belt.

'And you are a corrupt one. You were there to cure, not to inflict more misery.'

'Michael paid me well for my help. Had you been more sensible, you might have shared some of that money. As it is,' Zander went on, pulling something from his belt, 'you will get nothing beyond a last farewell.'

He moved forward so that Nicholas could see that he was holding a pistol. His hand was steady and he looked as if he was determined to shoot. Nicholas was tensing himself to leap at the man when Grammaticus flew into a panic.

'No, Emmanuel,' he cried. 'Do not kill him. Nick has helped me.'

'Do you want him to help you to a prison cell?'

'I'd rather that than stand accused of murder.'

'Out of my way,' snapped Zander. 'I'll be his executioner.'

'I'll not allow it!' yelled Grammaticus.

He grabbed the wrist that was holding the gun and there was a fierce struggle. Before Nicholas could intervene, the pistol went off and Grammaticus emitted a cry of agony before slumping to the floor. Bending over him, Nicholas saw that he had been wounded in the shoulder. He looked up at Zander.

'Now, doctor,' he said. 'Do you think that you can *help* a patient for once?'

Lawrence Firethorn berated himself for his own folly. Having won several games in a row, he knew that he should have quit the card table and returned to Shoreditch. But the hope of even larger winnings spurred him on. He soon began to falter. Though he had lost at the start of the evening, Philomen Lavery suddenly improved to take game after game. The money that Firethorn had won was slowly whittled away. By the time that the actor finally fled from the inn, he had barely enough coins in his purse to bribe the gatekeeper to let him out of the city through the postern. He rode home at a somnolent canter. When he got to the house in Old Street, he found it in darkness. Margery, it seemed, had either gone to bed or was waiting to ambush him again.

After stabling the horse, he approached the front door with furtive steps. Firethorn remembered how bitter his wife had been on his return the previous night. Rehearsing his excuses, he felt ready to withstand her fury again. But, when he tried the door, it would not budge. He pushed it, kicked it and even hurled his shoulder against it, but it had been bolted from inside and withstood all his assaults. He was about to yell up at the window of his bedchamber when he realised how futile that would be. Margery would not let him in and he would be telling the whole neighbourhood that he had been locked out. He wanted to save himself from that ignominy.

Firethorn ended the worst day of his life in the stable, sleeping in the straw.

Nicholas Bracewell was up at the crack of dawn. After an early breakfast, he did his best to reassure Dorothea Tate that he could cope with any dangers that lay ahead, and that the man who had violated her would soon be punished. As she saw him off at the door, Anne Hendrik was more composed. Horrified to learn that Edmund Hoode had been deliberately poisoned, she was relieved that he would soon be cured.

'When you see him today,' she said, 'give him my love.'

'Edmund will be back at the Queen's Head with us before long.'

'He's endured so much needless suffering.'

'I know, Anne,' he said. 'The culprits will be duly punished.'

He gave her a kiss and set off, walking briskly through the streets of Bankside and realising that he was unlikely to see them again that day. London Bridge was clogged with traffic as carriages, carts, and visitors on horseback or foot streamed into the city to buy or sell in the various markets. Nicholas had to dodge through the crowd to make any speed. Gracechurch Street was even more populous and he had to force his way through the press in order to reach the Queen's Head. As he turned into the yard, the first person he saw was Leonard, using his broom to sweep up horse manure. Nicholas waved to him and Leonard ambled over with a vacant grin of welcome.

'Good morrow, Nick,' he said. 'You are the first one here as usual.'

'We have a busy day ahead of us.'

'*The Knights of Malta* is a rousing tale. I've seen bits of it before.'

'You've never seen it like this, I fear,' said Nicholas, 'for we lack the costumes to dress the play in all its pomp. I came early to see what Hugh Wegges proposes to do.'

'Did that gentleman find you yesterday?'

'What gentleman?'

'The one who asked after you and Owen,' said Leonard. 'He wanted me to point you out but both of you had left by then.'

'Did he say what business he had with us?'

'No, Nick. He did not even know you were the book holder here until I told him.'

'How did he react to that?'

'It seemed to please him.'

'Did he ask after anyone else in the company?'

'Oh, no,' said Leonard. 'The gentleman was only interested in Nick Bracewell and Owen Elias.'

'Describe the fellow to me.'

Scratching his head, Leonard gave a rough and halting description of the stranger who had accosted him in the yard. Nicholas was disturbed. The man was clearly neither Joseph Beechcroft nor Ralph Olgrave, but the book holder sensed that he had been sent by one of them. That raised the worrying question of how they had linked his name to that of Elias and traced the both of them to the Queen's Head. Realising that they had both been misled by him, Beechcroft and Olgrave would want to strike back at Nicholas but he was relying on his ability to disappear into the crowd. All that they had was his name. How had they discovered his occupation?

Seeing the consternation on Nicholas's face, Leonard became remorseful.

'I did wrong, Nick. I can see that I did.'

'No, no, Leonard. You merely answered a civil question. I'll not fault you for that. But, should you see him again, I'd ask you to be wary of this man.'

'Why?'

'Because he's no friend of ours,' said Nicholas. 'Of that I'm certain. Do not point us out to him. Instead, warn us of his arrival.'

'Yes, Nick. I will.'

'Keep your eyes peeled for the fellow. I fancy that he'll be back.'

'No question but that he will.'

'How can you be so sure?'

'Because he said so,' explained Leonard. 'He told me that he had to see you both on urgent business. I asked him if I could carry a message to you but he gave me none. Indeed, he bade me not even mention that he was looking for you.'

'Why did he do that?' asked Nicholas.

'I think that he wanted to surprise you.'

Westfield's Men responded to the challenge with collective vigour. Not only did they arrive early for rehearsal, they brought with them a determination to wipe away the shame of the previous afternoon by giving a performance that would eclipse all else. Even with an attenuated wardrobe, they felt capable of reaching their best. Lawrence Firethorn was the last to arrive, riding into the yard with the hangdog look of a chastened husband, and highly embarrassed when someone pointed out that he smelt of horse dung and still had some wisps of straw stuck the back of his doublet.

Nicholas took him aside to tell him about the prospect of Edmund Hoode's swift recovery. Delighted to hear the news, Firethorn was soon bubbling with anger when he learnt of the way that Michael Grammaticus and Doctor Zander had conspired to bring the playwright down so that he was unable to work.

'I'll strangle the pair of them until their deceitful eyes pop out!' he vowed.

'They are beyond your reach,' said Nicholas. 'When the doctor had seen to Michael's wound, I took them both before a magistrate, where they confessed their crime. The law must take its course now.'

'The law will be too lenient, Nick. Deliver them up to me.'

'We are well rid of both of them, and we have Edmund back in exchange.'

'That gladdens my heart, Nick,' said Firethorn. His face darkened. 'But there's one loss we suffer. *The Siege of Troy* was a wondrous play yet we must disown it.'

'Why?' asked Nicholas. 'Now that we know who the true author is, we give him his due reward. We bought the play in good faith, remember. All that we have to do is to have the name of Stephen Wragby printed upon the playbills and justice will been done.'

Firethorn slapped his thigh. 'The Lord bless thee!' he shouted. 'You are right. The play is ours.' He embraced the book holder warmly. 'We owe this all to you, Nick. You saved Edmund from further misery and caught those two deep-dyed villains.'

'Margery's brother-in-law deserves our thanks as well.'

'What? That milksop, Jonathan Jarrold?'

'Yes,' said Nicholas. 'It was he who told me about Michael during his time at Cambridge. Master Jarrold knew him and his friend very well. That was what first set me wondering about how good a playwright Michael Grammaticus really was. But you must know some of this,' he went on. 'Did not Margery's brother-in-law mention that he and I had conversed at length about Michael?'

Firethorn shuffled his feet. 'I got back home too late to speak to him last night.' He recoiled from Nicholas's look of rebuke. 'Yes, yes, I know that I should not have gone anywhere near that card table,' he admitted. 'But I was tempted beyond my power to refuse. Still,' he said, cheerily, 'enough of my worries. Let's share the good tidings with the others. If this does not lift their hearts, then nothing will.'

Clapping his hands to get their attention, Firethorn called everyone together before handing over to the book holder. Nicholas gave them a shortened version of events, emphasising that their beloved playwright would soon be back in the fold. While the whole company was thrilled with the news, not one of them had any sympathy for Michael Grammaticus. They rejoiced at his downfall. It was Firethorn who pointed out the implications of it all.

'We have been through a dark night, my friends,' he declared, 'but we've emerged into the sunshine. Let us celebrate onstage this afternoon. Lord Westfield will be in his accustomed seat, our loyal spectators will be flooding into the yard and, before too long, Edmund will be here to take up his place once more.' Smiling broadly, he held out both arms. 'It will be just like old times.'

'Yes,' observed Barnaby Gill, grimly. 'Our landlord will soon be back.'

Eager to hear what he had learnt, Ralph Olgrave met him at a tavern near Bridewell.

'Well,' he said, 'What did you find out, Gregory?'

'More than I expected, sir. Both of them are employed by Westfield's Men.'

'Nicholas Bracewell is also an actor?'

'No,' said the other. 'He's their book holder and, according to the simpleton I talked to at the Queen's Head, he's held in high esteem there.'

'Did you get a sighting of him?'

'Neither of him, nor of Owen Elias. Both of them had left the inn.'

Olgrave handed him a purse. 'You've done well, Gregory,' he said. 'Take this. There'll be much more when we've seen this business through. So,' he added, sampling his wine, 'the two of them are yoked together in Westfield's Men, are they?'

'That makes our task much easier, Master Olgrave.'

'Did you find out where they live?'

'Alas, no,' said Gregory, slipping the purse into a pocket. 'The shambling oaf who spoke to me did not know their addresses. I doubt if he could remember his own. All that he could say was that Nicholas Bracewell lived in Bankside, and that the Welshman lodged somewhere near Coleman Street.'

'Now that we know where they work, we'll soon track them to their lairs.'

'They play *The Knights of Malta* this afternoon.'

'Do they? Is that a comedy or tragedy?'

'How would I know, Master Olgrave? I've never seen it acted.'

'Then we'll have to repair that omission,' said Olgrave with a chuckle. 'You and I will both join the crowd at the Queen's Head today. I'd love to see what Owen Elias looks like. If he's the only Welshman in the company, we'll pick him out by his voice.' He glanced across at his companion. 'Come well armed, Gregory,' he instructed. 'We may catch a glimpse of their book holder as well.'

While she did her best to look after her young guest, Anne Hendrik could not neglect her own work. She invited Dorothea to go with her into the adjoining house that morning but the girl soon tired of watching the industrious Dutchmen, even though the apprentice kept smiling up at her. Dorothea excused herself to return to the house. Preben van Loew, the oldest and most experienced of the hatmakers, waited until the girl had left.

'The child is too restless,' he commented.

'I was like that at her age, Preben.'

'I do not believe that you ever had time on your hands,' he said with admiration. 'You could not be idle if you tried. As for Dorothea, she needs employment.'

'I've tried to give her simple jobs to do.'

'Her mind is on other things.'

'She is beset with worries.'

Anne did not enlarge on her remark. The Dutchman was a good friend and a loyal servant but she did not wish to confide details of what had happened to Dorothea Tate. He would not be able to help the girl out of her predicament. Anne gave him a sketch she had made of a hat that had been commissioned by a mercer's wife in the city. Since it would be expensive and difficult to make, she assigned it to Preben van Loew. Staring at it with interest, he discussed its finer points with her.

It was half an hour before Anne was able to go back to her house. Letting herself in, she was surprised not to find the girl in the parlour. She went across to the stairs.

'Dorothea!' she called. 'Dorothea, are you there?'

There was no reply. She went quickly up the steps and let herself into the girl's room. Her worst fears were realised. The dress that Dorothea had been wearing had been discarded, and the tattered garments in which she had first arrived were missing. An upsurge of guilt made Anne cry out in alarm. The girl had run away.

In spite of their poor account of *Love and Fortune* on the previous day, Westfield's Men enticed a full audience into the Queen's Head that afternoon. Whether they had come to mock or to admire, it did not matter. The company had the chance to vindicate itself and it was resolved to succeed. Lawrence Firethorn, in the leading role of Jean de Valette, Grand Master of the Order of Saint John Jerusalem, led his actors as if he was a general, taking a real army into battle. His voice was like the boom of a cannon.

> *'No tyrant from the east shall conquer here.*
> *The Knights of Malta will protect the isle*
> *And fight with God Almighty on their side*
> *To bless their cause and urge them on to feats*
> *Of valour, acts of noble note, triumphing*
> *At the last o'er Turkish hordes, whate'er their*
> *Strength and purpose.'*

Firethorn had such spirit and authority that nobody in the yard seemed to notice that the cloak he wore over his armour was only a velvet curtain, borrowed from the house of a friend. Hugh Wegges had worked hard to transform the mass of costumes into something that looked vaguely appropriate to the play, and – apart from occasional moments of sartorial incongruity – nobody's appearance provoked derision. Barnaby Gill, as the jester, Hilario, was clothed in yellow from head to foot and, because the costume had been tailored to fit him perfectly, he was able to dance and turn somersaults with his usual freedom.

It was clear from the start that here was a performance of exceptional power and commitment. Having seized the attention of their audience, the company did not let it wander for a second. *The Knights of Malta* moved on with gathering momentum. Owen Elias had two parts in the play. Having first given a vivid portrayal of a Turkish spy, he changed sides to reappear in the final scene as Don Garcia de Toledo, Viceroy of Sicily, the man who raised the siege and liberated the gallant knights. But it was Firethorn who, having spoken the first lines in the play, brought it to a conclusion with a speech that thundered around the yard.

An ovation greeted the actors and everyone in the galleries rose spontaneously to signal their joy. Even Lord Westfield, their sybaritic patron, disentangled himself from the arms of his mistress long enough to get to his feet and applaud. When they surged back into the tiring-house, the actors were in a state of euphoria. Their only disappointment was that Edmund Hoode had not been there to share in the acclaim. Though *The Knights of Malta* had been written by another hand, it had been so greatly improved by Hoode's deft touches that he was looked upon as the author. In previous performances, he had always reserved the role of the Viceroy of Sicily for himself.

Firethorn was ecstatic. 'Did you hear that applause, Nick?'

'It was no more than you deserved.'

'Costumes or not, we set their hearts and minds alight today.'

'You have never played the part better,' said Nicholas with sincerity. 'Everyone in the company was inspired by you.'

'All but Barnaby. He gave us the same stale antics.'

'The audience loved him, as they should. Nobody can deny that.'

'True,' conceded Firethorn. 'When you've heard those jests as often as I have, you are bound to find them barren. I think our clown did very well.' He leant over to whisper into Nicholas's ear. 'But do not tell Barnaby that I said so.'

'An encouraging word from you would be savoured,' said Nicholas.

'That's why he must never hear it.' Firethorn's broad grin suddenly vanished. 'O woeful day!' he sighed, putting a hand against a wall for support. 'What a case I am in, Nick. This afternoon, I was Jean de Valette himself, lately Governor of Tripoli and Captain General of the Order's galleys, now the Grand Master. Yet this evening,' he said, lowering his voice, 'I must creep home to Shoreditch with my tail between my legs and try to make peace with Margery.'

'Do not call in on Master Lavery on the way,' counselled Nicholas.

'I'll not, you have my word on it!'

Firethorn moved away to take off his costume. Still carrying his sword and wearing his armour, Frank Quilter came over to speak to the book holder.

'When do you want us, Nick?' he asked, quietly.

'When everything has been cleared away.'

'James and I will be in the taproom.'

'I'll find you there,' said Nicholas.

'Does Lawrence know what we are about?'

'No, Frank. Nor must he, until it is all over. Impress that upon James.'

Quilter was puzzled. 'Why the need for secrecy?'

'You'll be told anon.'

It took some time for the yard to empty. Hundreds of spectators had hailed the play and some wanted to remain there to discuss it with their companions. Many people headed for the taproom to slake their thirst or to take the opportunity to have a closer look at the actors who had entertained them so royally. Up in the galleries, several of the gallants and their ladies lingered until the rougher sort had dispersed. Still seated at the rear of the upper gallery, two men watched as George Dart and the other assistant stagekeepers came out to take down the trestles. Ralph Olgrave and Gregory had enjoyed the play more than they expected, even though they had been distracted by the sight of Owen Elias in his contrasting roles. When a burly figure strode out of the tiring house to take control of the dismantling, Olgrave nudged his friend.

'That's him,' he said. 'Nicholas Bracewell.'

'He's a strapping fellow,' noted Gregory. 'Look at those shoulders of his.'

'A broad back gives you a bigger target.'

'What of the Welshman, Owen Elias?'

'Kill him first,' decided Olgrave. 'And do it as soon as you can.'

Chapter Twelve

The search was in vain. Though she spent a long time scouring the streets around her home, Anne Hendrik could not find any trace of the girl. Even when she widened the search, it was all to no avail. Anne was accompanied by her apprentice, Jan Muller, a sturdy lad whose muscular presence gave her the protection that she needed, and whose urge to find the missing girl was almost as great as Anne's own. Though he had only met Dorothea Tate briefly, the apprentice had warmed to her at once and he was distressed to hear that she had gone missing.

'Why should she run away?' he asked.

'I do not know, Jan.'

'I thought that she liked us.'

'Yes,' said Anne. 'I believe that she did. But Dorothea had a troubled mind. She may have gone somewhere to be alone with her thoughts.'

'If she had troubles,' he said, 'she could have turned to me.'

'That's kind of you to say so.'

'I was fond of Dorothea. We all were, even Preben.'

Anne smiled. 'Then she was indeed popular, for Preben is too shy even to look at most girls. But he noticed this one and saw how unsettled she was.'

'I hope she was not fleeing from *me*,' said Jan, seriously.

'No, no. You are not to blame in any way.'

'Where would she go?'

'I wish that I knew, Jan.'

'Does she not know how dangerous Bankside is, even in daylight?'

'That did not stop her from taking to her heels.'

'Let's move farther on,' he suggested. 'Along the river bank.'

'No, Jan. We've hunted long enough. Dorothea is not here.'

He was upset. 'You are going to stop looking for her?'

'We have to,' said Anne, resignedly. 'We are wasting our time here. I fear that she's gone back to the city.'

'Then we'll *never* find her.'

'No, but Nick might.' She pondered. 'Can you ride a horse?'

'Well enough to stay in the saddle.'

'Let's go back to the house, then,' she urged. 'And quickly. I'll write a letter and you can bear it to him at the Queen's Head in Gracechurch Street. Can you manage that?'

The lad stuck out his chest. 'If it will bring Dorothea back to us,' he said, bravely, 'I'll manage *anything*. Let's make haste.'

Joseph Beechcroft had regained much of his accustomed nonchalance. He was wearing his most garish doublet and his hat sprouted no less than four ostrich feathers. As he and Ralph Olgrave walked together around one of the courtyards in Bridewell, he was very encouraged by what he heard.

'You saw them *both* at the Queen's Head?' he enquired.

'We did,' replied Olgrave. 'The Welshman is a good actor, I have to concede that. Though he took two roles in the play, they bore no resemblance to each other. One moment he was a treacherous Turk, the next, the Viceroy of Sicily.'

'What of Nicholas Bracewell?'

'It was as Gregory told me. The man is the book holder, and reckoned to be a power in the company for all that he's only a hired man. We saw him when the performance was done, helping the others to pack their stage away.'

'How did two such people come to know Hywel Rees?'

'That does not matter, Joseph. They have to be silenced.'

'Yes,' said Beechcroft. 'They know far too much for my peace of mind. The last thing we need at the moment is for anyone to peep into our affairs. We've another banquet arranged for tonight and I wish to enjoy it without worrying about Nicholas Bracewell and his friend.'

'You shall, Joseph. And so shall I.'

Beechcroft smirked. 'Whom will you choose tonight, Ralph?'

'I've not made up my mind.'

'Joan Lockyer? She's always a favourite with our guests.'

'Then let them take her,' said Olgrave, holding up a hand. 'Joan is a comely wench but I'd hate to purchase a French welcome from between those ample thighs of hers. I'll look for safer company in my bed tonight. Someone younger and freer from disease.'

'Only a virgin would bring that surety, and we've few of those left in Bridewell.'

'Alas, yes. There's such a special pleasure in deflowering an innocent, especially if she fights as fiercely as Dorothea Tate. You missed a treat there, Joseph.'

'So you say.'

'And what *I* missed was the chance to close that pretty little mouth of hers for ever,' said Olgrave, bitterly. 'That would have saved us all his bother. Well,' he added, 'I'll make amends in due course. She'll not live much longer.'

'The two men are the greater danger,' said Beechcroft.

'I know that well.'

'What have you told Gregory?'

'To wait for his moment and strike.'

'And who's to be the first victim, Ralph?'

'Owen Elias,' said Olgrave, complacently. 'That vexatious Welshman. Even as we speak, he may already be dead.'

Owen Elias was in his element. Having adjourned to the taproom, he was celebrating the triumphant performance of *The Knights of Malta* with a tankard of ale and enjoying the admiration of the spectators who were gathered there. Adam Crowmere had been watching in the yard that afternoon and, at the landlord's instigation, Elias declaimed his opening speech as the Viceroy of Sicily. It earned him a round of applause. When he saw Nicholas Bracewell come into the taproom, the Welshman knew that his friend wanted a private word with him. Finishing his drink, he sauntered across to the book holder.

'Will you not have some ale, Nick?' he asked. 'You've earned it.'

'I need to keep my head clear.'

'When will you go there?'

'Very soon,' said Nicholas. 'First, I must pass on some disturbing news. A message from Anne was just handed to me, brought by her apprentice, Jan Muller.'

'Well?'

'Dorothea has vanished.'

Elias was rocked. 'She was kidnapped?'

'No, Owen. She ran away.'

'But *why*? The girl was safe with Anne. Why put herself in peril again?'

'Only she can tell us that,' said Nicholas. 'According to Jan, they searched Bankside for hours but saw no sign of her. The lad is clearly upset that she's gone.'

'So am I, Nick. What are we to do?'

'Try to find her ourselves. Keep your eyes open, and not only for Dorothea.'

'Who else?'

'That man I warned you about is here somewhere,'

Nicholas told him. 'Leonard saw him earlier on. He may well be lurking to waylay one of us. Take care, Owen.'

Elias patted his dagger. 'I will.'

After giving the two men a signal, Nicholas went out of the taproom with Frank Quilter and James Ingram, leaving Elias to order another tankard of ale and join in the merriment. The actor was soon singing a bawdy song to amuse the others. In the convivial atmosphere, he was completely at ease and could have stayed all evening, but he had other priorities. Downing his ale, he soon bade farewell to his friends and rolled out of the inn.

It was a fine, warm evening as he walked along Gracechurch Street in the direction of the river. By the time he turned right into Canning Street, he knew that he was being followed and even caught a fleeting glimpse of the man. Elias sauntered on at the same unhurried pace, listening for the sound of the footsteps behind him, and noting that his stalker was slowly gaining on him. Crossing the road, he turned left down one of the alleyways that led to Thames Street. Once out of sight, he darted towards a lane on his right and dived swiftly down it.

Gregory, meanwhile, increased his own speed. Spying his chance to catch his victim alone, he quickened his step until he came to the alleyway. But there was nobody in sight. Elias seemed to have disappeared into thin air. Had he let himself into one of the gardens that backed on to the alleyway? Or had he slipped down one of the lanes off it? Gregory tried each garden door as he passed but they were all bolted. When he came to the lane on the right, he sensed that Elias must have gone that way, trying to outrun him. Pulling out his dagger, he broke into a trot.

He did not get very far. As he hurried along the lane, he was suddenly grabbed from behind by Elias, who had been concealed in a doorway, waiting to strike. Before he knew what was happening, Gregory was slammed hard against a stone wall. His dagger was knocked from his grasp and Elias kicked it away. Seizing him by the throat, the Welshman pressed him to the wall and held him there by sheer power.

'Who are you?' he demanded.

'Nobody,' said the other, still dazed. 'I was simply walking to Thames Street.'

'Then you came the wrong way.' Elias unsheathed his own dagger to hold the point under the man's chin. 'Now, let's have the truth or I'll cut that lying tongue out.'

'I mean you no harm, sir.'

'Well, I mean *you* some harm. You followed me.'

'No, that's not true.'

'Then why did you have a weapon in your hand, you cur?'

'Dangers can always lurk in an alleyway.'

'Who sent you?'

'Nobody, sir.'

'Who sent you?' repeated Elias, jabbing the point of his dagger into the man's neck. 'Was it Joseph Beechcroft or Ralph Olgrave? Yes,' he said, seeing the look of alarm in the other's eyes. 'You know them both, I think. One of those rogues sent you to find us at the Queen's Head.' He jabbed the dagger again and drew blood. 'Which one of those monsters from Bridewell was it?'

Gregory was shivering. 'Master Olgrave, sir,' he bleated.

'What were your orders?'

'To follow you, that's all.'

'Oh, to follow me, was it?' said Elias with sarcasm. 'What did you intend to do when you caught up with me? Make a present of your dagger?' He tightened his grip on the man's neck. 'Who are you?'

'My name is Gregory Sumner,' spluttered the other.

'Where do you live?'

'Leave off, sir, or you'll strangle me!'

'Answer my question or I'll squeeze every ounce of breath out of you.'

'I dwell in the workhouse,' admitted the other. 'I'm a keeper in Bridewell.'

'Then you'll know what happened to my good friend, Hywel Rees,' said Elias, releasing his hold. 'You're to come with me, Gregory Sumner. I can see that you must be a religious man,' he taunted. 'I've a lawyer nearby who'll happily hear your confession.'

Still in pain, Gregory Sumner rubbed his neck ruefully but he was only biding his time. As Elias stepped back to look at him properly, the man came to life and tried to retrieve his discarded dagger. It was a foolish move. The Welshman was ready for him. Holding him by the scruff of his neck, Elias swung him round with vicious force and threw him against the wall, drawing fresh blood and knocking all the resistance out of him. Sheathing his own dagger, Elias tucked the other weapon into his belt then bent down to remove the shoes of the fallen man. Without ceremony, he tore off Sumner's hose and used it to tie the prisoner's hands behind his back.

'Come, sir,' said Elias, lifting the man up and putting him over his shoulder. 'I want you to meet a friend of mine. But I warn you now,' he added with a growl. 'Do not dare to bleed over me on the way.'

Edmund Hoode felt so much better in himself that he was able to read *A Way to Content All Women* once more. Indeed, by the afternoon, he had even made a tentative stab at writing a new scene for it. Doctor John Mordrake was responsible for his recovery. Having identified the poison that had been keeping the patient drowsy and confused for so long, Mordrake concocted his own remedy and administered it in person. As a result, Hoode's brain was functioning again. His body was still tired, but his mind was racing and eager to make up for lost time.

One of the clearest indications of his improvement was the return of his subdued lust for the landlady's daughter. When Adele came into his room that evening, Hoode hoped that she had come to change the sheets on his bed and allow him to watch her nubile body as it bent and swayed before him. In fact, the girl was only delivering a message. As she spoke, Hoode stared with idle pleasure at the expressive dimples in her cheeks and at the delicate arches of her eyebrows.

'There's someone below who would speak with you, Master Hoode,' she said.

'Did he give a name?'

'Yes, sir. It was Tom Rooke.'

'Tom Rooke?' he echoed. 'But that's the name of a character from a play of mine called *The Faithful Shepherd*. Are you sure that is what he is called, Adele?'

'I am,' she said. 'But this fellow is no shepherd. I can vouch for that.'

'What sort of man is he?'

'Not one that my mother would let into the house, sir. He's a scurvy beggar. But he insists that he's a friend of yours, and will not leave until he has seen you.'

Hoode was mystified. Outside of his play, he knew nobody by the name of Rooke and was not acquainted with any beggars. Curiosity took him down the stairs. When he reached the front door, he opened it to find himself looking at a bedraggled creature with a filthy cap, a patch over one eye and his arm in a sling. Either side of him was an officer but Hoode ignored them. His only interest was in the crooked figure who had sent up the name of Tom Rooke. He was certain that he had never seen the man before.

'Do you know me, sir?' croaked the beggar.

'No,' said Hoode, turning his head away in disgust, 'and I've no wish to know someone who stinks as much as you. Away with you, man!'

The beggar raised himself to his full height and lifted the eye patch up. Slipping his arm out of the sling, he put both hands on his hips and used his real voice.

'Will you deny me now?' asked Nicholas Bracewell.

Hoode was amazed. 'Nick!' he gasped. 'Is that you?'

'It is, Edmund. I did not think to fool you so easily, but it seems that I did. Had you looked at my companions, you'd have seen that they, too, are old friends.'

'Frank and James,' said the playwright, recognising Quilter and Ingram and shaking each by the hand. 'What mean these disguises?'

'All will be explained in time,' said Nicholas. 'I must be brief. I called simply to see how remarkable a recovery Doctor Mordrake has brought about, and to tell you what happened after I left here last night.'

'I thought that you went off to see Michael.'

'And so I did. By the time I'd delivered him and Doctor Zander to a magistrate, it was far too late to call back here. And today has kept me fettered to the Queen's Head.'

Hoode blinked. 'What's this about a magistrate?'

Nicholas gave him an abbreviated account of what had taken place in Cornhill. Hoode was extremely angry at Doctor Zander but, in spite of what had been done to him, managed a vestigial sympathy for Michael Grammaticus.

'Ambition is a cruel master,' he said. 'It drove Michael much farther than he was able to go. I've been at the mercy of that ambition myself. I know the overwhelming urge to see your play performed upon a stage. It's like a madness.'

'Michael will pay dearly for it,' said Nicholas. 'But we must away, Edmund.'

'Dressed in those rags? Will you beg in the streets?'

'We'll not allow that,' said Quilter sternly, taking Nicholas by the arm.

Hoode laughed. 'You'd make a good officer, Frank. But

do not treat my friend Tom Rooke too harshly. I need him for one of my plays. And when he's Nick Bracewell again,' he went on, grinning happily, 'I need him for *all* my plays.'

Nicholas slipped his arm back into the sling and replaced the eye patch. After giving the playwright a wave, he twisted his body into a grotesque shape and limped away between the two officers. Hoode went back inside and met Adele on the stairs.

'No,' he told her. 'He was no friend of mine. I've never set eyes on that mangy creature before.'

Lawrence Firethorn did not know what sort of reception he would get at home. On the ride back to Shoreditch, he was not certain whether his wife had mellowed or if a night apart from her husband had merely hardened her heart. When he reached the house in Old Street, therefore, he tethered his horse to the gatepost in case he needed to make a swift departure. Finding that the front door was no longer locked, he took it as a good omen and stepped inside.

'Margery!' he cooed. 'Where are you, my sweetness?'

'In the kitchen,' she announced in a rasping voice.

'I'm back early today, as you will see.'

He went into the kitchen where his wife had been talking to her brother-in-law as she mixed some dough in a bowl. Jarrold could see that Margery was throbbing with displeasure. Not wishing to come between the couple at such a delicate moment, he gave a nervous smile and tried to steal away, but Firethorn flung his arms around the man to embrace him.

'Thank God you came to stay with us, Jonathan!' he declared. 'You've been our salvation. Westfield's Men owe you so much.'

'They owe me nothing, Lawrence,' said the other man, quailing before the frank display of emotion. 'If anything is owed, it's my apology. I hoped to get to the Queen's Head this afternoon to watch the play, but I was detained by a bookseller with whom I was doing some business. Will you forgive me?'

'After what you did, I'd forgive you anything.'

'What are you talking about?' asked Margery, suspiciously. 'You've hardly had a word to say to Jonathan since he's been here, yet now you greet him as if he's the best friend you have in the world.'

'I do so on behalf of the whole company,' said Firethorn. 'Has your brother-in-law not told you what help he rendered us, Margery?'

'No, Lawrence.'

'How could I tell what I did not even know about?' said Jarrold.

'Have you ever heard such modesty?' cried Firethorn, taking him by the cheeks to plant a kiss on his forehead. 'But for you, Jonathan Jarrold, all would have been lost. But for you, Edmund would have languished in his bed forever. But for you, that wicked doctor would have gone on poisoning him while Michael Grammaticus reaped the benefit of his absence. You exposed their villainy.'

The bookseller was baffled. 'Did I? When was this?'

Firethorn explained how Doctor Mordrake had been

called in, and how Zander and Grammaticus had been arrested for their crime. Jarrold was shocked to hear that his former customer had been involved in such gross deception, but glad that the information he supplied about Stephen Wragby had been crucial. For her part, Margery was torn between joy and remorse.

'Edmund recovered?' she cried with delight. 'Back with us again?'

'He will be very soon,' said Firethorn.

'And this is where you were last night? Helping to catch those two villains?'

'Yes,' lied her husband, seeing a way to get off the marital hook. 'They fought hard, Margery. By the time that Nick and I hauled them off to a magistrate, the city gates had been closed. I know that I promised to be back early, but I had to look into the truth of what Jonathan told me about Michael Grammaticus.'

'I only spoke of him to Nicholas Bracewell,' said Jarrold.

'Nick and I have no secrets.'

'What will happen to *The Siege of Troy*? Michael claimed to have written it.'

'We'll perform it as a play by Stephen Wragby.'

Jarrold was about to ask another question but he was elbowed gently in the ribs by Margery. Realising that he was now in the way, he mumbled an excuse and backed out of the kitchen. She gazed up lovingly at her husband.

'It appears that I mistook you, Lawrence.'

'I bear no grudge, my love.'

'But I locked you out of your own house.'

'You felt that you had good cause.'

'Why did you not explain it all to me this morning?'

'Because I had to get to the Queen's Head early and did not wish to disturb you. As you've heard, my love, I've had much on my mind these past few days.'

'And all that I did was to add to your woes.'

'You were not to know, Margery.'

'I feel so mean and unjust,' she said. 'You've every right to despise me.'

He laughed artlessly. 'Why on earth should I do that?' He spread his arms. 'Come to me, Margery, and we'll say no more about it.'

She hurled herself into his embrace and surrendered willingly to his kiss, leaving the imprints of her flour-covered hands on the back of his doublet. After a moment, she pushed him away and wrinkled her nose.

'I can smell horse dung,' she said.

Dorothea Tate took some time to find her bearings. Having crossed London Bridge on her own, she searched for the place by the river where she and Hywel Recs had spent their nights when they first came to the city. It brought back some happy memories and she stayed to enjoy them until she was driven away by other vagrants who had claimed the refuge as their own. Dorothea wandered aimlessly, sorry that she had let everyone down by fleeing without explanation, but driven by the fear that she had been an unfair burden. She felt that it was wrong of her to impose on compassionate people like Anne Hendrik and

Nicholas Bracewell. Now that they had helped her over the death of her friend, it was time for her to stand on her own feet again.

When she grew hungry, she begged some stale bread off an old woman in the market and drank water from a pump. It tasted brackish. Dorothea spat it out. Recalling the meals she had been served in Bankside, she was full of regrets but she did not even think of returning. Since she had run away, she believed, they would not have her back again. Theirs was one world, hers another. She trudged on until her feet brought her to a building she recognised with a tremor of fear. The façade of Bridewell towered over her and seemed to crush her spirit. It was then that she realised why she had come. An unseen hand had guided her to the workhouse. This was where she could get revenge.

Deep in her pocket, her hand gripped the large stone that she had picked up from beside the river. Dorothea had grabbed it as a means of defence, but it could also be used in attack. She felt the rough contours with her fingers. They would never anticipate an assault from her. If she could somehow get close enough to Joseph Beechroft – or, better still, to Ralph Olgrave – she could dash out his brains with her weapon. Finding a place in the shadows, she sat down to watch and wait.

Dorothea was still keeping Bridewell under surveillance when two officers dragged a beggar into view. The man was lame and had his arm in a sling but that earned him no sympathy. The officers pulled him to the gatehouse then pushed him to the ground. Knowing what lay ahead for the beggar, Dorothea wanted to reach out and comfort him. One more anonymous victim was about to suffer an ordeal.

Nicholas Bracewell cowered before the gatekeeper's searching gaze. One of the officers hauled him to his feet while the other handed over a writ.

'What's his name?' asked the gatekeeper.

'Tom Rooke,' replied Frank Quilter, 'but it might as well be Tom o'Bedlam for he talks nothing but nonsense. He's been whipped at the cart's-arse so we've no more use for him. Lock him up and throw away the key.'

'We'll want work out of him,' said the gatekeeper. 'One arm may be useless but we'll find labour for the other. Leave him to me, friends. I'll take care of Tom Rooke.'

Quilter and Ingram nodded a farewell and set off again. After checking the writ that committed the prisoner to Bridewell, the gatekeeper wrote details of the newcomer in his ledger. He then summoned another man, who promptly punched the beggar to make him move. Nicholas scrambled forward through the main gate.

'What's your name?' said the keeper.

'Tom Rooke, sir,' croaked Nicholas.

'You'll be plain Tom in here. Remember that.'

'I will, sir.'

'What's wrong with your arm?'

'I cut it badly, sir.'

'Every beggar pretends to have a bad arm or leg or foot,' sneered the keeper, tugging the limb free of the sling and producing a yelp of pain. 'It's an old trick to get out of doing heavy work.'

He examined the arm. Nicholas had bound it with filthy strips of linen that had been soaked in pig's blood beforehand. His fair beard was grimed and he had rubbed dirt all over his face. Leonard had given him some sour milk from the kitchen at the Queen's Head and he had poured it all over his ragged clothes. The keeper reacted to the stench.

'You stink of foul vomit,' he complained. 'We ought to toss you into the Thames to clean you off, you leprous scab! Put that arm back in the sling and follow me.'

Nicholas did as he was told and went across the first courtyard, taking careful note of its design and dimensions and seeing that Dorothea Tate's description of the place had not erred too much. When they went through into the next courtyard, he saw young boys helping to unload boxes of food from a cart. The keeper turned on him.

'That's not for the likes of you,' he said, 'so you can look away.'

They went through a door and climbed a winding staircase. Nicholas was led along a passageway to a large oaken door that the keeper had to unlock. Both of them entered a long, narrow room with a number of soiled mattresses along one wall. There was little in the way of furniture beyond a small table and a single stool. The keeper pointed to the mattresses.

'You'll sleep in here,' he told Nicholas. 'Choose someone else's mattress and they'll soon let you know it with their fists. Tomorrow, we'll put you to work.'

'How many of us are in here?'

'Enough.'

'Will I be fed today?'

'No,' said the man, gruffly. 'Only those who work can eat in Bridewell.'

The keeper went out and locked the door behind him. Nicholas was able to straighten up and lift his eye patch so that he could inspect the room in more detail. It was not difficult to identify the mattresses that were in use. Meagre belongings lay beside each of them. Since the mattress at the far end of the line was the dirtiest and most shredded, he knew that it would be his. Light flooded in. The three windows all overlooked the courtyard where the boys were still unloading produce from the cart.

According to the sketch that was drawn from Dorothea's memory, Nicholas was in the same room where Hywel Rees had been kept. It was from one of the windows that he must have seen the girl being taken reluctantly to the feast in the hall. If that was the case, Nicholas wondered how the Welshman had been able to get out in order to go to the girl's rescue. The window was too high from the ground for him to drop down with any safety, and the door far too solid to force.

Nicholas remained at a window to watch. There was no sign of either Joseph Beechcroft or Ralph Olgrave, but a number of other people came into view. Some were obviously inmates, forced to do whatever chores were necessary, and there were several keepers on duty as well. But he also noticed a few men who came and went from doors on the opposite side of the courtyard. They moved around with complete freedom and, judging from their attire, they could hardly be described as paupers. Nicholas asked himself what function they had in Bridewell.

When the cart had been unloaded, one of the boys was clipped around the head by the keeper and sent through an archway to do another task. The keeper then took the second boy towards the door through which Nicholas had come. Leaving the window, Nicholas went to the last mattress and dragged it away from the others, then he put his arm back in the sling and arranged the patch over his eye. He crouched on his mattress and waited. After a while, the door was unlocked and a weary young boy came in, only to have the door locked immediately behind him. Seeing Nicholas, the boy stopped.

'Who are you?' he asked, warily.

'My name is Tom Rooke,' said Nicholas, in the cracked voice he had practised earlier. 'I'm convicted of vagrancy and sent here. What do I call you, lad?'

'Ned. Ned Griddle.' He approached slowly. 'What's wrong with your arm?'

'I was stabbed in a brawl, and lost a lot of blood.'

'They'll want you to work in here.'

Nicholas held up a hand. 'Stay back, Ned. I do not smell too sweet.'

'Have you been in Bridewell before?'

'Never,' said Nicholas, adjusting his sling, 'but I had a friend who was sent here recently. I hope to see him again.'

'Who is he?'

'A young Welshman by the name of Hywel Rees. Do you know him?'

'I did,' said the boy, sadly. 'I liked him. Hywel was discharged.'

'So soon? Why was that, Ned?'

'They said he caused too much trouble. There was a girl he knew, she was in here as well, but they would not let him see her. So Hywel escaped.'

'How?' asked Nicholas. 'If he'd jumped from the window, he'd have broken his legs. There's no way out.'

'Hywel found one,' explained Griddle. 'He climbed on the roof and worked his way along until he came to an open window. He went through it. That room was not locked because I later saw him run across the courtyard to the hall.'

'Brave man! The girl must have been Dorothea, then.'

'Did you know her as well, Tom?'

'A little,' said Nicholas. 'They'd not been in London for long.'

The door was unlocked again and four youths came into the room. Thin and dishevelled, they had obviously been working hard because they all dropped down on their individual mattresses. One of them fell asleep at once, the others barely gave the newcomer a glance. Ned Griddle's mattress was the one next to Nicholas. He squatted down on it and slipped a hand inside his shirt. Making sure that the others did not see him, he passed Nicholas a piece of the bread he had scrounged from the kitchen. Both of them munched in silence for a few minutes.

'How many of us are there altogether?' said Nicholas at length.

'No more than fifty or sixty in all,' replied Griddle, 'most of them girls.'

'I heard there were the best part of two hundred people here.'

'There are, but they're not all sent for punishment. Many of them live here.'

Nicholas was surprised. 'They *live* in a workhouse?'

'Master Beechcroft rents out rooms to them,' said the boy. 'He makes more money that way. He sells what we make but it brings only a poor profit.'

'What sort of work do we do?'

'We make nails, draw wire, cut timber to size. When my brother was here, they had him unloading supplies on the wharf. We've no skills, Tom,' he complained. 'Hard labour is all we're fit for. Those with skills are the ones they treat much better.'

'Skills?'

'Look at Ben Hemp, for instance. They'll never let him out.'

'Why not?'

'He brings in too much money,' said Griddle, resentfully. 'That's why he has a room of his own to work and sleep in. Ben is a cunning forger. He makes false dice and packs of cards for cony-catchers. He was taught by the best in the trade.'

'Oh,' said Nicholas. 'And who was that?'

'A fiendish clever fellow, according to Ben. A true master of the art.'

'What was his name?'

'Lavery,' said the boy. 'Philomen Lavery.'

Philomen Lavery dealt the cards with nimble fingers and shared a disingenuous smile among the people sitting at his table. Because it was his last night at the Queen's Head, he had invited some of those who had played regularly with him to partake of food and drink in his room. It had put the visitors in a pleasant mood. They were sorry that Lavery would be leaving and taking his cards with him. None of the actors was there but Adam Crowmere had drifted in to play for a while. He soon accepted that he was not going to win. After losing every game in a row, he rose from the table with a chuckle.

'I'm not going to let you rob me of my last penny, Master Lavery.'

'Sit down again, Adam,' coaxed the dealer. 'You may yet have good fortune.'

'Not at cards. Everyone at the table has better luck than me tonight.'

'It was not always so. There was a time when you emptied all our purses.'

'Then lost the money the next night,' said Crowmere, amiably. 'A card table has too many risks. To tell the truth, I prefer dice. Real skill is involved there.'

'Yes,' said one of the other players. 'I'm a man for dice as well.'

'Nothing gives me the same thrill as a game of cards,' argued Lavery. 'Turn one over and it could mean the difference between wealth and beggary.'

'The same is true of dice,' said Crowmere. 'One throw could make you rich.'

'Or very poor, Adam, if you do not have the knack of it.'

'I have that knack, Master Lavery. At least, I used to have.'

'I confess that I do not possess it.'

'Then you must stay with your beloved cards. I know that you feel much safer with them, and they clearly favour you this evening. Dice would give the rest of us more of a chance to win back what we have lost.'

Lavery blinked up at him. 'Do you really believe that, Adam?'

'Yes, I do,' said the other.

'You feel at a disadvantage with cards?'

'Only when I play against you.'

'Yet you'd be prepared to wager on the throw of a dice?'

'Time and again.'

'Then we'll put it to the test after this game,' decided Lavery, looking around the table. 'As it happens, I do have some dice with me somewhere. If we can find them, we'll see if our cheery landlord really does have the knack of which he boasts.' He beamed at the others. 'Are we all agreed?'

Standing at the window, Nicholas had counted four carriages. One by one, they had rolled into the courtyard to disgorge their raucous occupants. All the visitors were men and they were welcomed at the door of the hall by Joseph Beechcroft. Other guests arrived on horseback and a few came on foot. Arrayed in their taffeta, the women soon came out to join them. Nicholas gazed around the room. Most of his companions were fast asleep, uninterested in a banquet from which they were excluded and too exhausted to remain awake to talk. Ned Griddle was the only one whose eyes were still open. He crept across to the window.

'Get some sleep while you can, Tom,' he counselled in a whisper.

'I like to watch,' said Nicholas. 'Who are these people?'

'Friends of Master Beechcroft's or Master Olgrave's. They eat well.'

'By the sound of them, they've already drunk well. How long will they stay?'

Griddle yawned. 'I've never stayed awake long enough to find out.'

The banquet was under way. Almost thirty people were seated at the long table and all them were relishing the occasion. Three musicians played in the background and their lively airs caught the spirit of the evening. The food was rich, the wine plentiful and the guests blandished by the women in their gaudy plumage. Seated at the end of the table, Joseph Beechcroft and Ralph Olgrave looked on with satisfaction.

'How much have we made this evening?' asked Olgrave.

'A handsome profit. When men are drunk, their purse strings are much looser.'

'They get their money's worth, Joseph.'

'Oh, yes,' said Beechcroft, looking down the table to see one of the guests fondling a swarthy young woman with large, round breasts spilling out of her bodice. 'I think that Master Greatorex will be pleasuring Joan Lockyer tonight. He cannot keep his hands off her.'

'Is it not strange?' said Olgrave with a grin. 'Master Greatorex would never dare to venture into the stews of Clerkenwell Street, where Joan and her sisters ply their trade, yet he'll play with her paps for hours in here.'

Beechcroft smirked. 'Bridewell is a palace, remember.'

'And we are its kings.'

A servant filled their cups with wine and Olgrave joined in the noisy badinage. His partner was more circumspect. While he was delighted that yet another banquet was such a success, he remembered what had happened the last time that the hall had been filled with guests. When there was a lull in the general hilarity, he turned to Olgrave.

'The girl still worries me, Ralph,' he confided.

'Forget her, man. She belongs in the past.'

'Not while she's still alive to accuse us.'

Olgrave sneered. 'Who will listen to the word of a beggar?'

'Nicholas Bracewell did.'

'And he'll pay for his folly, Joseph. When that Welsh friend of his has been dispatched,' he explained, 'Gregory will follow the book holder to his lodging, for that's where Dorothea will be hiding, I feel certain. Gregory has orders to kill them both.'

'Good,' said Beechcroft, reassured. 'He's a ready assassin.'

'The fellow has never let us down before.' Olgrave let his gaze travel up and down the table. 'Now, then, which of these fine ladies shall I take tonight?'

'Choose two, Ralph. There are more than enough to spare.'

'One is all I need before I go home to my wife,' said the other, as his eye settled on the youngest woman in the room. 'Nan Welbeck tempts me, I must confess.'

'She's clean and fresh enough.'

'And more than willing. There'll be good sport for both of us, I fancy. Nan is no Dorothea Tate,' he added with a lecherous cackle. 'I'll not need Gregory Sumner to hold her down for me.'

Bruised and bloodied, Gregory Sumner sat in a chair in the lawyer's office. His legs were bare, he wore no shoes and his hands were still tied behind his back. Owen Elias was a menacing presence behind him but it was Henry Cleaton who asked all the questions, and who noted the answers down on a sheet of paper. Sumner was amazed at how much the two of them seemed to know about the death of Hywel Rees and the violation of Dorothea Tate. Involved directly in both crimes, he did his best to shift the blame entirely on to Beechcroft and Olgrave. Encouraged by an occasional sharp prod from Elias, the man tried to save his own skin by incriminating others and new facts tumbled out of him.

Henry Cleaton read carefully through what he had written down.

'We have enough,' concluded the lawyer. 'Let's take him before a magistrate.'

Ned Griddle slept as soundly as the others in the room until the breeze picked up and brushed his face and hair. He came awake to see that one of the windows was wide open. He turned instinctively to the man who had slumbered on the mattress beside him but Tom Rooke was not there. Griddle sat up and rubbed his eyes. Even in the gloom, he could see that the newcomer was no longer in the room. Casting aside his tattered blanket, he scampered to the open window and looked out. A scraping sound took his gaze upward and he gaped in wonder. Silhouetted against the night sky, the crooked beggar who had earlier had his arm in a sling, and a patch over his eye, was now moving with remarkable agility along the roof.

Nicholas Bracewell had no fear of heights. His years at sea had accustomed him to climbing the rigging even in the most inclement weather, and his time in the crow's nest of the *Golden Hind* during a heavy swell had prepared him for anything. It was a fine night and he was clambering over a solid surface. He felt completely secure. All that he had to do was to find an open window through which he could re-enter the building. Sling, eye patch and anything else that might encumber him had been cast off so that he could move freely.

He first climbed to the apex of the roof, to take his bearings and to survey the whole building. With the sketch of Bridewell in his mind, he tried to work out where Ralph Olgrave's bedchamber was situated. Dorothea had said that it was somewhere above the main hall. Nicholas edged his way forward in that direction. To his left was the forbidding outline of Baynard's Castle. Down below, the River Fleet gurgled along before merging with the Thames. To his right was Greyfriars, the ancient monastery now converted into living quarters, its church renamed, its function changed forever. Ahead of him, across the water, Anne Hendrik would be asleep in Bankside. Nicholas had no idea where the girl was.

Easing himself down the angle of the roof, he reached one of the gables and felt his way around it. The window was locked. It was the same with the next gable and the one beyond it, but a fourth proved more amenable. Not only was the window wide open to admit fresh air, a candle had been lighted in the room, enabling him to see that it was unoccupied. In a manoeuvre he had used hundreds of times at sea, he grabbed the side of the gable and swung himself in through the window as if descending to the deck of a ship. Nicholas was back inside the building.

After taking a quick inventory of the room, he padded across to the door. It was locked and would not give way to his shoulder. He would need another point of access. Before he went in search of it, however, he looked around the room more carefully. A large table stood in the middle of it with two chairs beside it. Ledgers, books, papers and a series of letters were stacked neatly side by side. Using the candle to illumine the items on the table, Nicholas realised that he must have stumbled into the room that was Bridewell's counting house.

He picked up a piece of paper and saw that it was a receipt for money paid in rent at the workhouse, clear proof that those who ran the place were breaking the terms of their contract. Nicholas's curiosity was whetted. He leafed his way through some of the other documents and found further evidence of the misuse of Bridewell. Sitting on one of the chairs, he opened a ledger and saw that it was the account book for the institution. He studied the most recent entries. Income and expenditure were listed in parallel columns, but there was no mention of any rental money. Instead, the income appeared to come entirely from what was manufactured by the inmates and sold at a commercial price.

When he flicked back through the pages, Nicholas saw a convincing record of what seemed to be a legal enterprise that fulfilled all the requirements enjoined by the city authorities who leased the workhouse to Beechcroft and Olgrave. Anyone looking at the accounts would congratulate the two partners on the way that they had kept the institution, and balanced loss so punctiliously against profit. It was obvious to Nicholas that what he held was a counterfeit ledger, carefully devised to appease any inspectors who might pry into it.

Putting the book aside, he reached for an identical ledger that had been beneath it. When he opened it to examine the most recent entries, he found a very different story. Income was now vastly in excess of expenditure, and it came from a variety of sources. Bridewell was the home for dozens of residents who paid a considerable rent for their rooms and who, in some cases, worked at skilled trades within the building and gave a percentage of their earnings to Beechcroft and Olgrave. A name that caught Nicholas's attention was that of Ben Hemp, the forger. The sale of marked cards and loaded dice brought in an appreciable sum.

There was an item that had especial interest for Nicholas. Under the heading of entertainment, the costs of food and drink were set down. Listed opposite them was the amount of money that guests paid for the pleasure of enjoying one of the regular banquets. The ledger was quite specific. Those who wanted more than a delicious meal in congenial surroundings were charged extra for the company of one of the prostitutes. Every penny clearly went into the coffers of Bridewell rather than to the women themselves. Nicholas thought about Dorothea Tate, dressed to entice the men then hustled along to the hall with dire threats to bring her to heel.

On its own, the second ledger was enough to reveal the fraudulent operation run by Beechcroft and Olgrave, and to ensure their conviction, but Nicholas wanted more than that. Murder and rape had also occurred, and he knew the victims of each. It was time to go in search of those responsible. Before he could do so, however, Nicholas heard footsteps coming along the passageway outside the door.

When a key was inserted in the lock, he had no time to flee through the window. Replacing the ledgers as he found them, Nicholas dived behind the arras and held his breath.

Two people came into the room and closed the door behind them. The heaviness of their tread suggested to Nicholas that they were both men. He listened to what sounded like a large bag of money being dropped onto the table. Coins were emptied out and someone began to count them. Hidden from sight, Nicholas hoped that he could stay where he was until the two men left the room, but his stench gave him away. The rags that he wore were impregnated with sour milk and its reek had not been dispelled by the breeze that blew in through the open window.

While he was still hunched behind the arras, it was suddenly pulled aside by Joseph Beechcroft. He held a dagger in his other hand and the keeper who accompanied him was carrying a cudgel. Both men glared accusingly at him. Nicholas shrunk back and brought his arms up protectively. Beechcroft brandished his weapon.

'Who are you?' he demanded. 'And how on earth did you get in here?'

Chapter Thirteen

Dorothea Tate kept a lonely vigil outside Bridewell. A number of people had gone in through the gate, some in carriages, others on horseback, but nobody had come out. As evening shaded into night, she began to wonder if Joseph Beechcroft and Ralph Olgrave were even inside the workhouse, but she did not abandon her post. The hope that one, or both of them, would ultimately appear, kept her huddled in the doorway on the opposite side of the road. The heavy stone in her pocket, she believed, would help her to avenge the murder of Hywel Rees. Once that had been achieved, Dorothea did not care what happened to her. She would be content.

Her position had rendered her vulnerable to various hazards. Stray dogs had bothered her, children had mocked her and a parish constable had chased her away for a while, but she quickly returned to her chosen spot. One passer-by had even tossed her a coin. As light began to fade, there had been less traffic on the street and the two watchmen who went past on patrol did not even notice the bundle of rags in the doorway. Obsessed by one ambition, Dorothea was not frightened to be alone on the street at night. Indeed, darkness helped her to merge with the stonework all round her and more or less disappear from sight.

She was not free from regret. Dorothea was sad that she had to flee from people who had befriended her at a time when everyone else turned away. Anne Hendrik and Nicholas Bracewell would doubtless be anxious on her behalf, and she was sorry about that, but she consoled herself with the thought that she was doing the right thing. Why should she expect others to exact justice for her when she could do so herself? She simply had to confront her detractors. That was the only way she would get true satisfaction.

She felt another pang of regret when the genial face of Owen Elias came into her mind. Delighted to hear another Welsh voice in the capital, it was he who had first come to their aid when Hywel's performance as a counterfeit crank had been exposed. Her disappearance would disappoint and hurt Elias. He was bound to feel betrayed yet that could not be helped. Had she turned to him – or to Nicholas Bracewell – she knew that neither of them would have condoned what she was now planning to do. On the contrary, they would have done everything they could to keep her well away from Bridewell.

At long last, the gate was opened and a man emerged,

leading a horse. Dorothea was on her feet at once, pulling the stone from her pocket in readiness. As soon as he mounted, however, and she could see him in profile, she knew that it was neither of the men for whom she lay in ambush. She returned to her place in the doorway and settled down once more. Her moment, she was certain, would eventually come.

Nicholas Bracewell's disguise was effective. Even at such close range, Beechcroft did not recognise him. When the beggar flinched and spoke in a cracked voice, he was taken for what he appeared to be. The keeper raised his cudgel to strike.

'What's your name?' he demanded.

'Tom Rooke, sir,' croaked Nicholas.

'When were you admitted to Bridewell?'

'Today, sir.'

'How did you get in here?'

'I lost my way.'

'He's lying,' snarled Beechcroft. 'The room is always kept locked. He must have sneaked in earlier when I was in here myself.' Sheathing his dagger, he stood back and snapped his fingers. 'Beat him hard for his impudence.'

'I'll do so with pleasure,' said the keeper.

Nicholas was forced to act. If he took the punishment, he knew that he would be beaten senseless then locked up more securely. Defence was vital. As the man wielded his cudgel for the first time, therefore, Nicholas dodged the blow, grabbed the tapestry and tore it from its pole so that he could wind it around the keeper. The two men then grappled fiercely. Beechcroft was astounded. The cowering beggar had suddenly turned into a vigorous man, who was patently getting the upper hand in the brawl. Beechcroft pulled out his dagger again and tried to stab Nicholas, but the latter simply twisted the keeper around so that he felt the point of the weapon in his shoulder.

Letting out a yell of agony, the keeper stumbled back, enabling Nicholas to wrest the cudgel from his grasp. Beechcroft continued to jab away without success. Nicholas pushed the keeper roughly to the floor and used the cudgel to knock Beechcroft's dagger from his hand. When the latter made a dash for the door, Nicholas grabbed him by the arm, spun him round then shoved him with force against the wood. Panting with fear, eyes bulging from their sockets, Beechcroft had the uncomfortable feeling that he could identify his attacker.

'I think I know you, sir, do I not?' he said.

'My name is not Tom Rooke,' said Nicholas in his normal voice. 'That much I'll freely confess.'

Beechcroft goggled at him. 'Nicholas Bracewell!'

'The same.'

'What are you doing here?'

'I came to talk about the murder of Hywel Rees, and what that partner of yours did to a defenceless creature named Dorothea Tate.'

'I had no part in that! I swear it!'

'The girl told me that two men were involved. One of them held her down.'

'That was Gregory Sumner, a keeper here. He assisted Ralph, not me.'

'Yet you were the one who beat Dorothea,' said Nicholas, holding the cudgel over him. 'You pummelled the girl until her friend came to her rescue.'

'I did not mean to hurt her,' claimed Beechcroft, starting to tremble.

'Then I'll not mean to hurt *you*, when I beat the truth out of you.'

Beechcroft cringed against the door. 'No!' he begged. 'Do not strike me!'

'Then tell me what you did to Hywel Rees.'

Nicholas made the mistake of taking an eye off the wounded keeper. The tapestry in which he had been caught up had saved him from serious injury, muffling the impact of the dagger thrust. Blood had been drawn but it was only a minor flesh wound. Throwing off the tapestry, the man soon struggled to his feet. He dived at Nicholas from behind and got an arm around his neck, pulling him backward across the room. Beechcroft needed no second invitation to escape. He was through the door in a flash and locked it behind him. Nicholas, meanwhile, had to contend with a strong arm across his throat, squeezing the breath out of him. He pumped away with his elbows to wind his adversary then stamped hard on his toe to produce a howl of rage. The man released his hold. Spinning round, Nicholas cracked him on the head with the cudgel and sent him to his knees. A second blow knocked the man unconscious.

There was no sense in remaining in the room. Beechcroft

would soon be back with armed men and Nicholas would be trapped. He collected the fallen dagger and stuck it in his belt. Apart from saving himself, Nicholas also wanted to take the two ledgers with him as additional proof of the mismanagement of Bridewell. Left in the room, they could always be hidden or even destroyed. Wrapping the books in the tapestry, therefore, he took them to the window and swung them up behind the gable. He then clambered after them and made his way along the roof, wedging his cargo behind one of the chimney pots, out of reach of any but the most intrepid climbers.

From down below, he heard the sound of the door being unlocked and of many feet rushing into the room. Beechcroft's roar of anger was clearly audible.

'Where the devil has he gone *now*?'

The banquet in the hall had reached the stage where couples were starting to peel off and adjourn to nearby rooms. Music still played, wine still flowed but only half of the guests remained at the table. While his partner went off to count the evening's takings, Ralph Olgrave decided to sample the charms of Nan Welbeck, a sprightly young woman with long fair hair, who still had something of a bloom on her. He beckoned her over, took a first kiss then eased her onto his lap. Caressing her with one hand, he held his cup of wine in the other and took a long sip before handing it to her. Nan Welbeck drained it, laughed merrily then gave Olgrave a long, luscious, searching kiss on the lips.

It was not a moment when he wanted to be interrupted.

Seeing his partner come bursting into the room, Olgrave was very annoyed and tried to wave him away, but Beechcroft was determined. He had an air of desperation about him.

'I need to speak to you in private, Ralph,' he said.

'Not now, please.'

'I must insist.'

'And I must insist that you leave Nan and me alone,' said Olgrave, glaring at him. 'There's nothing so important that it cannot wait until later.'

'Yes, there is.'

'Find yourself a woman and leave us be.'

'You must come *now*,' warned Beechcroft, grabbing him by the arm. 'We have an unwelcome guest, Ralph. I've seen him with my own eyes.'

'Oh, and who is that?'

'Nicholas Bracewell.'

Olgrave sobered at once. 'How ever did he get in here?'

'By posing as a beggar by the name of Tom Rooke.'

'Excuse me, Nan,' said Olgrave, moving her off his lap and getting up. 'This business will not wait. Do not go away, my sweet, for I'll soon be back.' He blew her a kiss then hurried for the door with Beechcroft. Once outside, he turned on his partner. 'Now then, Joseph. What's this all about?'

'Our survival.'

'Do not talk such nonsense. What can one man do against so many of us?'

'He broke into the counting house. He has our ledgers.'

'What?' cried Olgrave. '*Both* of them?'

'Yes, Ralph. He stole them and hid them. I've hunted everywhere.'

'Are you *sure* that it was that book holder from Westfield's Men?'

'As sure as I am that he holds *our* books now,' said Beechcroft. 'If the aldermen should ever see those accounts, we are both condemned.'

'Calm down, Joseph. It will not come to that.'

'I think that we should run for it while we can.'

'No!'

'Divide the money and get clean away.'

'That's lunacy.'

'It's the only way out. Stay here and we'll both be arraigned. There's more than enough for the two of us, Ralph. Come and take your share.'

'I'll not dream of it.'

'But it's what we'd always planned to do if we were found out.'

'We've *not* been found out, you idiot,' said Olgrave, taking him by the shoulders to shake him. 'We have an interloper in Bridewell, that's all.'

'An interloper in possession of evidence that could send us both to prison.'

'Only if he gets that evidence out of here. And how can he do that?'

'I told you that this man would be a danger.'

'Not when we've done the job that Gregory was sent to do,' asserted Olgrave, taking out his dagger. 'If this meddling fool is inside Bridewell, there's no way that he can get out again. All the gates are locked.'

'He managed to get in, Ralph.'

'He'll live to regret that, I warrant you. Now, where is the rogue?'

'That's the problem we face,' wailed Beechcroft.

'What is?'

'Nicholas Bracewell has vanished.'

As long as he stayed where he was, Nicholas felt safe. Having climbed to the apex of the roof, he now lay on the outward slope so that he was invisible from the courtyard. The ledgers were stuffed up against a chimney and, even if it rained, they would be protected. Their disappearance was causing unrest. When he peeped over the ridge tiles, he could see a group of people in the yard, some with blazing torches, taking orders from Ralph Olgrave. The keepers dispersed to carry out a methodical search, leaving Olgrave alone in the courtyard with his partner. Their voices were raised in argument but Nicholas could not hear all that was said. Beechcroft pointed up at the counting house then ran towards the door that would give him access to it.

Bearing torches, other keepers came trotting up to help in the search for the fugitive. Olgrave sent all but two of them to explore the rooms on the ground floor. Looking upwards, he studied the gable window of the counting house and reached a decision. When Nicholas saw him point to the roof, he knew that his hiding place had been discovered. He had either to find an open window on the exterior of the building, or wait to be caught. Lowering himself to the edge of the roof on the side above the Fleet, he went carefully along the edge from gable to gable, trying each of the windows. He soon found one that was open but, before he could swing down into it, a keeper came into it and saw his legs dangling down.

The alarm was raised at once. Nicholas had no means of escape. All that he could do was to scramble back up to the apex of the roof. Sitting astride it, he looked down into the courtyard where Olgrave was still standing. The latter could see his outline against the night sky.

'Give yourself up while you can!' he yelled.

'No,' replied Nicholas, boldly. 'You'll have to come and get me.'

'You are trespassing on private property.'

'My crime pales beside those that you have committed, Master Olgrave.'

'Watch what you say, sir!'

'Your days in Bridewell are over. You and your partner will be thrown out of here like the villains that you are. You'll hang from the gallows – both of you.'

'Seize him!' shouted Olgrave.

Nicholas looked along the roof and saw that a short, stocky man was climbing out of a gable window some ten yards away. When the man got on to the tiles and steadied himself, he pulled a dagger from his belt. Making his way up the incline, he reached the apex and cocked a leg over it. Nicholas expected the man to move towards him but the keeper had another plan. Without warning, he suddenly hurled the weapon at Nicholas. The book holder swung quickly to the left but the dagger still grazed his arm. Though it was only a scratch, he put a hand to it to stem the trickle of blood.

Encouraged by his success, the man moved a few feet closer to his target before taking a second dagger from his belt. He was confident of hitting him this time. As the keeper raised his arm to throw, Nicholas snatched out his own weapon and used it to parry the missile that came hurtling towards him. It clattered down the roof and fell harmlessly into the river below. Nicholas then did something that amazed Ralph Olgrave and the others who were watching from the courtyard. Standing up on the ridge tiles, he stretched out his arms to aid his balance then walked nimbly along them as if strolling on firm ground. He threatened the keeper with his dagger.

'Get down while you may,' he ordered.

'Keep off!'

'Go now, and you'll not be harmed.'

The man tried to obey. Losing his nerve, he tried to lower himself swiftly down the roof but his hold slipped and he tumbled backwards, rolling down the incline until he dropped over the edge. He let out a long scream of despair as he plummeted downwards. When his body hit the ground, there was an awesome thud, followed by a long silence. It was eventually broken by a command from Ralph Olgrave.

'Fetch guns!' he ordered. 'Shoot him off the roof.'

Joseph Beechcroft heard the scream and rushed to the window of the counting house to look down. By the light of the torches, he could see the keeper's body, twisted into an unnatural shape as it lay on the ground. Their interloper was still at liberty. Beechcroft did not wait any longer. Sensing that their reign at the Bridewell was nearing its end, he unlocked a cupboard and took out several purses, stuffing them into a leather satchel as fast as he could. Leaving his partner's share of the booty intact, he locked the cupboard again and fled through the door, hurtling down the staircase. When he came out of the door at ground level, he had to step over the body of the dead man.

'What are you doing?' asked Olgrave.

'Leaving while I can, Ralph. You should do the same.'

'But we have him cornered. A pistol or a musket will soon bring him down.'

'Yes,' said Beechcroft, looking up. 'In front of witnesses. There'll be faces watching from every window. What they'll see is murder. I'll not stay.'

'Hold!' said Olgrave, grabbing his arm. 'We can face this out.'

'No, Ralph. It's too late. The game is up.'

'Why throw it all away?'

'Let me go,' insisted Beechcroft.

Pulling his arm free, he fled across the courtyard in the direction of the main gate.

Though she became increasingly weary, Dorothea Tate did not dare to fall asleep. Concealed in her doorway, she did not shift her gaze from Bridewell for a second, hoping and praying that her chance would somehow come. She reflected on the horrors she had suffered inside its walls, and thought once more of her dearest friend, stolen from her forever because he had tried to protect her. Dorothea also thought fondly of those who had given her succour in the wake of her loss. She was jerked out of her reverie by the sound of the gate of Bridewell, creaking back on its hinges. She was on her feet in an instant. Her eyes were now accustomed to the dark and she was able to pick out the shape of the rider who came out through the gate. Her spirits lifted. Revenge was at hand.

Certain that it was Joseph Beechcroft, she ran to the middle of the road and pulled out her stone, flinging it hard at the rider as the horse cantered towards her. It struck Beechcroft in the chest, making him fall back and pull involuntarily on the reins. Skidding to a halt with a neigh of protest, the horse reared and threw him from the saddle. Dorothea dashed across to him and began to punch him with both fists. Beechcroft was dazed by the fall but was not badly injured. He soon recovered enough to defend himself, seizing her by the wrists to stop her assault. It was then that he recognised her.

'We should have killed you along with your friend,' he growled.

'Murderer!' she cried and spat in his face.

'You little devil!'

He flung her away, wiped the spit from his eyes then got to his feet. When he saw her trying to pick up the stone again, he rushed across to twist it from her hand, then raised it high to dash against her head.

'Stop!' yelled a voice. 'Leave the child alone!'

Beechcroft turned to see a group of men, hurrying towards Bridewell with lighted torches. One of their number, a stocky Welshman, was racing towards him.

'Owen!' cried Dorothea.

'Is that *you*, girl?' he asked in astonishment.

'This is him. This is Master Beechcroft.'

'Leave him to me, Dorothea.'

Dropping the stone, Beechcroft took to his heels but he did not get far. Elias soon overhauled him and jumped on his back to bring him down. Hitting the hard road with his forehead, Beechcroft was too stunned to fight back. Elias turned him over as two men arrived to shed light on the scene with their torches.

'Arrest this one first,' said Elias, 'before I lose my temper with him.'

The commotion in the courtyard had aroused many spectators. Windows were opened so that inmates, and those who rented rooms at the workhouse, could see what was going on. Some of the guests had stumbled out of the hall to watch from the doorway. Ralph Olgrave tried to persuade them to go back to their banquet, but they were too inquisitive. They wondered why he was holding the musket that one of the keepers had fetched, and they were even more curious when they saw the corpse on the ground.

Nicholas watched it all from the apex of the roof, knowing that time was running out for him. Every means of escape has been cut off. The gable windows below him were either locked or guarded by keepers. It was only a matter of time before someone was brave enough to come after him. Nicholas might be able to dodge, or ward off, a dagger but he had no protection against a musket ball. Someone who could handle a gun could easily pick him off. Beechcroft may have fled in panic but his partner was still in charge, and there was no point in trying to reason with him. Olgrave wanted him dead.

Nicholas soon had vivid proof of the fact. A man emerged from one of the gable windows and pulled himself up with care onto the roof. Nicholas was close enough to discern the musket that was slung from his shoulder. He suspected that the keeper would have a pistol in his belt as well. All that he could do was to scramble as far away as he could. The man, meanwhile, groped his way up to the apex of the roof and sat astride it. He could now see his prey, moving away from him in the gloom. He reached for the musket. Nicholas looked back and saw the weapon being levelled at him. Flattening himself on the tiles, he tried to present as small a target as he could.

Tensing himself, he waited for the loud report as the musket was fired but the trigger was never pulled. Instead, a familiar voice reverberated around the courtyard as a trained actor opened his lungs to the full.

'Where are you, Nick!' shouted Owen Elias.

Nicholas looked down and saw uniformed men, coming into the courtyard with torches. Their sudden arrival had made the keeper with the musket hold his fire. The man did not dare to shoot while officers of the law were watching from below. Nicholas sat on the apex of the roof.

'Is that you, Owen?' he called. 'I'm up here.'

'*Diu!*' exclaimed his friend, looking up. 'What are you doing on the roof?'

Nicholas laughed with relief. 'Waiting for you to come,' he said.

'Joseph Beechcroft has been arrested, and we have a warrant to search Bridewell and take his partner into custody. Where would we find Ralph Olgrave?'

'Down there!'

Nicholas pointed at the man but Olgrave did not wait to be apprehended. Pushing aside the guests who stood in his way, he darted into the hall and slammed the door shut before locking it from the inside. Some of the officers ran to the door but their concerted strength could not force it open. Nicholas remained where he was. He knew that Olgrave would understand the folly of staying on the premises when a warrant for his arrest had been issued. The man would surely bolt. Soon afterwards, he saw a figure rush out of a rear door and make for the wharf. Olgrave was hoping to escape by boat.

Nicholas was off at once. Balancing on the roof tiles, he walked along them for several yards. Then he sat down and slid on his backside until he reached the gable window through which the keeper with the musket had climbed. He took a grip, swung down into the room then sprinted through the door. Descending the stairs at speed, he went along a passageway and tried every door to the rooms facing the Fleet River. When one finally opened, he found himself in a storeroom and he felt his way across to the window. He was through it in seconds and dropped to the ground.

Olgrave was a blob in the darkness, rowing frantically down river. Nicholas ran to the wharf and jumped into another boat that was moored there. Using an oar to push himself away from the bank, he gave chase. Olgrave heaved on the oars with all his energy but he was no sailor. The boat zigzagged its way crazily through the water. Behind him, Nicholas settled into a steady rhythm. Using the power of his thighs as much as the strength of his arms, he was soon rowing in a relatively straight line. While Olgrave splashed his way along, Nicholas made sure that the blades of his oars entered the water cleanly at the right angle to give him maximum thrust. He soon began to gain on the other man.

Helped by the current, Olgrave contrived to maintain a reasonable speed. He believed that, by the time that the officers had broken into the hall and searched that part of the building, he would be well out of their reach. But he had reckoned without the man on the roof, who had witnessed his flight. A shape slowly emerged out of the gloom behind him. As he struggled to guide his own boat, Olgrave saw to his horror that he was being followed by a stronger and better oarsman. He could not hope to stay ahead of him. Sweat was already dribbling down his face and moistening his shirt under the armpits. Fear made his heart pound like a drum.

Olgrave used one oar to turn the prow of his boat towards the shore, then he put all his effort into reaching it before he was caught. Nicholas changed course as well, gaining on him with every pull of the oars. He was less than fifteen yards behind now. Looking over his shoulder, Olgrave saw a landing stage ahead that served the stately residence of Durham House. When he got close, he let go of his oars and turned round to stand up in the boat. As soon as it thudded into the timber, he flung himself at the landing stage and tried to drag himself up.

Nicholas was soon after him, tying his own boat to one of the iron rings before jumping ashore to give pursuit. Breathing heavily, Olgrave swung round to confront him, tugging a dagger from its sheath and holding it aloft. The only way to shake off his pursuer, he accepted, was to kill him. When he recognised Nicholas, his desire for blood was quickened.

'Give up your weapon,' said Nicholas, as the other man circled him slowly. 'You heard what Owen told me. There's a warrant for your arrest.'

'I'll not be taken,' snapped Olgrave.

'There's no way out for you.'

'Or for you, sir.' He slashed with the dagger but Nicholas eluded the blade. 'You should have kept your nose out of our affairs, my friend. It will cost you your life.'

'I think not,' said Nicholas, dodging another thrust. 'I'm not like Hywel Rees, You and your partner cannot bludgeon me from behind and throw me in the Thames.'

Olgrave smirked. 'No, but I can stab you through the heart and watch you die at my feet,' he said. 'It's no more than your meddling deserves.'

Nicholas danced out of the way as the dagger was aimed at his heart. He still had Beechcroft's weapon tucked in his belt, but he did not even think of drawing it. He wanted to take Olgrave alive so that the man could be convicted of his crimes. To dispatch him now in the darkness would be to let him escape the full rigor of justice, and that had to be avoided. Nicholas reminded himself that here was a man who had raped an innocent girl without mercy and helped to murder her friend.

Jabbing with the dagger, Olgrave tried to move him backward towards the river so that the available space was cut down. He was only a tailor by trade but he still felt able to dispose of a man who appeared to be unarmed. He did not realise that Nicholas was a veteran of countless brawls with sailors. That experience had sharpened his instincts. Every time that Olgrave thrust his dagger, Nicholas seemed to know exactly where it would go and evaded its point. However, he was being manoeuvred slowly backward.

Olgrave ran out of patience. Unable even to wound his man, he suddenly dived forward to grab him by the shoulder, intending to ram the dagger into his body with the other hand. Instead, Nicholas caught him by the wrist and tried to twist the weapon from his grasp. Olgrave reacted swiftly, tripping Nicholas up so that fell down and pulled his attacker on top of him. They grappled furiously. Olgrave's wrist was still held in an iron grip but the point of the dagger was only inches away from Nicholas's face.

'I'll blind you first and kill you afterwards,' boasted Olgrave.

'Your luck has finally run out, I think.'

'You are the one in need of luck, my friend.'

'I doubt that, Master Olgrave.'

'Die, you rogue!'

With a surge of strength, he pressed down hard but Nicholas was too quick for him again. He flicked his head aside so that the dagger embedded itself harmlessly in the timber, then he rolled Olgrave over and sat astride him to deliver a relay of punches. Getting to his feet, Nicholas dragged his adversary up after him. Olgrave was not finished yet. He flailed away with both arms until Nicholas hit him with a fearsome uppercut that sent him reeling backward. The next moment, Olgrave had fallen off the edge of the landing stage into the water. As soon as he surfaced, he began to thresh about wildly.

'Help me!' he begged. 'I cannot swim!'

'What help did you give to Dorothea Tate?'

'For the love of God, get me out of here!'

'Confess your crimes first,' said Nicholas. 'Did you violate the girl?'

'Yes, yes.'

'And did you murder Hywel Rees?'

'No, I swear it!'

'Then stay in the river and drown.'

'Spare me. I'll tell all.'

'Then say how he was battered to death.'

'Three of us did it,' admitted the other, expelling a mouthful of water. 'My partner and I were helped by a man named Gregory Sumner.'

Nicholas was satisfied. 'Then come out and join them in court,' he said.

He retrieved one of the oars from his boat and offered the blade to Olgrave, who clung on tightly as he was pulled out of the Thames. Sodden and spluttering, the man was soon twitching on the landing stage like a giant fish.

'Let's get you back to Bridewell,' said Nicholas.

Anne Hendrik was so thrilled to see Dorothea again that she kissed her on both cheeks. The girl burst into tears and gabbled her apologies. It was late when Nicholas arrived back in Bankside with her, but Anne did not mind being roused from her bed to welcome them. To have them both safely returned was more than she had dared to hope. Dorothea began to tell her story until exhaustion made her eyelids droop. Anne put her to bed then came back into the parlour, where Nicholas was still sitting.

'I never thought that we'd see her again,' she said.

'I am sorry to bring a problem back to your door, Anne.'

'It relieves my mind to know that she is alive and well. And Dorothea may not be a problem for long. I've a neighbour who is looking for a servant girl. If we can teach her what to do,' suggested Anne, 'we may find a new home for her. And she will not lack for a young friend. Jan Muller, my apprentice, is quite smitten with the girl.' She sat beside Nicholas. 'Now, then,' she said. 'Tell me what really happened.'

'Owen is the hero, Anne. He rescued both Dorothea and me.'

'What was she doing outside Bridewell?'

'Remembering what happened inside the place.'

Calmly and with typical modesty, Nicholas told her about his own adventures in the workhouse, and the subsequent arrest of Beechcroft and Olgrave. He recalled the fight on the landing stage.

'Is it not strange?' he said. 'Ralph Olgrave was so afraid of drowning that he would rather be hauled out of the water to face certain death on the gallows.'

'You mentioned something about ledgers.'

'They were account books for Bridewell. One was accurate, and the other a tissue of lies concocted to fool any inspectors. When I got back there, I collected them from the roof where I'd left them. Yes,' he added with a laugh, 'and I helped down the poor keeper who was stranded up there. He managed to get up on the roof with a musket to shoot me, then lacked the courage to climb down again.'

'You should have left him there, Nick.'

'I saw one man fall to his death. That was enough.'

'All is now settled, then.'

'Not quite, Anne.'

'What more remains?'

'Some unfinished business at the Queen's Head,' he said. 'I'll need to borrow your horse again for I have to be at the inn soon after dawn. Otherwise, I may miss him.'

'Who?'

'A man who was hoping to sneak away tomorrow with a large amount of money in his purse that he obtained by trickery.'

'Trickery?'

'Cards and dice, Anne.'

'What's the fellow's name?'

'Philomen Lavery.'

Philomen Lavery was up early to eat a frugal breakfast before packing his bags. There was a tap on the door of his room and the landlord let himself in. He pumped Lavery's hand appreciatively.

'I am sorry to see you leave,' he said.

'It would be foolish to stay any longer, Adam.'

'Where will you go next?'

'Back to St Albans, I think. Then on to Bedford.'

'Do not forget us in Rochester,' said Crowmere. 'It's two years since we last saw you at The Red Lion. I expect you back again one day.'

'I'll be there,' promised Lavery. 'How much do I owe you?'

'Nothing, my friend. All debts are settled.'

'Then I'll bid you farewell and steal away.'

'Let me help you,' volunteered the landlord, picking up one of the bags.

'Thank you, Adam.'

Lavery reached for the other bag and the large satchel beside it. When the two men turned towards the open door, however, they found their way blocked by Nicholas Bracewell. Quite unperturbed, Lavery produced one of his innocuous smiles.

'If you wish to play cards,' he said, softly, 'you come too late. I must away.'

'We need to have words, Master Lavery,' said Nicholas.

'About what?'

'A pupil of yours, now working in Bridewell.'

'A pupil? I'm a merchant, sir, and not a schoolmaster.'

'Yet you taught this particular lad well,' said Nicholas. 'His name is Ben Hemp and you instructed him in the art of making false dice.'

'Dice?' repeated Lavery in surprise. 'But I know nothing of dice. I devote myself to a pack of cards, as many of your fellows will testify.'

'I'm told that dice were also rolled on your table last night, Master Lavery, and that you won game after game. When you faltered,' Nicholas went on with a meaningful glance at Crowmere, 'your confederate inherited your good fortune.'

'Are you accusing *me*, Nick?' said the landlord.

'The two of you worked together from the start.'

'I'd never even met Master Lavery until he turned up at the Queen's Head.'

'Oh,' said Nicholas, 'I suspect that you and he are old partners. You bring in the gulls and your friend cleverly fleeces them. By using an accomplice, he makes it appear that he does not win all the time. That would only attract suspicion.'

'These are vile allegations,' warned Lavery with vehemence. 'Especially when you have no proof to back them up.'

'It lies in one of those bags. Wherever you keep your marked cards and your false dice, there's proof enough of your villainy. Be glad that I'm the one to find it, Master

340

Lavery,' said Nicholas. 'Were some of my fellows here instead, you'd not escape without a sound whipping.' He turned to Crowmere. 'Neither of you.'

'I thought that we were friends, Nick,' protested the landlord.

'It was only a counterfeit friendship.'

'Did I not arrange a feast for Westfield's Men?'

'You did,' agreed Nicholas, 'but you made us pay for it ourselves when you stole the takings for one of our performances. And your friendship was seen in its true light when you made off with half our wardrobe.'

Crowmere turned puce. 'I deny it!'

'Then perhaps you can explain this, Adam.'

Nicholas stepped into the room so that the massive frame of Leonard could come into view in the doorway. Across his arms, he was holding a velvet cloak, two velvet gowns and a mayoral robe.

'There's much more besides in that chest,' he announced.

Crowmere flared up. 'What were you doing in my room, you oaf?'

'Searching the one place that you somehow forgot to search,' explained Nicholas. 'Leonard acted on my instructions. I thought that our wardrobe might still be here somehow, and you were the only person who could possibly have it. Just think, Leonard,' he said. 'If you had not found these costumes, you would have carried them downstairs in that chest when the landlord left us. We'd never think of looking for them in his tavern in Rochester.'

'Let me say now that I had nothing to do with the theft of your wardrobe,' declared Lavery, righteously. 'That was Adam's idea.'

'Be quiet, Philomen!' said the landlord.

'I'll not be arraigned for *your* crimes.'

'You've committed enough of your own,' noted Nicholas. 'I fancy that the Queen's Head is only the latest inn where you have tricked money out of honest purses. I hope that you enjoyed your stay here.'

Lavery grinned unashamedly. 'It was a profitable visit.'

'Then you'll have some pleasant memories to take with you to prison.'

Crowmere thought only of himself. His confederate was too puny to fight his way out but the landlord was a strong man. Pretending to concede all the charges against him, he offered his hand to Nicholas in congratulation then brought it up suddenly to push the book holder in the chest. He lunged for the door but Leonard stood in his way. When he tried to shove him aside, Crowmere had the costumes thrust in his face. He was then lifted bodily by Leonard and tossed back into the room with ridiculous ease. Falling to the floor with a thump, he stared up resentfully at the man he used to employ.

'Why did you do that, you lumbering fool?' he demanded.

Leonard shrugged. 'Nick is my friend,' he said. 'You pushed him.'

Lawrence Firethorn could not remember a time when he had been so happy. Reconciled with his wife, he was the manager of a theatre company that had its wardrobe restored, its stolen money repaid, its playwright returned from his sick bed and its book holder back in charge. It even had an exciting new play, *The Siege of Troy*, to present that afternoon. The final rehearsal went so well that the diminutive George Dart only dropped his spear once by mistake, and took four minor roles without ever getting them confused. As they broke for refreshment, Firethorn came bounding over to Nicholas Bracewell.

'I sense another triumph in the air, Nick,' he said, confidently.

'I always thought it a fine play.'

'Thanks to you, its fine author now gets credit. Otherwise, we would be staging a tragedy by a counterfeit playwright. The real tragedy is that Stephen Wragby was the one to die while Michael Grammaticus lived.'

'Wish no man to an early grave, Lawrence.'

'Why not?' said Firethorn. 'I'd happily dig the graves of Philomen Lavery and that crafty landlord, then bury their bodies while the two of them were still breathing.'

'They are not here to vex us any more,' observed Nicholas.

'Thanks to you again.'

'Leonard helped me, remember. He discovered our wardrobe.'

'Hidden away right under our noses,' said Firethorn, snorting. 'Have you ever met a more audacious rogue than Adam Crowmere?'

'Yes, I have. Two of them, in fact.'

'What are their names?'

'Joseph Beechcroft and Ralph Olgrave,' said Nicholas. 'Both of them, born liars, cheats, thieves, lechers, embezzlers, murderers and much more. It gives me great pleasure to send them to the gallows.'

Firethorn was vengeful. 'I'd have Crowmere and Lavery dangling beside them,' he said, bitterly. 'Yes, and if there was any rope left, I'd make a noose for Michael and that poisonous Doctor Zander.' He put a companionable arm around Nicholas's shoulder. 'You've had a busy time of late, Nick, filling the city's prisons.'

'Each one of those villains deserves his new residence.'

'Yes,' said Owen Elias, overhearing them. 'Do not forget to include Gregory Sumner. He's behind bars as well. His confession will drown out all the lies of his egregious masters. We did the city good service by revealing what was happening behind the walls of Bridewell.'

'I know,' said Nicholas. 'But only because we met a counterfeit crank.'

'What we met was a true Welshman. No man can counterfeit his nation.'

'We'll need to do so this afternoon,' argued Firethorn. 'I'll be a warlike Greek and you'll be a worthy Trojan. Beware, Owen. I'll besiege your Welshness.'

'Never!' said Elias.

'I'll pelt your Celtic heritage.'

'Over my dead body!'

'Let's move this quarrel into the tiring house,' said Nicholas, easing the two men away. 'We need to clear the stage. Our audience will be here ere long. Do not let them see you in costume until the play begins or you rob us of surprise.'

'True, Nick,' agreed Firethorn. 'But Owen and I will not quarrel.'

'No,' said Elias. 'We'll settle this dispute with swords.'

'Swords or leeks?' taunted the other.

'Both, Lawrence!'

Still bickering, the actors went off, leaving Nicholas to make sure that everything was ready for the performance that afternoon. When the stage had been set for the first scene, he checked that the gatherers were at their posts, and that all the properties stood in readiness in the tiring house. Returning to the yard once more, he saw that the first two spectators were already taking their seats in the lower gallery. Anne Hendrik had brought Dorothea Tate to take her first excited look at Westfield's Men.

An hour later, they were only a tiny part of the large crowd that had descended on the Queen's Head to watch *The Siege of Troy*. Surrounded by his entourage, Lord Westfield was in his usual place, quite unaware of the vicissitudes endured by his company. Two people who did have some insight into what the troupe had suffered sat side by side in the upper gallery. Doctor John Mordrake and Margery Firethorn made an unlikely couple but they had been invited along at the suggestion of Nicholas Bracewell to see a new play being launched upon the choppy waters of a demanding audience.

Margery's principal interest was in her husband, but Mordrake was more concerned to see how his patient fared. Recovered enough to take a supporting role, Edmund Hoode was overjoyed to be back with his fellows and, from the moment that he entered in a black cloak to deliver the Prologue, it was clear that his doctor had effected a remarkable cure. Like *Caesar's Fall*, by the same author, *The Siege of Troy* recounted a story that had been told on stage many times. Where it outshone rival versions, and where it rose above Stephen Wragby's other play, was in the quality of its verse, the delineation of its characters and the sheer verve of its action.

A decade of war was displayed at the Queen's Head. Lawrence Firethorn was a wily Ulysses, spinning seductive webs of words, while Owen Elias was a defiant King Priam. Richard Honeydew found pathos and cynicism in the role of Cressida. James Ingram was a commanding Agamemnon and Frank Quilter, a bellicose Ajax, teased and tormented by Barnaby Gill's prancing clown. Mistakes were inevitably made but they went unnoticed by the audience as the play swept on from scene to arresting scene. In the final act, when the huge wooden horse made by Nathan Curtis was wheeled out of the stables where it had been concealed, it earned the biggest cheer of the afternoon.

Appropriately, it fell to Edmund Hoode, who had suffered the worst ordeal because of his unique position in the company, to deliver the Epilogue that he had written to replace that by Michael Grammaticus. Standing in the centre of the stage, relishing his moment, he declaimed the speech to the sound of music.

'Our tale is told of Trojan and of Greek,
Of ancient malice, treachery and meek
Surrender to a wooden horse, a toy
Whose silent neigh brought down the walls of Troy.
Upon these boards, false Cressida has walked,
Ulysses hatched his plots, Achilles stalked
The gallant Hector with a shameful plan
To murder him by ambush. Every man
Was traitor or betrayed. This self-same flower
Of perfidy and lies has left its dower
To each succeeding age. It charms our mind
And with its scent makes all of us go blind.
We do not see what stands before our eyes
Until it is too late. Deceit now thrives
And forgery runs wild. This Grecian trick
Has spawned a thousand ruses just as quick
To steal our purses or to take our lives.
The innocent go down, the cheat survives.
For proof of this, behold our little stage,
Where you have seen the bloody battles rage
And mighty generals meeting face to face
While cunning politicians swift embrace.
You let illusion take its benefit
For we, your actors, did but counterfeit.'

Alexander Marwood was a picture of dejection. The high
hopes that had taken him to Dunstable had been dashed.
After sitting interminably beside his dying brother, he did
his best to put aside old enmities, only to learn, when the

will was finally read after the funeral, that he had been left nothing at all. Accompanied by a vindictive wife, who blamed him for wasting their time, he travelled back to London in great discomfort on their cart. Not even the sight of the capital could inspire him. Having left a brother who had betrayed him, he was going back, with a wife he feared, to an inn he hated and an occupation that he despised.

They reached Gracechurch Street towards the end of the afternoon, just in time to watch the happy crowds pouring out of the Queen's Head to remind the landlord that he would have to contend with the actors who loathed him almost as much as he detested them. It was a heavy cross to bear. He and Sybil drove into the yard in grim silence, furious at the noise of revelry that was coming from the taproom. It sounded as if a riot was taking place there. Marwood jumped down from the cart and rushed off to save what he could of his inn before what he believed was an unruly mob got completely out of hand. But, when he charged into the taproom, a miracle occurred.

The noise ceased instantly and everyone turned to look at him with a respect that bordered almost on reverence. During his absence, Westfield's Men had been assailed by a whole series of setbacks, testing them to the limit of their tolerance. Much of their suffering had been inflicted by Adam Crowmere, the very man engaged to replace their old landlord. He and his false friendship had now gone. Alexander Marwood was back to revile them as before but they found that strangely reassuring. Whatever his faults, the landlord was sincere. He was no counterfeit.

With a spontaneous release of affection, the whole company clapped and cheered him to the echo. Lawrence Firethorn even went so far as to hug the man warmly and kiss him on his pate. Marwood was overwhelmed by his reception. Against all the odds, he was wanted. As the ovation continued, and as the actors patted him warmly on the back, he was caught up in the spirit of the moment. For the first time since his wedding night, he put back his head and laughed with unreserved joy.

If you liked *The Counterfeit Crank*,
try Edward Marston's other series...

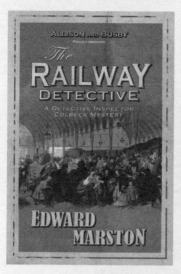

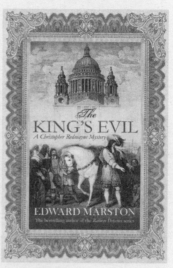

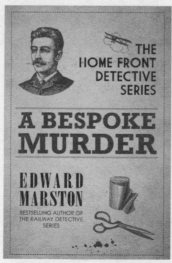